Marshall P Stafford

The Life of James Fisk, Jr.

A Full and Accurate Narrative of his Career, his Great Enterprises...

Marshall P Stafford

The Life of James Fisk, Jr.
A Full and Accurate Narrative of his Career, his Great Enterprises...

ISBN/EAN: 9783744751902

Printed in Europe, USA, Canada, Australia, Japan

Cover: Foto ©Raphael Reischuk / pixelio.de

More available books at **www.hansebooks.com**

JAMES FISK, Jr., Jobber in Silks, Shawls, Dress Goods, Jewelry, Silver Ware and Yankee Notions.   [See page 6.]

THE LIFE

OF

JAMES FISK, Jr.,

A FULL AND ACCURATE NARRATIVE OF HIS CAREER, HIS GREAT ENTERPRISES, AND HIS ASSASSINATION.

BY

Marshall P. Stafford.

PUBLISHED BY THE AUTHOR.

New York:
POLHEMUS & PEARSON, PRINTERS, 114 FULTON STREET,
1872.

that his declared intention of withdrawal has naturally aroused expectation and hope in other quarters. Indeed, no political leader more accurately apprehends the situation, or is more honorable and generous in his feeling toward all his fellow-Republicans. But as the time approaches for definite consideration and consultation in regard to the nominations, and as there is naturally the most general desire among Republicans to understand precisely the feeling of the Vice-President, we are very sure that we are not wrong in saying that if the Convention should [illegible] what he says; and if he does not, no rules which depend upon his will could be sufficient. The Chicago *Times*, a rebel newspaper during the war, and which, therefore, hates the General who received the sword of LEE, says that "Mr. GRANT, as Mr. GRANT'S record shows, can lie and will lie." That paper, therefore, thinks the President's scheme "thin twaddle." So it is, if its view of him be correct. But the Chicago *Times* no more speaks for honest American citizens·now than it did when it was cheering rebels, and trying to destroy the Union in order to perpetuate slavery.

A LIFE OF

JAMES FISK, Jr.

CHAPTER I.

CHILDHOOD AND SCHOOL-DAYS—HIS EARLY HOME—A VERMONT PEDDLER—HIS FIRST SENSATION.

James Fisk, Jr., was born in Pownal, near the historic town of Bennington, in the southwestern part of Vermont, April 1st, 1835.   At the time of his birth his father peddled from this point as a centre, visiting the adjacent country in all directions with one of those carts which were much more frequent before the revolutions caused by railroads than they now are, being a small variety store upon wheels, and carrying nearly everything that a rural community ordinarily puchased, from a silk dress to a jewsharp.   While the son was still a small child the father moved across to the east side of the Green Mountains, and established the base of his operations at Brattleboro, in the southeastern corner of the State, on the Connecticut River.   It was here in one

of the loveliest spots in the " Switzerland of America," in
the heart of the Green Mountains, in the midst of scenery
generally supposed to foster and develop some of the finest
traits of character, that passed the childhood and youth of
the man whose career is the greatest wonder as well as
one of the most significant commentaries of the times.
Here, in the little "deestrict" school, he received all of the
very limited education he could be induced to take in;
here still live many of the friends and companions of his
young days, who have watched his career with the greatest
wonder and amazement and now talk of it with deepest
interest; from here he has taken not a few of the play-
fellows and acquaintances of his early life to fill places of
various kinds that have since been at his disposal; here
he grew up to manhood, was married, and first entered
into business on his own account; and here he first displayed in the same marked way, though on a smaller
stage, the same striking traits which make him so conspicuous now, and exhibited abilities so marked as to lead
to his being called to other and larger spheres of action.

Should you enter the Revere House at Brattleboro and
casually remark to the affable clerk, " I believe this is the
town that has the honor of having produced Jim Fisk ?"
he will answer you, " Yes, this is the very house where he
used to live. His father built it, and sometimes used to
run it himself when a satisfactory tenant could not be
found. Jim himself used to wait on table in that room
right in there," pointing to a room beside the office, now

used as the general room for reading, writing, private conversation, etc. You will at once perceive that you have touched upon a subject in which your interlocutor takes much interest, if not pride, and about which he delights to talk. He will lead the way to the room previously designated as the scene of Jim's first services to the public in the capacity of *garçon*, the character in which he vented his first puns and *jeu d'esprits*, thereby rendering himself no small favorite with the guests. Your attention will here be called to one of the walls of the room, now become a "Neptunian wall" or a kind of "Poets' Corner," being set apart for a collection of memorials and souvenirs of its hero, consisting of the cartoons and caricatures which have appeared from time to time illustrative of the various episodes of his career—the whole forming a not uninteresting epic, told in rough legendary art of the pre-Raphaelite type and making a quite unique adornment. But there is one piece in the collection, one chapter in the story thus told, that would now undoubtedly have for the world at large a much greater interest than all the rest. It is the smallest and oldest of the collection. It is of Mr. Fisk's own design and was executed at his own order and expense while as yet he had no dreams of the life that awaited him beyond the hills or of the peculiar interest that would one day flow back from him and hover around this earliest embodiment of his artistic and æsthetic sense. It is one of the original business cards with which he brought himself to the notice of the public in his grand peddling enterprise.   The frontispiece cut is a fac-simile.

It is only quite recently that this house ceased to be the home of the family, they having always retained rooms here and made it their headquarters ever since it was built by the senior Fisk.   But they are all gone from it now, the settlement of the two children elsewhere having broken up the family nucleus, leaving only its traditions to cluster about the homestead.   The father was for a time concerned in some of the speculative schemes of the son, but ill health and·the increasing weight of years having incapacitated him for the cares of business, he now lives a life of retired leisure upon the competence which he amassed during his many years of business.   Mr. Fisk's own mother died when he was a small child.   His father soon married a second wife, a Brattleboro lady who was always much esteemed in the village where all her life has passed.   His half sister was a very pretty and pleasing young lady, much liked and highly regarded by all who knew her down to the hour she was married and left her native village.

The old residents of the place, the eye-witnesses of his childhood's days as they flowed quietly away, who can still vividly recall his boyhood, speak of James as having always been a pleasant, kind-hearted boy, with no bad traits, a general favorite, always wide-awake and lively, boiling over with animal spirits and fun, "rather rattle-headed and always full of his traps," always on hand and conspicuous if anything was going on, and so well known for being quick-witted and sharp at repartee, that his advent in any circle was ever a signal for getting the laughing apparatus ready for use.

Having no inclination to books or school, but being impatient to enter the arena of active life and commence his battle with the world, he began while yet a boy to accompany his father in his peddling trips. This life had a great charm for him then, suiting his disposition and inclination exactly, and he at once displayed such a natural aptitude for it that his father soon consented to let him have a cart by himself and make trips alone over some of their routes. A very few of these trips sufficed to show the son the better peddler of the two. By this division of their labor, acting upon separate lines, the amount of their sales was greatly increased, and it was not long before the father gave the son an interest in the business. He then immediately began to manifest the traits which have been so striking throughout his career and make him so conspicuous at the present time The carts were more gaudily painted, more spirited horses were driven and more showy harnesses were used. But the conservative nature and old-fashioned notions of the father repressed these inclinations and greatly hampered their full play. It was not long before their ideas as to the proper manner of conducting their business were radically different and inharmonious. The son favored great innovations and an extension of their operations, while the father was naturally contented with things as they were and regarded the schemes of James as boyish, wild and all nonsense. Dissatisfied with this state of things and impatient of the restraint which his father exercised over his burning ambition and projects, James, Jr., as the easiest remedy for all his difficulties and as the best and most effective way of settling all their differences, boldly proposed to buy out his father's interest in the business, boss it himself with undivided authority and conduct it wholly in accordance with his own ideas. Satisfactory terms were offered, a bargain was struck on the spot, Fisk senior came down from the cart as a partner and remounted it as his son's hired man at a very liberal salary. Instantly the whole appearance and organization of things was changed as if by magic. The sole proprietor now determined to extend his operations, employ several men and send them out with carts as branches of his establishment, and reduce the business to a regular organized system. Two new four-horse carts, the most elegant that could be procured, one for himself and the other for his father, replaced those they had been using. Eight horses, the most showy and spirited that could be obtained in the region famed for the finest "Blackhawks" and "Morgans," were secured for them; and harnesses of the finest material with the most elegant and glittering mountings were made to order to be in keeping and complete the turnout. The carts used by his subordinates, though of course much smaller and less pretending than these two grand establishments, were yet all after the same neat style, much more elegant than those ordinarily used by peddlers and such as to give a proper reflection of the grandeur of the resplendent central orb.

When everything was ready for the first campaign under the new *régime* and all were drawn up together ready to start at the word of command, the quiet villagers of Brattleboro, — those who had ever been the playmates of the youthful commander, or given him a bloody nose in boyhood's battles; those who had sat round the hotel fire with him many a winter evening whittling sticks and getting off gibes; his first little snub-nosed loves with whom he had sat on the front seat in the little schoolhouse and played puzzles with one eye on the teacher and to whom he had written and slyly passed along many such communications as, "Sal du me this er sum, look out not ter let ole specs kech yew duin it ur he wil swot my ers J, F, Jr, p s i luv yew an ma i go hum with yew arfter skool ter nite;" those who had always spelt him down to the foot of his class on such words as peddler, cart, honor, modesty, shame, and judge, which he always spelt pedlur, kart, onur, mudesty, sham and jug; those who had seen him tumble down and bump his nose in his first efforts to stand alone and walk; the young and the old—all crowded round in their garb of many cuts and colors, with eyes and mouth agape in mingled admiration and amazement and feeling not a little pride that the very neatest thing they had ever seen before,

even in the grand procession of Dan Rice's circus entering
the village with the great brass band in a gorgeous chariot
at the head, was now so completely eclipsed by their own
modest little town. When the eyes of his fellow towns-
people had gloated and been dazzled by a minute inspection of every detail and he had drank sufficiently deep
of the glory of the occasion, the great lion of the hour
mounted his grand cart, drew up the reins over his four
nervous steeds, brought a graceful flourish of his long whip
to an end .in a loud snap and dashed out of the village of
quaint beauty followed by his glittering retinue. James
Fisk, Jr., had created the first of his long series of grand
sensations. How vast have been the contributions levied
from many fields to feed the ever-growing flame lighted by
that early scene in his village home, the world knows but
too well; but in all the many grand *tableaux* of which he
has been the central figure—whether as admiral, resplendent in gold lace ; as colonel, the centre of a sunset pageant
at Long Branch, or astride his mettlesome charger leading
his regiment of braves up Broadway ; or as *impressario* in
his private box or standing at the head of the grand entrance staircase in his marble palace as the throng flow in
and out on successful nights in his theatre, the largest and
most brilliantly gilded in America—it is doubtful if he has
over tingled in every tiniest nerve with such a keen relish
of gratified pride and self-importance as on that bright
morning when those whom he had always known gathered around him in their homely attire—perhaps the most

respectable, honest and worthy company he has ever drawn together. The keen and delicious edge of the first enjoyment was more than sufficient to counterbalance the grander proportions of each succeeding repetition, and, moreover, there was a genuineness and sincerity in that first demonstration, while a mawkish curiosity and a smile of contempt have been the chief ingredients in all its successors, and no one knows better than Mr. Fisk how to appreciate this difference, notwithstanding that in the absence of the genuine he glories in the spurious.

When the pageant had passed away and the gathering had scattered to their work and to talk over the great event, not a few of the staid old rustic spirits shook their heads dubiously, sagely predicting a disastrous end to such extravagance and giddiness, and slept the more soundly that night from the consciousness that they were not the young man's creditors, nor had their names on the back of any of his I O U's. But the subjects of these gloomy forebodings and misgivings saw not the clear vision and perfect confidence of the guiding spirit, which is the main element in every enterprise, nor foresaw the favorable consequence of conducting the business with admirable organization and system.

Mr. Fisk gave to each of his subordinates explicit directions as to the road to be followed for a week, and the route for each was laid out so that they would all come together and meet their commander every Saturday afternoon. Each then gave an account of his stewardship for the week, and made known his wants in the way of new stock, etc. Some large town on the railroad, to which new goods could be ordered in advance to meet them from market, was always selected for the weekly rendezvous. The time from Saturday to Monday was devoted to balancing accounts, refurnishing supplies, mapping out the courses and giving directions for the ensuing week. The smaller carts were sent out as skirmishers on either side to visit the more secluded regions and smaller villages, the main lines of travel and larger towns being reserved for the visitations of the two larger and more imposing establishments. The amount of business done and the account sales for each week under this plan of operations were many times as large as those of an ordinary country merchant. Indeed, many of the latter class of tradesmen bought much of their stock of Mr. Fisk instead of going or sending to market themselves, so that he was in reality, and to no small extent, what his card announced—a "jobber" in the trade.

When on the road in these trips he always drove in a dashing style at the rate of ten miles an hour and never failed to attract everybody's attention. Men working in the field rested from their toil to watch him as he passed; the inmates of every house ran to the windows to catch a sight of the grand turnout and held up their babies to look and cease crying. As he came flying into a village and drew up at a store or tavern, all the children gathered round at once to gaze in admiration—every boy resolving that when he grew up to be a man he would have *just* such a cart and go peddling, every girl feeling sad at the misfortune which shut her out from all the pleasure of the same ambition and resolve and left her only the cold comfort of vowing it should be a man who looked and did just like that she would have for her husband. Country lasses peered coyly through the shutters or from behind the curtains, wondering if he would call at their house, their innocent hearts. rising to the mouth and falling back again with the alternations of increasing prospect or parting hope. The women admired, men envied and were deferential, and he in turn was gracious and affable, always jocose, scattering pennies and candy among the children, bewitching smiles among the sweet-sixteens, and consternation among their mammas. In a word, he was a great gun generally—the biggest gun ever seen in the towns he visited. And now that he is so famous and his early career is known to thousands by hearsay quite as well as by those who witnessed it, it is surprising how many there are in every town within a hundred miles of which he ever travelled in those days who have a most vivid remembrance and give the most minute description of just how he looked and the appearance and sensation he used to make when he drove by on their road, though he never set foot in the town.

It is the fashion with certain journalists to refer to this period of Mr. Fisk's life in a sneering tone, as though it implied disgrace or discredit, and to indulge little flings

about "peddling shirt buttons," etc. · The sneer is a mean
and unwarranted one, and destroys the force of whatever
is said in connection with it by disclosing an unworthy
animus and a disinclination to "give even the devil his
due." There may have been some dealings on a petty
scale in his business at this time, as there are in the dealings of nearly every tradesman in the world, not except-
ing those whose palatial stores cover acres of ground, employ armies of clerks, and constitute an object of pride to
the largest city on the continent, as being without an
equal in the world. There is more petty dealing in the
business of nineteen out of every twenty tradesmen in
the world than there was in Mr. Fisk's peddling business,
so the fling cast at him applies with greater force to them
and should be used only when it is intended to express
contempt for all tradesmen as a class—a thing which the
said journalists would not dare to do. The influence of
such a training upon the mental, moral and social traits is
undoubtedly very different from that exerted by a college
course and the liberal professions; but if this be a fault
or just cause for a sneer, it applies to the vast majority of
men—including many great journalists as well; and certain it is that if all the little affairs in the past private
life of certain exceedingly snobbish "renegade English-
men," who seem to take most delight in these flings, and
think there is great force and virtue in them, were laid
bare to the public they would be much more obnoxious ·
to sneers and have much greater cause for mortification

than has Mr. Fisk for anything in his Brattleboro record. There is no other period of his career so free from taint, so much to his credit. He drove the best bargain he could, as do all tradesmen, for that is their business; but no charge of unfair dealing was ever made against him at this time. It is but fair to accept the opinion entertained of a man by those with whom he has lived and dealt and who know him most intimately; and when Mr. Fisk left Brattleboro no damaging reputation or gossip attached to his name but he left behind him a good record in all his relations to life and society. It is as unjust as it is unnecessary to fling mud upon such a record for anything that has since happened.

CHAPTER II.

The drygoods used by Mr. Fisk in his business at
Brattleboro were purchased of the young Boston house
of Jordan, Marsh & Co. This firm was not only impressed by the frequent large bills of goods which their
young customer from Vermont purchased but was also
struck by his general bearing and manner of doing business. Detecting in him abilities worthy of a higher and
larger sphere of action, and perhaps spurred on by the more
self-interested desire to secure the abilities of such a
stirring man in their firm, they suggested his abandoning peddling and entering their establishment as a
salesman. There was much about his peddling business
that was very congenial to such a nature as his and he
liked it not a little. There was constant change, variety
and moderate excitement in the life, constant opportunity ·
for indulging his inclination to sport and jokes; he was

his own master, wholly independent; and, above all, he was very conspicuous, the cynosure of all eyes, the centre of an almost constant sensation—an aliment indispensable to his contentment. But his style of living and conducting his business was extravagant for such a trade. He hated and would not practise that rigid economy which alone could make it a paying enterprise. His expenses were so great that the promise of pecuniary success was not good. For this reason, as well as for the attraction there naturally would be for a man of his temperament in passing from a peddler's cart to a very large wholesale house, and from a home in the country to life in a great city, the proposition of the Boston firm was at once accepted. With that promptitude which is one of his most marked traits, he wound up his business at Brattleboro immediately and entered the house of Jordan, Marsh & Co. on a salary.

The inexorable laws of his nature here exhibited themselves very strikingly at once, and in a manner as unexpected to himself as to his employers. The salesman seemed entirely out of his element. The young man's energy seemed to have suddenly collapsed. "Drumming" customers was a work he instinctively recoiled from and could not do. Exhibiting goods and talking a man into a purchase suited him no better. It had an air of pettiness, servitude and dependence that grated harshly upon every fibre of his spirit. There was no *éclat* or dash about it. It was a fall from the position he

had enjoyed in the country, where people came to him
and wanted to buy, where he bossed and gave orders and
managed things with a great flourish, and was looked up
to by all as being a grand affair. Now he was insignificant, swallowed up in a great establishment with
many gradations of clerks, where he was bossed and had
to take orders. He felt the change. Leaving the country for the city seemed to have been a great mistake.
The prince of country peddlers had been spoiled to make
a very poor city salesman. In short, his first six months
in Boston were a complete failure and at the end of that
time the firm advised him to return to his peddling business as being that for which he was best adapted, and
in which he would meet with most success. But here
another marked trait of his character and nature asserted
itself and appeared in bold relief. He is not a man to
acknowledge failure in anything he undertakes. His is
one of those spirits that much prefer to fight on undaunted against every obstacle rather than brook such a
thought as returning to what has once been laid aside to
go up higher. In this first trying circumstance of his
life he acted from that impulse and instinct within him
which has ever been his trusted and unquestioned guide,
the one light by which his steps have been directed
through all his remarkable career. To the suggestion
of the firm he replied " Give me a fair chance, Mr.
Jordan. Don't be discouraged too quick. Try me six
months more. If you are dissatisfied at the end of that

time, I shall be glad to quit. I'm not particular about any salary. I'm willing to accept a commission on my sales for my pay. Only let me have a fair chance." There was something in his manner that inspired hope and confidence and his request was readily granted. He had not the slightest tangible reason except the vague but potent something within, like Sheridan's "It's *in* me and it *shall* come out!" for indulging such hope and cherishing such faith. He had not the remotest definite idea how his salvation was to be wrought out. His hour came, however, and then he speedily justified his wisdom in following impulse.

The war broke out. He saw in a flash that this was his opportunity and he instantly embraced it. The government must have large supplies of woolen and cotton fabrics and there were large and very profitable contracts to be given to *somebody*. This was enough for him to know. Here was attractive game, a foeman worthy of his steel. The spirit that chafed at being an inconspicuous salesman and felt humbled and ashamed to go about "drumming" small purchasers, here saw something the management and securing of which would make him a man of some importance both with his firm and with those whom he had to approach. It required abilities, tact, liberal ideas, was on a scale sufficiently grand to gratify vanity, the profits sure to be derived were immense, and when once secured he would only have to give orders and directions and not attend personally to small affairs of detail. For these prizes Mr. Fisk was one of the earliest, most active and most successful contestants. He foresaw all, scented his trail, and set about accomplishing his design before anything of the kind had occured to the firm. He soon secured several large contracts for his house and they speedily changed their opinion as to the advisability of his returning to peddling.

The man's peculiar genius

> "—— for ways that are dark,
> And for tricks that are vain,"

came into full play and shone in all its brilliancy in securing the first contract. It is said that a Boston lady, through the influence of one of the Massachusetts Senators, had obtained a large contract for supplying underclothing for the army and had already disposed of a portion of the contract to a prominent Boston house. Mr. Fisk at once set to work to secure a graceful introduction to this lady of much consequence, succeeded, and ingratiated himself with her so speedily that he induced her to annul the sub-contract she had already given out and award it to his rival firm instead. Other contracts soon followed from the same source and the profits accruing to Jordan, Marsh & Co. therefrom were immense.

This stroke, though brilliant and successful, was soon quite eclipsed by another. The firm had quite a large quantity of blankets that had been on their hands for a long time and which were now stowed away in one of the lofts and regarded as dead stock. An idea struck James one day. He went immediately to the head of the firm and simply said "Mr. Jordan, I'm going to sell those blankets up in the loft." Nothing more explicit in regard to his designs or the idea he had conceived could be got out of him; but it had now begun to be felt that when James said he was going to do anything he would do it, and so, with a smile that was a mixture of hope and incredulity, he was answered, "All right! Go ahead and sell them for anything you can get." The next train for Washington carried James Fisk, Jr., among its passengers. The next morning of course James Fisk, Jr., was registered at Willard's. Of course he had one of Willard's best suites and lived in as free and sumptuous style as Willard's generous larder and capacious wine cellar permitted. It is of course that he did all this, for he never had done, and by the laws of his nature never could do, anything on any other than a grand scale, in the best style, in a manner sure to attract attention. Strange though it may seem, the doors of that suite of rooms were not closed to quartermasters, congressmen, or any one of position or influence among the powers that were. If any such came they were admitted as readily and made as welcome as any one else to all the hospitalities. There was great popping of corks, the sparkling goblets passed freely round, the landlord filled the flowing bowl and kept it running over, everybody enjoyed life, and

"Jim Fisk is a jolly good fellow"

was nightly sung with great gusto by a company in the

usual hilarious mood in which that tune becomes a great
favorite. Tho host while overseeing every desire supplied, joined in tho " flow of soul," got off innumerable
puns as if freo from every care,

> " And he smiled as ho sat by tho table
> With a smile that was child-like and bland."

At length, as one of those incidents in which conversation
around the social bowl is ever fruitful, it casually leaked
out that there was great need of blankets of a certain
kind for tho army. As a most fortunate coincidence, Mr.
Fisk happened to havo a hundred or two with him as
samples of somo he could furnish to supply the pressing
want. He produced them for inspection with an air of
much indifference and, as ho did so, facetiously quoted
Artemas Ward's famous pill-box label, " For such people
as like this kind of pills, these aro just the pills they
ought to take." A joke and a laugh is said often to go
much further than logic in swaying a jury. Whether
facetiousness bo equally potent with quartermasters is
not so well settled, but there is in this case some further
indication that human naturo is ever tho samo under all
circumstances—whether in tho jury box or under a
quartermaster-general's uniform. Happy result — all
those old blankets stowed away in Jordan, Marsh & Co.'s
loft were not only disposed of for three times as much as
tho firm would gladly have taken for them, but they
also got a contract for a further supply of a million or
more dollars in value. and their house must have realized

between two and three hundred thousand dollars as the result of this little pleasure trip to Washington.

It will readily be surmised that Mr. Fisk was not a man that would be likely to overlook the fact that he who could secure for his employers contracts from which the larger portion of their profits was derived, contracts for which any number of houses stood ready to pay an immense sum, was a man of no small consequence to the firm and had some rights which they were bound to respect, nor was it at all unnatural under the circumstances that he should feel it might be just as well for him to turn the opportunity to his own behoof. In short, soon after securing his earliest government contracts, the quondam country peddler boldly announced to the firm one morning that he had a no less ambitious and presuming desire than that of being immediately admitted into the partnership. The members laughed. It was one of James's little jokes, they thought, and was very good in its way. Of course it was too preposterous to be intended seriously, thought they. A joke? Not a bit of it!—unless they made it so, and then it would be a joke the humorous side of which they would not at all relish. They speedily woke to a consciousness that James meant business. They found he held the balance of power, saw his opportunity, and had the disposition and nerve to make the most of it. He had been shrewd enough to secure certain contracts in his own name instead of the name of the firm, consequently he could dispose of them as he pleased. If *they* would not, there were other first class houses that *would* gladly give him a partnership for the contracts he could secure for whatever house he was with, so they could have their choice between taking him in as a partner or seeing contracts worth hundreds of thousands of dollars carried off from their door to some rival house. *He* did not care. It was only to oblige them, not himself, that he wished to become a member of their firm. But from his ultimatum there was no escape. *Aut Cæsar aut nullus !* A partner or quit ! The comic smile which the preposterous demand at first raised disappeared instanter. A little consultation was held in which nothing of the humorous entered, and soon the crisis was settled. A new name, James Fisk, Jr., was thenceforth included in the elastic " Co." of Jordan, Marsh & Co.

The new sense of dignity, importance and power which naturally came with the consciousness of being a partner in one of the largest establishments in New England, in no wise diminished the confidence, zeal and boldness of the new member. Large contracts continued to flow in to their house as the fruit of his tact and energy, and very soon the business of the firm showed various signs of the infusion of new blood into its veins. Mr. Fisk, never having studied Bowen's Political Economy, was happy in the possession of a mind wholly unclouded by any befogged metaphysical abstractions about the beauty, simplicity and great advantage to humanity, resulting from the division of labor, and he therefore clearly saw that by manufacturing their own goods, instead of buying them from manufacturers and agents, his firm could add the manufacturer's profit to their own, and would also in that way be able to undersell rival houses that bought instead of manufacturing their goods, and thus largely increase the amount of their sales and profits. Accordingly he urged this course upon his firm. At first it was looked upon skeptically, but was tried in a small way as an experiment. The experiment was a grand success. The new member stuck a new red feather in his cap and was in his glory. The firm now bought several cotton and woolen mills, built as many more new ones, operated them at a profit that seemed almost fabulous in some cases, and thus for other hundreds of thousands of dollars were indebted to the originality and quick perceptions of the man whose name still rested in the oblivion of the now important "Co."

A single stroke at this period of his career disclosed all those striking mental qualities which have conduced so greatly to his later exploits—an intuitive perception of a whole situation almost instantly, an immediate resolve, a nerve and daring to do anything, and the greatest celerity of action. Being in New York on one occasion, and snuffing afar off the first indications and knowledge that there was likely to be a great demand soon for a certain kind of goods, and knowing or learning that there was but one mill in the country where such goods were manufactured, he immediately telegraphed his firm

to send an agent to Gaysville, Vt., to buy that mill at any
price demanded, and at the same time he bought up all
the goods of that kind to be had in the market. The firm
had now learned to obey the laconic and even mysterious
directions of James as unhesitatingly as Napoleon's subordinates obeyed his every word. The agent was sent as
the telegram ordered and the coveted mill was purchased
at a fair price. In less than an hour after the bargain was
closed, the former owner received a telegram from New
York offering him $5,000 more than the price at which
he had sold it. But it was too late. Fisk had been too
quick for them. Jordan, Marsh & Co. had an entire
monopoly and controlled the market. James Fisk, Jr.,
had got up his first "corner" and engineered it through
to entire success. After running the mill some two
years at an annual profit of upwards of $100,000, the
Boston firm resold it to the former owner.

Another project, and one which, in point of ethics, the
difficulties besetting it and the means by which it was to
be accomplished, savored more strongly of the character of
his later and well-known exploits, now suggested itself to
the versatile drygoods man. Cotton was selling in New
York and Boston at $1.70 to $1.80 the pound, and there
was but very little to be had even at those figures. Yet
within the Confederate lines cotton was abundant and
was a dead weight which the owners were as anxious to
dispose of as the New England mills were to obtain, and
that at figures almost as far in one extreme as the ruling

prices outside of the Confederacy were in the other. Query in Mr. Fisk's mind—how could these two facts be made to work together for good to those who loved the fortune lying between? Two difficulties were in the way. To most minds they would have seemed wholly insurmountable; but not so to the man to whom nothing seems impossible when only human beings are to be managed. All sentimental nonsense about there being a moral element in the problem, the right and wrong of giving aid and comfort to the enemies of his country, violating the laws of blockade, etc., Mr. Fisk dismissed at once in great contempt as worthy only of some brain-cracked lunatic, and immediately addressed himself to the practical questions, how to get cotton through the lines without its being seized by the government authorities as contraband, and how the delicate and perilous business of buying and forwarding inside the Confederacy could be conducted. He paid a visit to Tennessee, the point where the lines must be passed and the region where cotton was plenty. The government superintendent of the railroads here happened to be a man that he had formerly known in Boston. This was most fortunate. The tarry at Memphis was brief and he returned with a mind evidently at case on one point. The hare *could be cooked*, and in this case that was more difficult than to catch it. Boring a tunnel through Hoosac Mountain requires ten years or more, and many lives. The seemingly impassable barriers between two hostile territories engaged in a life and death struggle

Mr. Fisk pierced in a day and night so as to let the golden light shine through. The machine by which this unparalleled feat of tunnelling was accomplished has never been patented—perhaps for the reason that no one but the inventor could ever use it, so a patent would be useless. Its exact nature is therefore wholly a matter of inference. The remaining branch of the problem was now taken up and in the solution of this there was displayed a knowledge of human nature as keen and sagacious as that which is supposed to have carried General Grant through at the head of our armies so triumphantly. To buy cotton inside the rebel lines under such ticklish circumstances required a person of great tact and intuitive judgment of men and circumstances, and for this duty a woman admirably adapted to the purpose was employed. To collect and forward it when purchcsed was a work still more thickly beset with difficulties and pitfalls at every step, to elude the suspicions flying in front and rear, run the gauntlet of wary sentinels and get the forbidden fruit safely through to some market in the North. A single false step might defeat the whole project, sink all the capital invested, and involve the person found thus engaged in no slight danger of his personal liberty for a term of years. To brave all those risks and dangers and undertake these delicate duties, Mr. Fisk secured the services of his own father. The venture is supposed by those who pretend to know, to have been a very profitable one pecuniarily.

One of the noblest and most inspiring spectacles ever

witnessed in Boston, and one which those who witnessed it will never forget, was largely due to the originality and exertions of Mr. Fisk. The news of the battle of Antietam, in September, 1862, reached Boston on Sunday morning. When the Sabbath school bells rang on the bright lovely morning, all hearts were appalled by tidings that sent tho death shadow into many a homo and told of thousands of brave men suffering the agonies of a bloody battle field. Mr. Fisk and his partner, Mr. Jordan, conceived the idea of having the churches suspend services and devote themselves to the practical religion of relieving the suffering of the men who had fallen for them. The idea caught like magic. Tho churches wero closed, the citizens forgot self and put forth every exertion to mitigate tho suffering of tho wounded and dying. Tremont Temple was transformed into a dépôt for the collection of hospital supplies. Delicate ladies worked all the day long with tho devotion and enthusiasm peculiar to the sex in tho hour of great trials and suffering. Lint, bandages, and the necessities for binding up the gaping wounds, wines and all the delicacies that could mitigato the sufferings of tho fallen in tho hospital, poured in from every direction, each household contributing according to its means. It was a scene which made it hard for any beholder to repress tho tears, and suddenly throw into bold relief all tho noblest traits of humanity. By nightfall many carloads of supplies were on their way to the field of suffering. Mr. Fisk worked in this as he does in everything, with all his might, superintending and directing; and when this (perhaps his noblest) day's work was done he said, with an excusable pride and satisfaction, "There! what will New York say of Boston *now?*"

During these years and enterprises, Mr. Fisk was of course quite prominent after his peculiar fashion, always living in the sumptuous, regardless-of-expense style, and it was at this period that he saw the best society he has ever mingled with familiarly. His contempt for the most cardinal laws of decent social life had not then been openly manifested. He maintained a respectable attitude to the relations deemed most sacred by all decent people, and the doors of society of the middle class were open to him and his family. When General McClellan visited Boston on his tour to New England soon after receiving the famous order to report at Baltimore, Mr. Fisk was quite conspicuous and active in doing the honors for Boston on that occasion, met the distinguished visitor on quite familiar terms, and is said to have ingratiated himself not a little with the hero of the Chickahominy Swamps.

The house of Jordan, Marsh & Co., already prominent among the Boston firms when Mr. Fisk entered it, had, during the four years of his connection with it, rapidly grown to be one of the very foremost and probably now stood at the head of the list in extent of business done and profits realized. They not only gathered the same rich harvest in the doubling, trebling, quadrupling or more, in value of the large stocks of goods on hand, but they had also secured in addition to their regular business many enormously profitable government contracts, and had engaged extensively in manufacturing at just the time when this was most remunerative and when a single mill brought a fine fortune annually. For many of the richest contributions to this immense pool they were indebted directly and solely to Mr. Fisk, and it is probable that his abilities had a greater influence than those of any other one man in the firm, if not more than all the rest united, in swelling the grand total of wealth they had accumulated during these four eventful years. However this may be, it was not long before it became evident that, at the rate things were going, the firm of Jordan, Marsh & Co. would soon come to mean what the Erie Railway has since come to mean and just what everything with which this spirit is connected is sure soon to mean—James Fisk, Jr. A man of such strongly marked individuality cannot be long kept in a position of secondary authority and influence in anything he is connected with. His voice must be the potent one, his will the·ruling force, or else there will be trouble at once. While the era of government contracts and large outside speculative enterprises continued, this was his special field, and while thus engaged he was necessarily away much of the time at a distance that lent enchantment and was not brought into such close personal contact with the other members of the firm daily as to make his peculiar propensities felt unpleasantly ; but as this era waned he was brought more constantly in personal contact with his partners. The very qualities which had made him their most valuable man when government contracts were plenty, stocks rising, and a smile of prosperity rested over everything, were precisely the most dangerous ones to be influenced by now when business had become unsettled and hazardous, making it necessary to take in much of the sail that had been spread before the favorable and reliable breeze and manage all affairs with the utmost care and caution. His bold, venturesome, impulsive spirit now clashed at once with the cautious counsels of his partners and the man's individuality and dominant traits were at once felt in their full force. His native confidence, self-assertion and persistence in his own impulses and will, were not lessened of course by the consciousness of the important part he had played in the very successful career of the firm. It became evident at once that either the men whose names alone appeared upon the sign boards, must change place in importance with a single name covered up under the " Co.," and they be forced to accept a back seat while that ruling spirit stood chiefly at the helm, or else that spirit must be exorcised from the concern entirely. The latter was the alternative chosen and this proved not to be difficult of accomplishment. The firm freely admitted the great value Mr. Fisk's services had been to the house and they were willing to deal generously with him if he would now withdraw. He, on the other hand, confident of his own fertility of resources under any circumstances, cared not a rush about remaining in the firm provided he were paid what he deemed a fair sum to quit. Such being the spirit on either side, the question was easily settled and the man who had entered the establishment at one end as a salesman four years ago now made his exit at the other end as a partner, retiring with what he would have considered a princely fortune in his peddling days, and also carrying with him the satisfaction of knowing that he had been the most important element in the unrivalled success of a great firm during four most eventful years.

CHAPTER III.

A DRYGOODS MERCHANT—UNSUCCESSFUL VENTURES—A ROLLING
STONE—MISFORTUNES THICKEN—A FORETASTE OF RUIN—
THE GODDESS SMILES AGAIN—THE APPROPRIATE SPHERE AT
LAST—A MILLIONAIRE.

Mr. Fisk withdrew from the firm of Jordan, Marsh &
Co. possessed of what would have been quite a comfortable fortune to retire upon for a man having no heir
apparent. But he was not one of the retiring kind.
Activity and bustle as a man of affairs are as neccessary
to his contentment as is oxygen to his lungs. He
immediately resolved to continue in the trade and
establish a business of his own that should rival that of
the house in which he had served such a brilliant appren-
ticeship. In a surprisingly short time a large new sign
bearing the name of James Fisk, Jr., appeared over the
doors of a fine large store at the corner of Sumner and
Chauncey Streets—a conspicuous building in a conspicuous part of the city, within a stone's throw of the house
from which he had just separated. To build up a drygoods jobbing business by himself would not have been

an easy matter under any circumstances, and it was especially difficult just at that period. The constant and rapid rise in the price of fabrics, which had made the business so very prosperous and safe during the past four years, had reached its climax and the ebbing tide had set in and raised the reflex wave that introduced such great uncertainty and hazard into the trade and was destined to bury not a few beneath it in its fitful motions. The task that had been undertaken was as difficult as to stand on a barrel and roll it with the feet. Government contracts, in which his previous success had largely consisted, were no longer to be had, for the authorities were now confident of a speedy termination of the war and were retrenching expenditures. Manufacturing was at a standstill or was prosecuted only at a loss. Building up a regular legiti-mate jobbing trade was not at all in Mr. Fisk's vein. He felt for its duties the same aversion he had felt for "drumming" during his early months in Boston and let it alone in the same way. His attention and efforts being thus left unengrossed by the undertaking he had proposed for himself, he engaged in various speculative enterprises, not only such as were partially allied to his ostensible business (as cotton) but in anything that suggested itself to him or was presented in a favorable light and promised the requisite elements of diversion with a fair chance of profit. But everything was paralyzed and stagnant under reaction from the stimulant which the war had afforded, and all business that required the investment of capital seemed destined to entail loss. It was the most critical period of dread suspense when everything was unsettled and under a lowering future, and a tremor was running through all business in expectation of a great financial crash. Drygoods began to tumble at such leaps that any considerable stock on hand meant a small fortune lost every month. His speculative ventures rarely proved successful, often were bad failures. After a few months of this precarious fortune, again yielding to impulse and instinct rather than convictions reached by reflection and calculation, he resolved to close up his business and go out of the trade. This resolution to discontinue was executed with the same celerity as had been the former one to start by himself. The fortune drawn out from the firm of Jordan, Marsh & Co. had melted rapidly in the unprosperous months succeeding, but he settled up all his affairs leaving no unpaid obligations.

There is a certain famous being or character, half historic, half fabulous, favored in the fancy of both poet and theologian, who, it is positively alleged, is always sure to claim his own sooner or later. James Fisk, Jr., went to New York. He allowed "natur" to take its course now, and as naturally as the needle dips to the pole or the force of gravity draws all things towards the earth's centre, he brought up in Wall Street—the favorite haunt of the worst breed of gamblers the world has yet produced—men whom one who knows them best* has

* Vanderbilt

called "a set of thieves and cutthroats," every one of whose transactions leaves the world so much the worse off, and whose most fitting and forcible commentary is to be read in the fact that if every one of them were to drop out of existence instantly society and every honest calling would be greatly benefited. It was with the men of this ilk that the ex-drygoodsman now proposed to put his lance in rest and measure swords. All the world will admit the wisdom and appropriateness of the course selected as one for which he was eminently adapted. It was just the course Fowler would have advised him to pursue had he gone to him and had his head examined. In fact, so very natural and appropriate seems this migration to the great focus of respectable gambling and legalized robbery that the only wonder is that he did not gravitate to the genial clime and kindred, though inferior, spirits immediately on leaving Jordan, Marsh & Co. instead of first attempting to found a drygoods establishment. He has taught them many a lesson at their own tricks and it is questionable if the world at large does not owe him more gratitude than execration for the deeds that have made him

"By merit raised to that bad eminence"

among such leeches and pests.

It was in the waning months of 1864 that the resolution was taken to shake off the Puritan dust and pass from the shadow of Bunker Hill to that of Trinity Church. He still had sufficient capital to operate quite extensively on a "margin," the broker's most cunning decoy duck to bring game within his reach. He took offices on Broad Street and furnished them in the most sumptuous style, the man's individuality providing some original features found in no other office. He launched out boldly and almost haphazard in all the leading stocks and most active speculative enterprises, putting up his margins in pretty much the same way that he would place his "chips" in roulette or faro, thus at once disclosing his just conception of the character of the business. But in his first experience in the new field there seemed to hover over him the same untoward fortune that beset his last months in Boston and the proverbially fickle goddess seemed to have turned her smile and face from him entirely. He was not yet fully awake to the genius of the guild

"—— for ways that are dark"

and the artful dodges by which things were moved in Wall Street. He had heard of "honor among thieves" and in his unsophisticated confidence in human nature could not suspect that his new associates were sunk so far beneath even faro bank and roulette keepers in point of honor as to play with stacked cards and loaded dice. The scales had not yet all fallen from his eyes. He still had some lingering, verdant, boyish, Puritan, nonsense about there really being such things as honor and honesty, actually believed that there was such a crime as robbery or fraud known to the law and that it would lead a man to the State Prison. His senses must be quickened in the severe crucible of burnt fingers before he could fully emerge from these hallucinations imbibed in his early country home and understand that all this was but a name, a poetic fiction, a ridiculous Yankee notion probably invented by the same man who first sold wooden nutmegs. He is one of the aptest scholars in such a school and he plunged his fingers into the molten metal so boldly that he was not long in dispelling the clouds of rustic innocence that obscured the light. He made some successes, as all do; he made many more losses, as most do. It was but a few months before his margins were all swept away, his bank account cancelled, and the remnant of a once comfortable fortune which he had brought from Boston had wholly disappeared—gone the way of so many others before and since. The young man who had always had means and known plenty proportionate to his position and needs, who had constantly risen in worldly condition till his days had passed in familiar contact with men of high position, authority and influence and he felt himself a man of consequence and power established on a secure pedestal that could not be seriously shaken by fickle fortune, suddenly found himself penniless when his daily wants had grown to be very large, his fancied power and security broken and gone in a flaw of wind, despair driving its pitiless arrows through his breast, helpless and unresisting in the surging tide that was sweeping him down in its merciless whirlpool—*ruined!*

Such a spectacle is always sad and touching. No matter who or what the man in whose breast the terrible emotions of such an hour are passing, they touch a responsive chord of sympathy in the great heart of aggregate impersonal humanity as though it saw its own uncertainties and possible misfortunes typified therein. It is a situation whose agony in all its fullness can be but faintly imagined by one who has never felt the dread creeping coil of misfortune and ruin closing silently and fatally around, want, suffering and all the horrors of poverty gathering on every side, gnawing ceaselessly at the very vitals of the inner life and making death at one's own hand the one welcome relief from despair. It is a situation to be met with only in the life of a great cosmopolitan city.

For a moment (and perhaps it is the only instance in all his life) this man of singular experiences knew the keenest pangs of despair, became pensive and introspective and indulged a momentary meditation upon the vanity and mutability of human affairs. But it was only for a moment. His is not a spirit to sit down and acknowledge irretrievable failure. *Nil desperandum!* "Never say die!" is his motto and it is one to which he is eminently entitled. As he sat overlooking the street of world-wide fame and gazed down upon its hurrying throng, of which but yesterday he was one, half dreaming what to do, the pangs of failure piercing him, the spectre of want glaring at him, suddenly, as if himself unconscious of his words, he blurted out,—" *Wall Street has ruined me, and Wall Street shall pay for it!*" At the time, the words seemed the weak ravings of a mind in despair—a vain boast that might well provoke a smile. But that the threat of vengeance has been well redeemed Wall Street bitterly knows and will not soon forget. Jena was not more thoroughly avenged at Sedan, the mortification of Berlin not more thoroughly atoned by Bismarck and the troops of Fatherland marching in triumph through the gates of Paris. Nor rests Wall Street in a feeling of assurance that the thirst for revenge is even yet fully sated. At the moment of uttering these words he of course had as little idea as any one *how* they were to be made good. He had not the most remote conception of any plan for recuperating his broken fortune but, genius-like, confidence of a power within him to do it, though vague, was there. The threat was hardly cold upon his lips ere he bade adieu—" for ·a season "—to the threatened street, packed a carpet bag, which sufficed his purpose now, and started for Boston, aimless except to get away from the scene of his disaster.

On this journey to " the Hub " the victim of Wall Street did not sit in moody silence moaning to himself over his bleeding wounds but presented an unruffled surface as though everything was all right, mingled in conversation with his usual spirits and puns, and made

chance acquaintances as every one does when travelling
Among those with whom he thus got to talking was a
young man who seemed sorely troubled and dejected.
Perhaps it was animal magnetism that drew the two together, for however calm the surface with the late operator in stocks he was probably somewhat bilious down in
the depths. The two spirits naturally waxed communi-
cative, and soon the young stranger told his story. He
proved to be one of the quite numerous class of pitiable
mortals that nearly everybody has seen something of—a
man laboring in distress with the elephant of a patent
on his hands and brain. He had invented it, got it
patented, and spent all his own means and as much
more as he could borrow, endeavoring to get it before
the public and reap the fortune he had dreamed
would surely flow to him from it. He, too, was going
back to his home, dejected and crest-fallen, for his
enterprise had been ill-starred, his exertions and expenditures had all been in vain, and the dreams that
had sustained and lured him on so long had now all van-
ished, and he must carry disappointment to those who
had helped him. Like all men with patents, he was
ready and eager to explain its great merits and value and
talk about it and nothing else as long as any one would
listen. He explained its nature and utility to his fellow
miserable, who listened attentively, at first because he
was quite as eager to forget his own sorrows as the young
patentee was to expatiate upon his, but very soon because

a sudden ray of light beamed upon his vision. Mr. Fisk saw at once that tho patent was of valuo and that the young man's dreams of tho fortuno thero was in it had been far from bascless; but, strango to say, ho did not give his now acquaintanco the consolation of suspecting this new-born conviction. However, ho induced tho dojected spirit to go on to Boston instead of stopping at homo, philanthropically encouraging him to hopo that they might possibly pick up somo greenhorn thero who could bo wheedled into giving a littlo somothing for it, and whatever ho could get now would be so much cloar gain of courso, as ho was going homo to throw it up entirely. Arrived at their journey's end, the young man gladly disposed of his patent-right for a comparative triflo and went homo somowhat less heavy hearted. The purchaser that had been wheedlod into buying it was not, however, so much of a greenhorn as might be. Fisk nudged tho young inventor in tho ribs and chuckled with him over tho sharp manner in which they had duped somo unwary wight and when he had got him to feeling niccly ho loft him and hurried away to reap tho benefit of tho largo interest which ho had taken good earo to securo to himself. Tho patent was a small improvement of great utility and extensivo application in machinery used in cotton and woolen mills, proved to bo of immenso practical and pecuniary valuo, and brought tho now owners a handsomo incomo.

The downward tide in Mr. Fisk's fortunes was stemmed.

Confidence and courage were replenished, and with the possession once more of capital sufficient for quite extensive operations on a margin, his longing turned to Wall Street again. But before starting back he learned that some parties in Boston were desirous of buying the Bristol line of steamers running on Long Island Sound. It occurred to him that he might turn this circumstance to some account for himself and this was the pretext of his next visit to New York. His first business was to secure a letter of introduction to the president of the company owning the coveted line of steamers. This he readily procured and presented. The person to whom he was thus introduced was the celebrated Daniel Drew. But for this meeting the world would probably never have heard of James Fisk, Jr. That event constitutes the most prominent and important landmark in his life and turned his career into the course that has conducted him to his present position. The presidency of the Bristol Line Steamboat Company was but one small bob on the Drew kite. Already past his three score and ten, he wore the scars of many fierce battles, some of which were still fresh and scarcely cicatrized. Born a farmer's boy, at Carmel, on the Harlem road, he had been successively a drover, proprietor of the Bull's Head Tavern (of great fame in the olden time), and a large owner in steamship enterprises. In this last character he came into contact with Vanderbilt and the two had since been life-long rivals. He had been the Commodore's great antagonist in the then recent Harlem "corners"—the pioneer *coups-de-main* in Wall Street stock jobbing operations, and in these had been badly worsted by his veteran foe. He was now the great Mogul of Erie—one of its directors, its treasurer, its sole manipulator, the first to use his position to gamble in the stock of his own corporation, already dubbed the "speculative director," and the acknowledged leader of Wall Street's "bear" brigade. Drew was much pleased with his new acquaintance, was quite surprised and fascinated with the grand and liberal ideas which the young man very freely ventilated on the question of steamships and affairs generally, and immediately authorized him to act as his agent in negotiating the sale of the Bristol steamers. This trust was executed in a manner that confirmed and heightened the old gentleman's first impressions and gave him entire satisfaction at the same time that it put a nice little sum into the skillful agent's pocket as his commission for conducting the transfer.

Mr. Fisk now looked upon Wall Street as his headquarters again, but as he had learned that the game there was played with stacked cards and loaded dice he sagely concluded it would be much safer to have a finger in the stacking business or be privy to its manner, and make himself master of the magic cubes, instead of having them played on him again. He is not to be caught twice in the same trap. He had seen those "twenty-four jacks" fall out of Ah Sin's sleeves in their first hand of euchre and he was not going to sit down to the game again till he had a pair of sleeves just like Ah Sin's—only a little larger—and they should be well filled with right bowers. Drew, in the first flush of his admiration for the young man's bearing, spoke the necessary words of encouragement, and shortly after the sign of a new firm of brokers appeared bearing the firm name of Fisk & Belden. They made a specialty of dealing in Erie and soon became known among the fraternity as Drew's brokers. The head of the firm being a special favorite, confidant and *protégé* of the crafty director and treasurer, it is more than probable that he was privy to sufficient information and "points" not for general use, to enable him to operate on his own account with all desired safety and make much more than a simple commission as broker for others. It was in the spring of 1866 that Drew executed his first great master-stroke in bear operations, inaugurating a system of manipulations wholly original and unparalelled, making the entire bull clique writhe under his goad, and finally strewing the pavement with their skulls and bones, establishing for himself an enduring fame in the history and traditions of Wall Street. Fisk, being fully behind the scenes in this campaign, enjoyed the sport immensely and turned his opportunity to much substantial account. He was immoderately amused at the mad boundings and bellowings of the rampant animals, shook a red flag before them to incite them on and cried "*Habet! habet!*" in delight as his uncle Daniel poured in the final broadside and sent them reeling to the ground. This was an excellent school for the apt pupil. He took to its ways with a readiness that showed a genius for the science. The briefest period of tuition sufficed to make him master of its entire curriculum. All the scales having now fallen from his eyes, he resisted a longer pupilage and came forward at once as a professor. Having caught the principle and spirit of the process by which puppets were made to dance on the Wall Street stage, he immediately saw that many improvements could be made in the *modus operandi* of his instructor and felt he could play upon the magic keys much more deftly than he saw it done by the fingers clumsy in size and stiffened by the toils and chills of more than three score and ten winters. His subsequent career speaks for the close attention he paid during his brief term of schooling, and no one can testify better than the teacher how thoroughly the lesson was learned both in letter and spirit, for the pupil soon repaid the debt of gratitude, principal and interest, to his instructor by teaching him in turn many tricks at his own trade. But the improvements were of a nature requiring a cunning of hand which the veteran director could not hope to conjure in his weight of years, and it is more than doubtful if the instructor feels at all proud of his pupil, accurately as he has followed instructions and brilliant as his exploits flowing therefrom have been, for the teachings were returned in a practical way that was not highly appreciated, though its force was acknowledged. When the pupil had once seen how the cards were stacked he brought to the work such rare manual skill that he stacked them under his instructor's very eyes without his seeing it and played them upon him before he was aware of it. After this had been repeated a few times, the old gentleman rose from the table, offended at this disrespect for his years and refused to play any more. He now stands a looker on at the table at which he was once master and, with hands folded behind him, he gazes with an expression of mute curiosity at the grace and dexterity with which his pupil shuffles the cards and throws the dice.

With wind and tide both in his favor, Mr. Fisk very soon recovered what he had involuntarily lent to Wall Street, and it was but a few months before the man who had lost his last dollar again had a bank account of over a million.

CHAPTER IV.

"SHORT AND LONG"—"BULLS AND BEARS"—"OPTION"—
"CORNER"—"MARGIN"—"CARRYING"—GOLD EXCHANGE
BANK—THE GOLD ROOM.

Wall Street has a dialect peculiar to itself, concise and expressive, but utterly unintelligible to the uninitiated. Some of the terms are quite familiar to many who yet have but a vague idea of their exact meaning. As an accurate understanding of the terms employed and some of the machinery used by brokers will be necessary to an intelligent reading of some of the following chapters, a brief elucidation may not be unwelcome to some into whose hands these pages may fall.

Suppose the stock of a certain railroad is selling to-day at $90 a share. A, for reasons known to himself, thinks the price is going to fall soon. He meets B who thinks, on the contrary, that the price is going up. A owns none of the stock at present, but he agrees to deliver B 100 shares at 90 sometime within 10, 20, 30 or 60 days. A has now gone "short" of the stock, *i. e.*, he is under obligation to deliver at a future day, and for a fixed price, stock that he does not now possess; and B has gone "long," *i. e.*, he is under obligation to take the stock at a future day at a price already agreed upon. The two terms are correlative, the one always implying the other, it being impossible for one man to go "short" till he meets another who will go "long."

Of course A's design is to wait till the stock has fallen, say to 85, then buy a hundred shares at that price, carry them to B and make him take them as agreed upon at 90, and clear $500 by the operation. B's design is to wait till the stock has risen, say to 95, then call on A to deliver the 100 shares at 90, as agreed upon, sell them at 95 and clear $500 dollars by the operation. The essence of the whole matter is, A bets the stock will fall and B bets it will rise, the amount of the bet being left to be determined by the amount of fluctuation in the stated time. And as a matter of fact it often, if not generally, happens that none of the stock is ever bought at all, but one simply pays to the other the difference in price at the two dates. Thus if the stock falls, A does not buy 100 shares, pay $8,500 therefor, take them to B and get $9,000 for them, but B simply pays A $500, the sum he would make by the operation—what has turned out to be the amount of the bet. As B entered into the contract only on speculation and not because he wanted to keep the stock as an investment, he would only have to sell it again at the lower rate, and all this useless trouble of two actual purchases, transfers and deliveries is avoided and the same result attained by simply paying A the amount he would make.

When such an agreement has been entered into, of course it is for A's interest that there should be a fall in the stock of which he is short, for the greater the fall the greater will be his profit, and therefore he, now exerts himself to make it fall. Ho represents the stock as a bad one to invest in; hints that there is going to be an opposition road built, so the stock will soon pay smaller dividends or no dividends, and greatly decrease in value; that the road is being badly managed, its officers are dishonest, using it for their own personal ends, and there is danger of its becoming bankrupt; or that there has been an issue of new stock, etc., etc. Those who hear and believe these rumors naturally become afraid of the stock, are anxious to sell it if they own any, and unwilling to buy. It thus becomes plenty in the market, is depressed and falls. A in such a case is said to "bear" the stock or be a "bear." It being for B's interest that the stock should rise, he sets to work circulating rumors of just the opposite nature and influence, endeavoring to make the stock attractive and in great demand. He is then said to "bull" the market or be a "bull." Therefore a man who has gone "short" is naturally by interest a "bear" and a man who has gone "long" is naturally by interest a "bull."

When A and B have made an agreement as supposed it often makes a great difference which one of them has

the right of demanding its fulfilment any day within the
limit. For if A agrees to deliver the stock within 30
days and it should fall rapidly in the first five days and
get as low as he thinks it will go, he will buy at this low
price and, if he has the right of choosing the day for carrying out the agreement, he will force B to take it the day
on which it is lowest; whereas, if B has the right of
choosing the day, he will wait in the hope that the stock
will rise again during the remaining 25 days and will
call on A to deliver on the day when it is selling highest.
The transaction *must* be closed on the last day of the
limit. This right of choosing the day is called the
"option." It is always settled at the time of making the
agreement who has the "option" and it often makes a
great difference in the price whether the buyer gives or
takes it. Of course A can buy when the stock is low,
though the option is against him, and hold the stock till
B calls for it. In such a case he is said to "cover his
shorts."

As a man who sells short has none of the stock at the
time of contracting for its future delivery, it is easily
possible that contracts may be entered into for the delivery of a greater number of shares than can possibly be
had, or even than there are in existence. A shrewd
operator may easily find a hundred men each of whom
will go short a thousand shares; he makes a contract
with each without any of the others suspecting it and he
will thus have contracts out for the delivery to him of

100,000 shares of the stock within 30 days when, it may be, there are but 50,000 shares in existence. He now buys up the stock as quietly as possible at the present low price and before any of the shorts are covered or any one suspects what is going on, he may have the whole 50,000 shares locked up in his own safe. Men suddenly find that not a single share of the stock is to be had in the market at any price and yet contracts are out for the delivery of 100,000 shares. The operator now has the shorts in what is called a "corner." They must satisfy their contracts or fail. Stock cannot be had to fulfill the agreements, therefore they must make the best terms they can to be let off from their contracts. They are wholly in the operator's power and his demands will be limited only by what he deems the utmost each can pay without failing.

The capital required in manipulating such a plot being very large, there are but few single individuals of sufficient means to manage a "corner" operation alone, but combinations of several men are often formed for the purpose, each contributing his means to a general fund to be used in the operation and sharing a proportionate part of the proceeds. Such a combination is called a "pool."

When a man directs a broker to buy stock for him he does not supply the broker with money to the full value of the stock, but only a certain per cent. thereon—5, 10 or 20 per cent., as the case may be—so much as is deemed sufficient to cover any probable fall in the price. The *per cent.* thus deposited with the broker is called a "margin," it being the range or margin over which the price may fluctuate without risk to the broker. The rest of the money or credit needed is furnished by the broker, who charges interest thereon, keeps the stock in his own hands as security and is said to "carry" it for his customer. By this means a man with only five or ten thousand dollars can operate with a capital of a hundred thousand, and a man with a hundred thousand dollars can operate with a capital of two millions. Herein lies the great temptation to indulge in such speculations and the whole secret of the great power which a few men, or even a single man, can exert in such matters.

An active broker often buys or sells the same stock or gold several times the same day. One customer directs him to buy and he buys; another directs him to sell and he sells. If a stock rises rapidly the customer who buys early in the morning may sell again in an hour or less; if it falls rapidly the man who sells in the morning may buy again in a few minutes. Fluctuations in the price are often so rapid that a man may buy and sell the same hundred shares of stock or the same lot of gold half a dozen times in as many hours, making a handsome profit at every turn. This would make a great deal of work and require many clerks in a broker's office if there was an actual transfer of the stock and gold in every transaction. To simplify and facilitate this work, an institution to which all brokers belong has been established to manago this part of the business and superintend all the actual transfers of property. As soon as a broker buys, he sends a notice of the transaction to this institution. Five minutes after, he sells either the same or another stock or lot of gold and immediately sends the institution a notice of this transaction. And so on through the whole day till a quarter past two o'clock, when transactions through the institution close for the day. A statement of all the purchases and sales of the day is now made out and balanced and handed in to the institution. If the amount of the purchases exceeds the amount of the sales, the broker pays the institution the difference; if the sales exceed the purchases in amount, the institution pays the broker the difference; if the two are just equal, all his transactions for the day, amounting, it may be, to many millions, are completed by simply balancing the two sides of the account and without one cent having been used by him in the operation. By this means the same stock or gold may be sold a hundred times during the day and yet there will be only one actual transfer of it. A starts the transactions, selling to B; B sells to C, C to D, and so on through the whole alphabet till the close of the day; then A, the first seller, hands it into the institution and Z, the last purchaser, draws it out. All the others have both bought and sold it, therefore it is only necessary for them to balance their accounts and settle the *difference*.

This arrangement, which renders neccessary capital

equal only to the difference in the two sides of all the accounts for the day, supplements the "margin" and is to the broker what the "margin" is to the operator. The two form a system of compound leverage by which a hundred dollars is made to move a million, or any amount, the principle being the same as that which justified the boast of Archimedes that he would move the world if any one would give him a place to stand on. It was by this system of paying only the balance of their accounts that it was possible for the dealings of the gold brokers to amount to five hundred millions of dollars on Black Friday when there was not in reality twenty millions of gold among all the brokers in New York.

The stock and gold brokers have separate clearing houses or institutions for effecting their clearances, i. e., superintending the transfer and settlement of the balances. That of the stock brokers is called the New York Stock Exchange, and that of the gold brokers the Gold Exchange Bank.

It is important to note that the dealings of the brokers are so interlaced, as they appear at the clearances, that if any one firm fails to hand in a statement of its transactions the whole machinery may be clogged up and the clearing house unable to proceed with its work. The following is an actual statement of the transactions of the firm of Smith, Gould (Jay Gould) & Martin on Black Friday:

Received from—		Delivered to—	
Wm. Heath & Co.	$6,210,000	Lockwood & Co. .	$10,000
White, Morris & Co. .	400,000	Stout Thayer .	20,000
Dakin Gillespie .	984,000	Dzondi, Springer & Co.	50,000
E. K. Willard .	5,845,000	Carver & Co. .	430,000
Hodgskin, Randall & Co.	50,000	Gibson & Beadleston .	75,000
Budge, Schiff & Co. .	300,000	B. K. Stevens, Jr., .	25,000
Cushman & Hurlburt .	50,000	Lounsberry & Fanshaw	1,700,000
S. R. Jacobs .	100,000	Fanshaw & Milliken .	300,000
Lange, Bolle & Anning	50,000	Hallgarten & Co. .	35,000
Dean, Maginnis & Co.	95,000	Kamlah, Sauer & Co.	134,000
M. Morgan's Sons .	20,000	Parker, Bros. & Geston	15,000
Foster & Randall .	20,000	Fellows & Co. .	15,000
J. W. Seligman & Co.	225,000	Cunningham & Mead.	85,000
Hallgarten & Co .	200,000	Maxwell & Graves .	30,000
Domett & Nichols .	10,000	Norton, Haughton & Co.	50,000
B. Hall & Young .	500,000	Tansing, Fisher & Co. .	90,000
G. H. & H. Redmond	875,000	N. R. Travers .	50,000
W. C. Mumford .	50,000	Grey, Prince & Co. .	1,245,000
Meyer & Grevo .	200,000	Chapin, Bowen & Day	2,915,000
Kennedy & Hutchinson	100,000	Wm. Heath & Co. .	200,000
Robinson, Cox & Co .	30,000	Cushman & Hurlburt.	25,000
Lees & Waller .	200,000		
Reed, Leo & Content .	1,015,000		$7,499,000
Hagen & Billing .	200,000	Coin due dealer	13,151,000
E. H. Biedermean .	445,000		
G. P. Persch .	735,000		$20,650,000
Robert Wallor .	655,000		
Stout Thayer .	90,000		
	$20,650,000		

Here were fifty-one different transactions by one firm in a single day, amounting to $28,149,000 and they were all adjusted, so far as this firm was concerned, by the single act of drawing from the bank $13,151,000 in gold and handing in a check for the currency value thereof. Now if (as actually happened) this firm failed to hand in this statement the clearing house would be unable to adjust the accounts of any one of the nearly fifty firms appearing therein, and as each of these firms would have transactions with many others, the whole machinery of settling must come to a standstill till the statement of every one is in.

For its services in effecting these clearances the Gold Exchange Bank receives ten cents for every $10,000 cleared. This may seem a ridiculously small commission at first, but when it appears that the average annual amount of clearances has been about $20,000,000,000 and that even at this small commission the bank has received in the neighborhood of $200,000 annually for its services, the remuneration does not seem quite so ridiculously small.

The Gold Room is the place where the gold brokers meet at certain hours of the day to buy and sell, the price then paid being officially recorded and forming the "quotations" for the day. It is a dingy, dismal room of moderate size, entered from New Street by narrow, untidy wooden stairs and quite disappoints the expectations naturally formed from the fame of its doings. On one side is a large clock, over which is the indicator showing, in large figures moved by telegraphic wires, the price at which gold is selling. On the opposite side is a gallery for spectators and such as have not the counter-sign that secures admission within the exclusive circle.

The body of the floor is an amphitheatre, *i. e.*, in the form of a circle and descending gradually by steps from the outside towards the centre. A circle in the centre, about eight feet in diameter, is surrounded by a strong iron railing enclosing a fountain. The design of this ornament is quite unique, being a bronze statuette standing upon huge oyster shells and hugging a dolphin to its breast; a jet of water constantly spouts from the dolphin's mouth, falls back upon the bronze and babbles down into the reservoir at the base—the whole constituting a forcible and fitting satire upon the life and doings of the men who daily crowd around it and deport themselves in a manner vividly suggestive of Babel, Bedlam and pandemonium united.

It was this small circular pit that constituted the most sensitive pulse of the nation during the trying days of the rebellion. It was here that the news of Bull Run and the Chickahominy, Gettysburg and the Wilderness, was most quickly felt. At this point was dropped the pebbles that started the magic waves which broke only on the limits of the nation. It was the yells of the men surging within this circle, shouting and gesticulating like maniacs, that determined the figures so eagerly scanned from each morning's news as it reached the remotest hamlet. Here still these men keep up a fitful losing battle to prolong their calling, though the circumstances that gave it being and some small elements of usefulness have long since passed away.

CHAPTER V.

Mr. Fisk first became officially connected with the Erie Railway on the 8th of October, 1867, being chosen a director at the annual election held on that day. The campaign for this election opened with three parties in the field. The officers in control of the road, headed by Drew, sought reëlection. With this party Mr. Fisk was identified. Next came Vanderbilt, who, having made himself absolute and undisputed master of the Harlem, Hudson River and N. Y. Central roads, now sought to grasp control of Erie in like manner, that he might have despotic sway over all the roads connecting New York with the great lakes and make himself practical dictator of the material interests of the commercial metropolis. The third party was headed by John S. Eldridge and composed of men largely interested in the Boston, Hartford & Erie road—a line running from Boston through Connecticut and New York to Fishkill, where it meets a branch of Erie. This corporation was in a desperate struggle for existence and was in bad financial odor. The Massachusetts Legislature had voted to assist the company to the sum of $3,000,000 provided it would raise an additional sum of $4,000,000 elsewhere. The laudable purpose of this third party was to gain a controlling voice in the Erie councils in order to get this corporation to assist them to the much-desired $4,000,000. Under the Eldridge banner Jay Gould was training.

At these elections each share of stock entitles the holder to one vote, consequently a party must control a majority of the stock in order to carry the election. With three parties competing for possession, there was a fine prospect of a rapid and extraordinary rise in the stock, promising a lively time and a rich harvest for the brokers, operators, and owners of Erie. But before the contending chiefs had marshalled their forces and mounted their heavy guns for this great triangular battle, the Eldridge party resorted to diplomacy and secured a coalition with Vanderbilt. These two factions agreed to unite their forces in ousting Drew and electing a board of directors that would manage the road so as to secure both their interests. They knew that their united power made their victory certain in a square fight; but they also knew very well that it would not be a square fight if Drew was left with his peculiar fertility of resource untrammelled. They remembered the ingenious device by which he had supplied himself with 58,000 shares of Erie stock to meet an emergency the year before and they knew the same convenient machinery would be made to do service again and grind out any desired number of shares at the proper crisis and thus, after relieving them of several millions of their money, rob them of victory at the last moment. To guard against this favorite species of Drew tactics they resolved to invoke the majesty of the law. The necessary preliminary affidavits and papers were made out preparatory to obtaining an injunction that should effectively prevent Drew from using at the election or in the market a single share of stock beyond the already authorized capital stock of the company.

In this position stood matters the Sunday before the election. On that day Drew, as if troubled with premonitions of approaching discomfiture, called upon Vanderbilt at his residence. The Commodore kindly entertained his caller by relating to him the arrangements made to compass his overthrow and complacently read for his edification the legal documents that were to be used for his special behoof the next morning. Drew seeing at once that the elements were getting too strong for him and that he was doomed to take an unwilling leave of the helm whereat he had stood for ten years and retire to the quiet life of his native Carmel unless he could effect some compromise, and being ever ready to do anything to save and serve himself, immediately proposed to change front entirely, abandon his chronic antagonism and bear operations, unite in a movement for running Erie up as Harlem, Hudson River and Central had been run up before, become the sworn ally of his life-long rival and serve him in all his schemes, on the sole condition of being permitted to retain his position as director and treasurer of Erie. The Commodore was entirely disarmed by this unexpected tender of the olive branch. He saw this would relieve many millions of dollars that else must be used in getting and keeping control of Erie and he knew that no other ally could serve him so well. Besides, there may have been a touch of the poetic in feeling reconciled to a foe after long years of warfare and mutual scars, and a natural affinity and preference for an ally as venerable as himself in years. At any rate, without the slightest regard for the agreement made with the Eldridge party, he accepted the proposition at once, and these two inveterate enemies, on the eve of another fierce conflict, struck hands over the altar of friendship, buried the past and coalesced to serve each other, unmindful of pledges recently made, reckless of the interests of great corporations entrusted to their care, indifferent to the rights of the (to them) somewhat vague and mythical entity, the public. Beautiful is it to witness in declining years such reconciliations of the feuds of a long life! But the Eldridge party were so singularly lacking in appreciation and love for the poetic that they were actually displeased and disposed to be indignant at being thus slighted and shook their heads at the affecting *tableau* much as the evil one is said to do at the sight of holy water. They called upon Vanderbilt soon after Drew had taken his leave, and when he informed them that he had changed his plan and decided upon a course looking to the continuance in power of the very man whose removal had formed the keystone of their union, they were utterly astounded, shouted for the agreement as Shylock for his bond, and signified their intention of taking a very bellicose attitude in case of any bad faith with them. Their suave host mildly proposed an adjournment of the interview to the residence of Mr. Drew. This was agreed upon, and a few hours later in the evening these devout spirits met for their third Sabbath-day services. The Eldridge faction still wearing a very bellicose and uncompromising visage, Vanderbilt coolly proceeded in their very presence to talk with Drew upon the course to be pursued to secure the utter defeat of the presuming youths and shut them out of all power and influence in the control of the road. The Bostonians well knew that these two powerful veterans working together could have things entirely their own way without the slightest difficulty, and finding that they were only derisively laughed at when they suggested that agreements and promises were of any binding force in such matters, and that they must make a new tack or be

DANIEL DREW.

swamped, they speedily dismounted from their high horse, adopted that discretion which is the better part of valor, resorted to diplomacy once more, and manœuvred for a fusion and harmonizing of all opposing interests and purposes. The council was prolonged far into the night and finally resulted in a proclamation of universal amnesty and impartial suffrage to a degree of perfection that should satisfy even Horace Greeley. When the meeting broke up and the parties emerged from the mansion of the "speculative director" in the gray dawn of the morning, all was peace. The rumble of cannon, yesterday moving into position for a fierce triangular battle had, died away in the harmony of a magnanimous tripartite alliance. Once in a compromising mood, it had been found quite feasible to arrange for a mutual grinding of all their little axes and let Wall Street, the public and the Erie Railway bleed for all three parties instead of one. Drew was to be continued in his position and Eldridge was to go into the direction and become its president; the road was to be run in league and fraternity with the Vanderbilt roads and in accordance with his wishes, and give him the monopoly he desired over New York; the corporation was to provide the Boston, Hartford & Erie Company (of which Mr. Eldridge was also president) with the much desired $4,000,000; there was to be a grand combination to run up the price of Erie stock; and Drew was to be the great factotum of all these little matters, which would enable him to add to his millions

by judicious use of the power and private information
incident to the position.

This arrangement was eminently satisfactory to all
three of the parties, as well it might be, but the Eldridge
men foresaw that its execution involved one unpleasant circumstance for them. Opposition to Drew had been their
chief stock in trade from the start. They had professed
themselves greatly scandalized at his conduct in abusing
his trust to further his private schemes and speculate in
the stock in contempt of law and directly against the interests of the stockholders. "Down with the speculative
director!" was the motto they had inscribed on their ban-
ner to win favor, and upon this purpose they had based
their special claim to consideration and support. They
had not yet acquired the lofty contempt of their veteran
confederates for the opinion and esteem of both public and
friends provided they carried their point, and therefore
naturally felt a little squeamish at the thought of appearing before their friends with such a sudden abandonment
of the cause they had so loudly championed; their indignation and offended moral sense so inexplicably collapsed,
and advocating the reëlection of the man whom they had
so unsparingly denounced as unfit to be continued in
power. They dreaded the reproach of bad faith and
treachery which they felt would be deservedly charged
upon them by their friends and followers. Out of regard
to this mawkish sensibility it was arranged that a ticket
with Drew's name left off should be made up and elected;

but one of the men on the ticket should be an obliging man of straw who would kindly resign immediately after election, and then the remaining directors, in virtue of the power given them to fill any vacancy in their board, would choose Drew to fill the place resigned by the *locum tenens.* This would save appearances for the sensitive spirits and raise a dust that would conceal their "job" from the eyes of their friends till it was forgotten. By a most fortunate chance, too, this piece of strategy would have an incidental consequence not to be despised or neglected. These contradictory actions would produce violent fluctuations in the stock on election day, which those behind the scenes would know how to turn to good account. With all matters thus nicely cut and dried, the protracted meeting in the house of the distinguished Methodist broke up and this Gideon's Band came forth from the mansion of peace with serene countenances.

The first act in the programme thus settled upon was faithfully carried out. The election came off and the news reaching Wall Street that the great leader of the bears had been defeated and driven out of his fort, spread a panic among his followers and Erie bounded upward. Two hours later came the news that Mr. Underwood had resigned his place as director and that Drew had been chosen to fill the vacancy and was reinstated in his old place. This acted like magic on the bear brigade, which instantly became ascendant again, and Erie fell as quickly as it had risen. There was a difference of $8\frac{1}{2}$ per cent. in the extreme prices of the day, a fluctuation sufficiently large to yield a rich profit to those who knew beforehand how the wires were to be operated and thus were enabled to reap two harvests in a single day.

The strange course of things on election day puzzled and confused operators and brokers utterly, but the mysterious movement was soon forgotten in the sweeping tide of Wall Street and Erie settled down for a calm of a few weeks, remaining quite steady at about 70.

Among the new directors chosen at this election were Jay Gould and James Fisk, Jr., who met for the first time at the preliminary meeting of the new board. Mr. Fisk says the date of this election is well fixed in his memory, because it constitutes an "episode" in his life. He dates his grey hairs from that day, and says he saw more robbery during the next year than he had ever seen before in his whole life—a statement that will receive ready credence. But it is amusing to note that this date which is so indelibly marked in his memory he testified to be the 13th of October when it was in reality the 8th. He has also said he had not been in office fifteen minutes before he made up his mind there was going to be trouble.

The first act of the programme had been successfully performed and it was now time for the next. In pursuance of the agreement to run the stock up, a large "pool" was formed the last of November or early part of December and Drew was left in charge of the fund to engineer the movement. Besides their contributions to the pool many of the confederates made large purchases on their own private accounts, looking to a rapid rise. The prices did not make rapid leaps upward at once but fluctuated two or three per cent. "forward and back" rather mysteriously for four or five weeks. The members of the pool who had made outside investments being surprised that the stock fell back heavily after each advance instead of rising uniformly and rapidly as anticipated, applied to Drew for information and advice; but he, in his childlike innocence and simplicity, seemed more confused and puzzled than any of the rest and utterly at a loss to account for the strange manner in which their stock acted, yet felt sure it would soon move regularly under their purchases. With this assurance from their sagacious chief they made still further private purchases, some of them even borrowing some of the pool money from Drew to put up as a margin and in addition went "long" extensively. They were confident the looked-for bound upward must come soon, began to count the hours ere their fortunes would be reckoned in millions, and were already forming many little plans and dreams to be executed when they came in possession.. They continued their purchases while the stock rose four, five or six per cent. and then, to their utter amazement, it dropped heavily back to the starting point and was plenty to all purchases. They now became alarmed, for their "long" contracts were near maturity and but a few days remained in which to reap the golden harvest they had deemed as good as secured.

Tho day on which this decline occurred was one of those days at the close of which operators and brokers are too excited and anxious to go home. In the evening, the Fifth Avenue Hotel presented the appearance of an adjourned meeting of the Stock Exchange, the main halls, corridors and public rooms being thronged with the *habitués* of Wall Street, all excited and utterly confounded over the course of Erie that day. Standing by the grand staircase was an old gentleman with a peculiarly wrinkled face and brow, with an expression of the most artless simplicity upon his countenance as he surveyed the scene around him and watched the writhings of the bulls with mute curiosity, utterly unable to comprehend the meaning of the situation. A prominent broker approached him and said,—"Well, Mr. Drew, is Erie going to fall?" "Other folks think so, but I can't give you no 'pints' in it," was the reply of the old gentleman of childlike innocence and he continued his disinterested survey of the scene.

Renewed applications of the members of the pool to Mr. Drew for light on tho subject were like efforts to get blood out of a turnip, so blissfully ignorant was he and so sphinx-like were his responses. They then commenced making investigations through their brokers, endeavoring to trace the stock furnished them to tho source of supply. Their efforts had not been exerted long in this direction when they were suddenly stricken with horror—tho most sickening of gorgon horrors. Their blood was chilled, cold perspiration gathered on their brows and a tremor ran through their very bones. *Nearly every share of stock they had bought had been supplied by Drew himself!* through his various brokers. The truth dawned upon them. They had been betrayed and sold out by their own leader, and must lose thousands where they had counted upon making hundreds of thousands. Who could have dreamt of such duplicity and treachery? Who could have believed that the man who was wholly indebted to the pool for a recent new lease of power, who had been able to make terms only by promising to join efforts with the pool and work for its aim, who had been entrusted by the pool with the pool fund to manage their "bull" movement, who had been confided in by members of the pool for advice, and who had kindly loaned them some of the pool money to operate with privately—who could have believed that *this* man would deceive and dupe them? victimize them so treacherously while acting as their trusted ally and chief? That was what Daniel Drew had done. He had played the bear and duped his most intimate associates so long that the disease was chronic, a "second nature" with him, and the weak nerves of the poor old man could no more resist the temptation of such an unprecedented opportunity for duping a fine lot of confederates, playing such a comical trick upon the trust reposed in him and acting his normal character of bear despite all pledges and obligations, than water can help running down hill or sparks can resist flying upward. When Erie was low he laid in a large stock. When it rose he kindly furnished his friends with money to buy with and then, one good turn deserving another, he had kindly supplied stock for them to buy. He loaded the market till the price fell and then he bought again, sending the market up, when once more his friends borrowed money of him to buy his own stock. And thus while Erie had acted in a manner that puzzled and surprised not only the general dealers but even those who thought they knew all about it, the wily old man had been manipulating these moderate turns, duping his friends and making large profits for the pool in general and himself in particular.

As soon as these facts became known, a meeting of the pool was held at which the comical Drew coolly and and soothingly announced that the pool had made a handsome sum and proceeded to divide the spoil. The grim humor of this situation has but few parallels and will be fully appreciated by all the world now, though the humorous side of it was not at the time at all apparent to the members of the pool, except, perhaps, Fisk and Gould. These gentlemen have a very lively sense of the humorous, and as they were too sharp to get caught, and probably even profited by the proceeding, it is more than likely that they appreciated the position in all its phases.

The wrath of Vanderbilt knew no bounds and was something inspiring to behold, like the fury of a mighty storm. It was not that he had been duped. It was not at Drew's ingratitude and duplicity. It was not that his friends had been victimised, pledges broken and his aims momentarily thwarted. It was at himself for allowing it to be possible to be caught at all, for putting himself in the power of any man, for falling so unsuspectingly and unguardedly into the trap of his inveterate foe. His motto is, "Never put it in any man's power to ruin you." He was not ruined nor seriously harmed, but he had infringed the rule of his life and been caught napping for once by his enemy under the most irritating circumstances. Drew chuckled, looked innocent as a babe and felt many an old score wiped out. Fisk and Gould chuckled, thought it a huge joke and carefully treasured the moral thereof.

Vanderbilt was now determined that Erie should come under his power,—absolutely and beyond the will of any man or body of men to say him nay. He first submitted to the directors certain propositions expressing his desire as to the management of the road, and the rejection of these by the board showing him that he was not supreme ruler but had been duped all round, he drew himself up in all the majesty of his mighty power and resolved to make Erie his by main force, as he had done with the others. A new pool was immediately formed to do what the first one had failed to do. For reasons not necessary to mention, Daniel Drew was not a member of this pool. Jay Gould, however, was. All these scenes changed rapidly, noiselessly, and by unseen forces, and Erie had scarcely fallen back under Drew's last unloading upon his friends when it wheeled and shot up from 70 to 80 under the inspiration of the new combination and Vanderbilt's roused will so suddenly as to puzzle and confound brokers more than ever by the queer, unexpected and inexplicable movement. Drew, now left out in the cold, was sad visaged, the picture of childlike innocence and simplicity, and despondent, as usual, but—also as usual—he boldly sold short of Erie despite the upward bound, despite the combination which he knew had been formed against him, despite the bitter experience he had had in going short when Vanderbilt was opposed to him. His course seemed strange, reckless and rushing upon self-destruction, as viewed by the multitude, but the wary Commodore was quick to read its significance and act accordingly.

The law of the State forbade any increase of the capital stock of any railroad by a direct issue of new shares. But

"Danger deviseth shifts : wit waits on fear,"

and Drew's genius had devised a ready and easy way of getting round this little difficulty. The charter of the company does authorize the directors to issue bonds of the corporation for various purposes in the management of the road, and these bonds may be made convertible into capital stock at the option of the holder. The directors were only too glad to issue bonds in any amount whenever they could find any one to take them, and these being immediately converted into shares of capital stock at the demand of the purchaser, Mr. Drew gracefully raised his hat at the cobweb restraint of statutes and proceeded on his course. The principle is quite simple. A step thirty-six inches long being forbidden, the space is divided into two steps of eighteen inches each and trippingly passed.

It was by this simple machinery, then used for the first time, that Mr. Drew provided himself with some 58,000 shares of new Erie stock in the spring of 1866. In that instance, however, it was placed with him only as collateral security for a loan to the corporation, the directors not suspecting it was to be put upon the market. He nevertheless made use of it in his famous bear campaign of that spring and had thereby laid himself liable to legal proceedings and heavy damages. He had been left undisturbed, however, and after having sent the stock down from 95 to 50 under the staggering load of new shares, he bought his collateral back again at the lower figure and held it in reserve for any new emergency.

By a recent statute it was also permitted to a railroad to issue its own bonds in place of those of any road under lease to it. Availing themselves of the door thus conveniently opened, Drew and some of his fellow directors had purchased the Buffalo, Bradford and Pittsburg Railroad. It was a worthless road and was bought for $250,000. Immediately after purchasing it they issued bonds in its name to the amount of $2,000,000, then leased it, thus burdened, to Erie—*i. e.*, in their private capacity they leased it to themselves as directors of Erie— on such favorable terms that they, as individuals, made an annual profit of $140,000 by the transaction. Erie bonds were then issued in place of those of the leased road and immediately converted into stock.

With his 58,000 shares of "collateral" ready to be launched upon the market any instant; with the shares into which the $2,000,000 of bonds of the leased road had been converted, ready for use whenever the market was high enough; and with the simple machinery of the two unlim- ited sources of supply easily put in motion at any moment to turn out any desired amount of stock, well might Mr. Drew recklessly go short in Erie when it stood somewhere above 70, and continue to look despondent, "with a smile that was child-like and bland." However rash and suicidal his course might seem to Wall Street, he innocently felt confident that he could oblige the greedy Commodore with as much Erie as he would take.

Vanderbilt understood perfectly well this blind confi- dence that went short so boldly, unterrified either by his combination, his wrath, or his vast power, and he was not such a chicken as to put his foot in the trap of his enemies again. He bethought himself of maliciously breaking some of the small wheels in Mr. Drew's little machines, clogging them up, throwing them out of gear so they would not work, and absolutely spoiling the poor old man's pet plaything so fondly constructed to amuse himself with in the dull hours. He therefore ordered a halt in the operations of the pool and his brokers till he could cripple the process by which Erie stock might be dumped upon him by the cart-load when he had lifted it to a tempting figure.

It was past the middle of January, 1868, when Drew's treachery leaked out and the pool and Vanderbilt had found themselves sold. Three weeks had passed in the rearrangement of wires, laying new pipes and forming the new battle lines. They had been three weeks of that dark portentous calm that heralds the coming of a mighty storm. On the 17th of February Vanderbilt fired the opening gun. It was an injunction from Judge George G. Barnard, tieing up the 58,000 shares of stock held by Drew as collateral so effectually that they could not be put upon the market. Two days later came a second order from the same judge suspending Drew from the office of treasurer and director and ordering him to appear on the 10th of March and show cause why he should not be permanently removed from the direction of the Erie Railway. Drew was the leading spirit and great arch-enemy and it was felt that with him out of the way and his hands effectually tied, all would be well. The 58,000 shares which he held having been tied up by the injunction of the 17th, he induced the board of directors to pass a resolution to issue $10,000,000 of new bonds to supply various needs of the road. These were of course converted into shares at once, and so for the 58,000 shares which Vanderbilt had tied up 100,000 new shares had been manufactured. This brilliant stroke was achieved on the 19th, before Judge Barnard's order of that date, suspending Drew from office, had been served, and was of course kept a dead secret to all but the directors concerned, no suspicion of it reaching Wall Street or Vanderbilt. Therefore when the second injunction arrived, it was received with a smile more childlike and bland than ever and did not disturb the old gent's nerves in the least. He chuckled and said, "Fire away, with your injunctions, Mr. Barnard! Fire away! An innocent man like me has nothing to fear from the law." Fisk and Gould exchanged winks, chuckled and whispered to each other "What jolly sport to see these old bucks butt heads!"

Of the new shares thus issued, Drew took 50,000 and James Fisk, Jr., 50,000. Drew immediately divided his into small lots, placed them where they could be used at a moment's notice and waited developments. When the two injunctions had been served, Vanderbilt regarded the hands of Drew tied beyond the power of doing further harm and therefore gave orders for the pool and his brokers to move forward in the purchase of Erie. The order was obeyed with alacrity and the great railroad king was fast gaining possession of the coveted power. The stock was very active, the chief feature of the street and the price tended upward. Drew thought it time to pour in his first broadside, send the price down and cover his shorts. February 29th Erie was selling in the morning at 68¾ and the demand for it was strong. Drew gave orders to his brokers, among whom the 50,000 shares had been distributed in small lots, to sell, and the whole load was dumped upon the bulls and eagerly swallowed by them before they were aware of its source. Soon the rumor that there had been a large issue of new stock spread like wildfire, striking terror into the bulls, and in a few minutes Erie reeled and tumbled to 65. A howl of delight went up from the bears and nearly every one was expecting to see it fall to 50, when it as suddenly wheeled again and shot back to 73. Like a great general stemming a panic among his men and turning a rout into victory, Vanderbilt commanded his brokers to stand firm and buy every share of Erie stock offered. Something like $5,000,000 worth of it was loaded upon him that day, but he stood up under it all without the slightest sign of being heavy laden, holding it with ease and even sending the price up! The little bears were all scooped up in his net and the nerves of even their great leader himself were somewhat unsettled by this manifestation of tremendous power and determination. Drew had now flung upon the market all the stock he could command, and yet the price had gone up and left him with large short contracts uncovered. On the 3d of March his nerves received a further shock, for on that day, at the instance of Vanderbilt, Judge Barnard fulminated his third injunction, this time not against Drew alone but against the whole body of Erie directors, peremptorily forbidding their issuing or using any stock of the company in addition to the 251,058 shares outstanding at the last annual report. As 50,000 new shares were already on the market and they had got Vanderbilt's money therefor, they could not restrain a slight smile at the Judge and his patron for this injunction. But Drew could not join in this smile at all. He could think of nothing but "them shorts" and was alarmed lest this last move had placed him in Vanderbilt's power once more. Nor did any of them long indulge in humor over the comical phase of this last move, but they seriously addressed themselves to the problem of breaking the cordon that was gathering around them.

A week wore on. Vanderbilt pushed Erie steadily upward and it now stood at 78. During these days the directors came to the conclusion that "two can play at that game" of injunctions. The 10th was the day on which Drew had got to appear before Judge Barnard and show cause why he should not be turned out of Erie. He knew that the crisis of the whole situation must culminate on that day. But on the morning of the 9th the directors quietly went over to Brooklyn, and upon affidavits stating that a conspiracy had been entered into to injure the Erie Railway and speculate in its stock, and that Judge Barnard himself was interested in it and was using the power of his Court to help it on, an injunction was obtained from Judge Gilbert staying proceedings in all the suits that had been instituted, Judge Barnard being included in the restraint, and ordering the directors to proceed in the management of the road precisely as if no suit had been instituted. This placed matters in a very interesting position. On one hand Judge Barnard had forbidden certain things to be done and therefore if the directors proceeded that functionary would visit them with his mighty vengeance for contempt of his Court; on the other hand was the order of Judge Gilbert directing them to move forward in those same matters, so if they stood still they were equally liable to be punished by him for contempt of his Court. Drew, being a devout Methodist, probably never plays cards and so had most likely never heard of Hoyle's famous maxim, " When you are in doubt, take the trick;" but he had seen quite enough of law in his long life to know that a prisoner is always entitled to the benefit of any doubt, and Judge Barnard was the man the terror of whose process for contempt it was decided to brave. In this position the opposing forces rested on their arms facing each other the last night before the great decisive battle, knowing that on the morrow would come the final crisis of the campaign and that before the sun set again the laurels would be awarded to bull or bear, Vanderbilt or Drew.

It had been a case of "love at sight " between Fisk and Gould. They recognized at once the elements of strength which their union would have and had been putting their heads together through all these months to improve any opportunity that might arise. Gould had retained the confidence of Vanderbilt all this time and he now so far presumed upon this confidence as to suggest to Vanderbilt that as the day was to be one of much excitement in the Courts the bears might take advantage of it to depress Erie and it would therefore be advisable for the Commodore to give his brokers orders to sustain the market. Vanderbilt saw the propriety of the course suggested. Gould then played upon Drew's nerves by ominously hinting that Fisk was acting a little peculiar, might not put his 50,000 shares upon the market after all, and if he did not Vanderbilt would triumph and Erie might go to 200 or higher as Harlem did. This greatly increased the old man's alarm and his weak knees began to tremble badly.

The morning of the 10th dawned. Vanderbilt gave an unlimited order to sustain the market, then standing at 79. Drew scrutinized Fisk's actions and found they did look dubious, as Gould said. He was seized with a fear that he was going to be duped in the house of his friends as he had duped others, and immediately sent orders for his brokers to buy Erie to cover his shorts. This was the moment Fisk was waiting for. His 50,000 shares were immediately distributed among numerous brokers in small lots and orders given to sell when the word came. The stock board met at 10 o'clock, and the street was already tremulous with nervous excitement. The presiding officer commenced calling the list of stocks and all were passed quickly with scarcely any dealings or bids till he called "Erie!" At that word, before it was off his lips, the thickly packed crowd of brokers bounded as if a mine had been sprung beneath them. Their united yells rent the air of the large room as had not been done for many a long day. They shouted till their faces were as red as demons', each trying to make himself heard above the rest, gesticulating frantically to the utmost extent of their physical power. It seemed more like a mad-house filled with raving maniacs suddenly released from constraint than a gathering of rational beings. Erie changed hands by the five and ten thousand shares per moment. The battle raged madly for ten minutes and the stock was going at 80, when the presiding officer announced that dealings in Erie must cease and called the next stock on the list. Instantly the whole body now bolted from the room and poured down the long, large staircase into the street like a wild sweeping torrent, leaving the vice-president to go through the formality of calling the list to the end to an empty room. On the street the battle was continued and raged in still greater disorder, each of Vanderbilt's brokers forming the centre of an eddying circle in the grand whirlpool and quickly catching at all offers to sell, while Drew's men were equally busy and eager covering his shorts. The struggle was kept up with unabated fury till noon when Erie, under the combined purchases of Vanderbilt and Drew, touched 83. Fisk's men now received their word and flung his 50,000 shares. They were snatched up as beggar boys snatch at pennies thrown among them and still ask for more. Still the battle raged on till those who had purchased got a chance to glance at the shares that had been delivered to them. It was then suddenly discovered that large quantities of brand-new stock, clean and unrumpled, *issued to James Fisk, Jr.*, had been put upon the street that day. Instantly and like wildfire a panic ran through the heart of Wall Street. Here, even more than elsewhere, rumors gather volume as they fly, and rumor now soon had it that new stock had been dumped upon the street in unlimited quantities. The shock was like the work of magic. The antics of those who had gobbled down the new stock unsuspectingly now resembled the contortions of a gooso that has swallowed a piece of red-hot iron mistaken for corn. Their retchings and eructations in the effort to disgorge were a rare mixture of the comic and painful to behold. All were eager to expel the indigestible, burning foreign matter from their maws, and sold to the first man who would buy. The panic extended even to Vanderbilt's allies. The men who were concerned with him in the new pool and who had made large outside investments under their agreement to run Erie up became utterly demoralized by the rumors flying wildly around them. Sharing the general conviction that the Drew party had triumphed and Vanderbilt been beaten, and knowing that in such an event Erie must tumble to 40 or even lower, they made haste to sell ere the Commodore could countermand the order to sustain the market, and thus saddled all their loads upon their chief before the news of the situation reached him.

Under the panic Erie reeled heavily and made a sudden lunge down to 71—a fall of 12 per cent. in two hours. There it halted quite firmly, making the wonder of the day, not that it fell so quick, but that it did not tumble 50 per cent. further. The whole shock of the battle, the whole huge load of the market, was sustained by one man, standing alone in his mighty power, deserted by his allies, who had sold out upon him at the trying moment and skulked away. But his own brokers had already been much the heaviest purchasers, so the additional amount loaded upon him was not very large comparatively, and as they held a vast volume of stock and still bought as it fell, they were able to stem the tide at 71 and hold it firmly.

When the panic started news of the crisis was sent to Vanderbilt and he was asked if his brokers should sell. "SELL!! *you fool!* No!!! *Buy every share offered!*" was the response roared by the man who saw with the quick eye of genius. One moment of hesitation, one faltering word of command, one instant of wavering in his position, and his lines would be hopelessly broken; Erie, of which he now held millions, would break and tumble 50 per cent.; Central, Hudson River, and Harlem, all of which he carried on his shoulders, would follow in the panic and he would be hopelessly swamped. He took in the whole situation at a glance and knew that Erie must be sustained at all hazards now, and by the force of his will alone the tide was stemmed, the panic stopped short, and disaster stayed.

The battle was done. Fisk and Gould had triumphed over Vanderbilt, defeating his purpose and hopes while relieving him of some $10,000,000 of his money, and had also bitten Drew quite severely by the way—just for a little side diversion. Fisk's dubious looks ceased the moment they had produced their desired effect in leading Drew to give orders to cover his contracts, and when the old gent learned an hour later that Fisk was going to sell, he sent a fleet messenger to countermand his order to buy; but it was too late. His brokers had acted promptly and his shorts, contracted at about 70, had been covered at about 80. Still, the result of the whole battle of three weeks was such that the veteran leader of the bears was eminently satisfied, and he heartily joined in the chuckle that ran round the self-satisfied circle gathered at Erie headquarters in West Street that evening around the uncovered chest containing Vanderbilt's millions in exchange for the small slips of clean paper ground out by their little mill only a few days before.

The roar of the wild battle in Wall Street had completely drowned the loudest noise in the neighboring halls of justice that day, and Judge Barnard's deepest and most powerful pipes had been as the squeaks of a penny whistle beside a battery of booming cannon. Nevertheless he had piped away after his fashion, venting much righteous indignation, overflowing with a more than noble Roman's valor and virtue, concluding in shrill tones, "My voice is still for war." The man he had sternly ordered to appear before the majesty of his law that morning, shielded himself behind a judge of co-ordinate power with Barnard, found it inconvenient to attend and failed to put in an appearance. Moreover, as "his Honor" took his seat upon the bench that morning he was himself treated to a little taste of injunctions, being at that moment, without the slightest awe of his august dignity, diamond studs, frilled shirt front, and velvet coat, served with Judge Gilbert's order peremptorily forbidding him to take any further proceedings in the matter of the orders and injunctions he had so freely fulminated against Drew and the whole body of Erie directors. He was amazed at such an extraordinary act on the part of his Brooklyn compeer, promptly declared it utterly null and void, and proceeded to treat it with entire contempt. But while he himself thus treated with contempt an order of the Supreme Court on the one hand, on the other he proposed to visit summary punishment upon those who had presumed to disregard his own annulled orders. Drew had failed to appear. That was contempt despite an order of the Supreme Court staying proceedings and telling him he need not appear. That day's history in Wall Street had disclosed that the Erie directors had issued new stock after "his Honor" had enjoined them from so doing. That was contempt despite a subsequent order of equal authority authorizing them to do as they pleased about it.   At least, so thought the pure-minded and immaculate Barnard, consequently he suffered not the majesty of his law to be slighted.

Before the sun was well up the next morning the coat-tails of all the sheriffs and deputy sheriffs that could be found in the celebrated new Court House were stuffed full of formidable documents bearing at the bottom what those who claim to speak from acquaintance pronounced to be the sign manual of George G. Barnard, *judex*.   The said savage-looking documents with the formidable name at the bottom were writs for the arrest of the whole posse of Erie directors, including "the body of James Fisk, Jr.," for contempt, and "his Honor" now made these pellets of justice as plentiful around the City Hall as Fisk had made Erie stock in Wall Street the day before.   The Erie directors, after a night of rest and pleasant dreams of victory and new fortunes made, had assembled at their headquarters in West Street again on the morning of the 11th and were on their knees taking a fresh matutinal peep into the chestful of pleasing souvenirs of their friend Vanderbilt.   In this morning devotion they were sur-prised by the arrival of a messenger nearly out of breath from the haste he had made to warn them that a small army of Judge Barnard's minions was in eager search for them, armed with writs for their arrest and intending to drag their precious bodies before "his Honor" of the august and terrible shirt frill. Upon the explosion of this shell in their midst, the knees of Drew smote each other as might a sinner's at the sound of Gabriel's trumpet, his countenance assumed a most woe-begone expression, and ghastly spectres of Ludlow Street jail haunted his aged vision. Fisk's first thought was for the security of that chest. He hastily closed the lid and located himself with his two hundred pounds and more of flesh on top thereof, announced that he should not get off till Barnard's dogs took him off, and called a council of war to meet around him to deliberate on the situation.

At Brattleboro in his boyhood he had often seen persecuted individuals whom the sheriff wanted to see very particularly, run through the covered bridge which here spans the Connecticut and when they had safely reached the New Hampshire side, turn suddenly round, put thumb to nose and set their fingers in a lively wiggle at the Vermont sheriff and kindly inquire the state of his health. This early practical instruction in the complexity of American jurisprudence resulting from our political system had amused him too many times in his youth to be forgotten and his knowledge of law thus gained now served him a good turn. The Erie offices were close upon the river bank directly opposite the ferry to Jersey City. It immediately struck Fisk that it would cut the Gordian knot of their present predicament and be a good joke on Barnard to step aboard the next boat and take a little pleasure trip to the Jersey side of the Hudson. That being

the terminus of the Erie road, they could superintend
the affairs of their corporation as well there as in New
York; and close by the water's edge where the ferry
would land them stands Taylor's Hotel, an establishment
that makes excellent provision for all the needs of the
inner man. The proposition had so much to recommend
it to their urgent necessity and so few drawbacks that
it struck his fellow miscrables as a brilliant idea and
was immediately adopted by a unanimous vote. Hasty
preparations for the foreign tour were at once commenced. Fisk deftly removed his two hundred pound
corpus from the chest and Drew, as treasurer, placed
therein all the funds of the Erie treasury, locked
it securely and placed it in charge of two trusted
porters to be taken to the ferry. Having thus attended to his official duties, he proceeded to gather up
his private funds—the proceeds of his brilliant management as confidential agent of Mr. Vanderbilt's pool, the
reward of lending men money to buy his own stock,
selling out his most intimate friends and various similar
brilliant exploits—requiring several small trunks to hold
them, and sent them in the wake of the chest. Fisk proceeded to stuff the pockets of his coat, vest and pants with
the greenbacks gathered as the fruit of wearing a dubious
look in Drew's presence the previous morning, smiling as
he did so to note the mournful glances cast at his plethoric pockets by the despondent old gentleman. Haste
being imperative, the preparations were few and soon

made, and now the band, taking with them such of the books, papers and more important documents as they could easily carry, made for the ferry, Fisk being careful to fall in directly behind the chest, so small had grown his confidence in human nature in general and in Daniel Drew in particular. As the party emerged from the building to the sidewalk, three or four policemen happened to be conversing together on the opposite corner. This being the general employment of New York police, that circumstance should not have caused any alarm; but

"Conscience makes cowards of us all,"

and the absconding directors instinctively halted for a moment at the sight of the brass-buttoned Hibernians with *lignum vitæ* clubs, apprehensive lest they were stationed there in the service of Barnard and were waiting for this appearance. The strange *tableau* which the directors thus presented, with their confused countenances and furtive glances, naturally attracted the attention and fixed upon themselves the stare of the policemen. Their first apprehension now became certainty, and the instinctive impulse to self-protection and personal safety becoming dominant, they broke and ran,—not as sheep do, in a united band in the direction of the one that starts first, but some one way and some another. In their utter demoralization, they reverted to the condition of mind existing before the Christian era, when stranger and enemy were synonymous terms, and were now anxiously suspicious of every man unknown to them that they met, lest he should prove to be armed with one of Judge Barnard's writs for their arrest. The meandering lines traced by their flight under such circumstances, their sudden dodgings and duckings and turning of sharp corners, were comic in the extreme. A few of them only made at once for the ferry, but of these few Fisk was one. The porters bearing the chest of funds, conscious of no offence, had not been at all disturbed at sight of the policemen but had moved directly on to the ferry and so were somewhat in advance of the party who had halted from fear. The boat with the chest and porters on board was just starting when such of the fugitives as ran in that direction arrived upon the slip; but Fisk seeing that chest was like Hans Breitmann, the soldier in Maryland, when scouts came in reporting a rebel town near by in which there was lager bier.

> " Gottsdonnerkreuzschockschwerenoth!
> How Breitmann broked de bush!
> O, let me see dat lager bier!
> O, let me at him rush!"

He of the plethoric pockets made a desperate leap for the boat, successfully accomplished the hazardous feat and was safe—safe from the water ready to receive him, safe from the wrath of the virtuous Barnard, safe near that chest. He wiped his brow, puffed for a moment, then imitated those funny men he had seen pass so hastily through the bridge at Brattleboro years before.

The other directors made their way to Jersey in straggling parties as best they could. Some went by the ferry; others, fearing they would now be watched for there, got themselves privately ferried over in small row boats. By nightfall all but two of the most unoffending ones had succeeded in placing the Hudson between themselves and danger. The two luckless ones fell into the sheriff's clutches and were marched into the august presence of Judge Barnard but were released under heavy bail.

As soon as Fisk had reached the land of safety and taken some refreshments, he took up his position at the head of the slip in the ferry house and, as the successive boats came in, walked up and down with his hands in his trowsers pockets, one of Park and Tilford's finest *Havanas* in his mouth, overflowing with spirits and humor, and made many kind inquiries about his friends Barnard and Vanderbilt. He welcomed each small squad of his fellow exiles with much delight as they straggled in, taking them warmly by the hand with the cheery words "Well, boys, how's everything over'n York?"

With the first shades of evening twilight, March 11th, 1868, a merrier company than is often gathered around the festive board in Taylor's Hotel sat down for "a feast of reason and a flow of soul." United once more, with the exception of the hapless two, after many struggles and dangers,

> "—multum ille et terris jactatus et alto
> Vi Superum, *sævi* memorem *Barnardis* ob iram,
> Multa quoque et bello passus,"

a right merry band were they now. Safe from all harm or intrusion, protected by the broad ægis of the land of the Camden & Amboy Railroad, otherwise known as the State of New Jersey, the home of large mosquitoes, they recounted the incidents of the past three days with an abundant flow of wit and wine, enjoying that weird fascination and pleasure that hovers over dangers well passed.

CHAPTER VI.

When the exiled directors had fully vented their humor and were ready to turn their attention to the practical affairs of their trust once more, the first step was to secure a firm legal footing in their new abode. An agent was immediately sent to Trenton, a bill making the Erie Railway a New Jersey corporation was pushed through the Legislature in two hours, was soon signed by the Governor, and Erie was now perfectly at home in its new quarters.

Another practical question that immediately presented itself for settlement related to the division of the spoils of the recent campaign. Of course the $10,000,000 of new bonds issued had not been negotiated at par. For the $5,000,000 worth issued to Mr. Fisk the Erie treasury realized $3,625,000, and as the stock into which he converted his bonds had been disposed of for about

$4,000,000, there remained the sum of $375,000 to be divided among the parties to compensate them for their valuable services in getting the stock upon the market When it was decided to issue the $10,000,000 of new bonds, a written agreement was entered into by Drew, Fisk, Gould and another, as to the manner in which the profits should be divided; but Fisk having come to put little faith in Drew's agreements, even though in writing, declined to hand over to the keeper of Mr. Vanderbilt's late pool the $375,000 which he held as the profit of his half of the transaction, till Drew also accounted for his profits in the late campaign, in accordance with his agreement. The wrangle was finally settled by Fisk giving the treasurer his *check* for $375,000 instead of surrendering the cash in his possession. This check was uncertified, which of course made it nothing but a due bill, and therefore of just as much value as Mr. Drew's agreement, and no more. It was however accompanied by about $180,000 worth of stock, as collateral, and the amount realized on this may be taken as the treasurer's profits from this single item of the day's transactions, for history does not record that Mr. Drew ever got that check of James Fisk, Jr., for $375,000 cashed. Half that sum being equally divided among the other three parties to the agreement, Fisk and Gould must have profited upward of $60,000 each by this one item of the day's transactions, and they were not men that would fail to have several items of a like profitable nature.

JAMES FISK, Jr.

These two matters being settled, the next thing to be attended to was public sentiment. Their proceedings had been of a nature that would have created a very unpleasant odor around their names in Wall Street, even had they remained upon the field and exerted themselves to counteract an unfavorable judgment; and the evil wrought by their deeds had been greatly enhanced by the sudden withdrawal from circulation of so many millions of currency as they had carried with them to Jersey. Money had been made very scarce all at once, causing serious embarrassment in financial matters and still further depressing the stock market heavily beyond what was done by the demoralizing effect of the issue of $10,000,000 of new stock. Both wind and tide had thus been set strongly against them and the current was increasing daily as the evil effects of their doings developed. But far worse than all this was the stench of having fled the State. The public had long since grown so indifferent to the course of events in Wall Street that, whatever their exploits there, it would have been regarded only as a "diamond cut diamond" proceeding and after a little harmless noise of the bulls and bears and a few equally harmless newspaper articles, all would have been forgotten and their names would not have been materially injured. But they now rested under the stigma of being fugitives from justice, and that circumstance alone branded them with great disgrace in the public eye. Therefore they now exerted themselves strenuously to counteract all this

D

and turn the tide in their favor. To all the reporters, interviewers and committees that now visited them by the score from every quarter, they represented themselves as the most disinterested and self-sacrificing champions of the public interests against the monopolizing schemes of Vanderbilt and affirmed that all they had done was not only a justifiable but absolutely necessary means to that most desirable end, and their only way to defend the road committed to their trust. And instead of being fugitives from justice, they claimed to be martyrs to the public weal and persecuted victims of the most corrupt judge that ever disgraced a bench, alleging that Barnard was nothing but the obsequious tool of Vanderbilt, in league with him to speculate in Erie stock, and scandalously abusing his power and position as a judge to harrass them for thwarting his knavish schemes. As these allegations had a firm basis in the facts of the case, the position in which they pictured themselves was very plausible and the tub thus constructed to sail a stormy sea would have been an excellent one had it only had a bottom. But to think of Fisk and Gould in the character of self-sacrificing guardians of public and corporate interests strikes one as extremely comic, and how much they surpassed Vanderbilt in seeking the welfare of the Erie Railway and the commercial interests of New York the sequel has left no room to doubt; but their character was not then developed or known and Mr. Eldridge, their president, enjoyed a high reputation both as a railroad manager and a man of character. Their agreement with Vanderbilt at the time of their election had not yet leaked out to the public and their several purposes were not yet patent. Therefore their tub, bottomless though it was, sailed very well temporarily. None of their visitors departed hungry or thirsty. All left with a very favorable impression of the kind-heartedness of the exiles, and the spirit of hospitality and *bonhomie* that pervaded Taylor's Hotel distilled a gentle infusion of roses into the ink of the newspaper men, who now clearly saw two sides to the question and began to think the generous spirits chased out of New York by Judge Barnard not so black as they had been painted.

And now occurred a most ludicrous incident which served to help the exiles somewhat in turning sympathy in their favor. On the 16th, a large body of New York "roughs" of the worst type made their appearance in Jersey City, about the ferry house, Erie depot and Taylor's Hotel. The news immediately spread that Vanderbilt had offered a reward of $50,000 for Drew, Fisk or Eldridge and this party had come over intending to kidnap all the directors they could find and take them back within the jurisdiction of the terrible Barnard by main force and with as much violence to Jersey law as might be necessary. Great excitement ran through the city at the news and a large crowd soon gathered in the vicinity. A large number of Erie *employés* was immediately summoned from the work-shops and formed into a body guard to

protect the directors, and Taylor's Hotel was at once and
not inaptly dubbed "Fort Taylor." A heavy detach-
ment of police was detailed for service within and about
"the Fort" and the whole force of the city was
instructed that if a rocket were sent up any time during
the night they should regard it as a signal to hasten to
the threatened quarter. General fear of a riot prevailed,
the stores were closed in the evening, the streets in the
disturbed quarter were avoided and the militia was placed
under orders to rally at a signal. The excitement of the
situation was rather enjoyed by the directors, and
especially by Mr. Fisk, who now bustled about with a
most determined looking visage, mounted his guard,
issued orders, puffed away at his cigar, kept up a constant discharge of puns, vowed he would never be taken
alive, and braved all the terrors and hazards of the deep
and Judge Barnard's jurisdiction by daring trips across
the Hudson in a small row boat under cover of the
darkness and fog to act as a spy in the camp of his
enemies, à la King Alfred, and get something good at
Delmonico's and elsewhere. No demonstration whatever
was made by the roughs, most of whom returned to New
York within an hour or two after their first appearance.
Fort Taylor was kept heavily garrisoned, however, and
continued to wear on the inside the air of a besieged
fortress. New rumors of an imminent attack came into
camp at intervals of two or three days, to renew the
excitement and prevent the situation from becoming

monotonous. This state of things was kept up for two weeks, when, the novelty and excitement of the episode having grown stale, the self-imposed siege was raised without a single instance of disorder having occurred, all the roughs having long ago retired to their favorite haunts in the Five Points and elsewhere and quite forgotten the affair in their active training for Aldermen.

A great handle was made of this affair by the exiles to show the reckless character of their persecutors and turn sentiment against Vanderbilt, as it could only be a man whose schemes were villainous and who hesitated at no acts of violence and lawlessness, that would resort to the assistance of New York roughs to help him on. Of course Vanderbilt had no more to do with it than had the King of Siam and it was the height of absurdity to represent him as doing such a thing. It would be much more supposable that Fisk himself hired the men to come over and that the whole affair was a contrived plot to excite an unfavorable sentiment against Vanderbilt. At any rate this turn was given to it.

But, far more than by any of these means, a popular feeling in favor of the exiles and a disposition to look upon them as the opponents of monopoly and champions of the interests of the public and the Erie Railway, was created by their lowering the charges for fare and freight nearly one third, entering into a fierce competition with the Commodore and his Central and running their road at losing rates, which the money Vanderbilt had supplied them with easily enabled them to do.

In the midst of all these efforts to turn sentiment in their favor, a bill to prevent the consolidation of the Erie and Central roads under the control of one man, or parties in his interest, to guard against monopoly of railroads, to establish a broad gauge connection to the West, *and to legalize the recent new issue of Erie stock*, was introduced into the Legislature at Albany. Under the various influences the exiles had brought to bear, a strong sentiment now set in in their favor, and petitions and memorials and letters poured in from all parts of the State, especially from New York and all along the line of the Erie road, upon the grave law-makers at Albany, praying for the passage of the bill to defeat Vanderbilt's monopoly schemes, and a large portion of the press took up the cudgel on the same side. But Vanderbilt was no common antagonist. He had started with things much in his favor, or against the runaways, and had done nothing of a doubtful legal look. The New York Courts had given him their fullest sanction and the adverse order which the Drew party had obtained of the Brooklyn judge to serve their purposes of the 10th had been indignantly dismissed on the day for its hearing, the judge intimating that it had been procured in a scandalous and fraudulent manner, thus making it look that Vanderbilt's cause was wholly within, while that of the Drew party was wholly without, the pale of law. The sentiment and influence of

Wall Street, too, had been decidedly in favor of Vanderbilt at the first and had steadily increased, for matters there had been placed in a very trying and critical position by the action of the fugitives, and were daily getting worse. All stocks were falling, money was very scarce and commanded high rates of interest, many brokers were failing, and the turn which affairs should take in the crisis depended wholly upon the course of Vanderbilt. He was bearing a tremendous load upon his shoulders. All his stocks were falling, gradually but constantly. With the least sign of wavering or weakness, he would be swamped and there would result a greater crash in the stock market than had been known since the era of stock speculation commenced. In this hour of supreme trial the metal of which he was made gave no uncertain ring. His genius as well as the immensity of his resources now loomed up like the shaft of Bunker Hill. With unshaken nerves he issued instructions to his brokers, holding the market as he wished, went off for a drive with his fast horses in the afternoon, and played whist in the evening, the merriest and seemingly the freest from care of any of the company. But there were circumstances not known to the public that enabled him to see clearly and feel confident. The exiles took to their New Jersey life not unpleasantly at first, but the Pater Anchises of this epic soon grew lonesome, despondent and homesick in his expatriation and became anxious for some settlement of the difficulties that would allow him to return to his home and attend Methodist prayer meetings with his family once more. While the young and jovial Fisk continued in the finest spirits, Drew pined and refused to be comforted, and when the merry company gathered around their evening camp fires, smoked, listened to Fisk's puns, laughed and sung war songs, the old man broke in at intervals with the strangely discordant refrain, " I want to go home." Sunday disarms sheriffs and Judge Barnard, and, pleasantly as time seemed to hang on their hands, it was amusing to note the promptitude with which the whole party laid down their pipes and started for the ferry when the clock struck twelve Saturday night. They appreciated the blessings of Christianity or the institution of the Sabbath very highly now and improved the immunity it gave them to appear boldly in their familiar haunts. Fisk may have attended church but Drew embraced the opportunity to call on his friend Vanderbilt. Monday morning found them back at their posts with military promptitude. But Drew was now suspected. He was missed from barracks at night and Fisk detailed a detective to watch all his movements. He was followed up the shore to Weehawken ferry, thence across to the city and to the house of Vanderbilt. The detective returned and reported. It was as had been suspected. Drew was intriguing for a compromise and they knew he would do anything with his friends and Erie if he could only escape unharmed himself. Soon it was found the funds of the Erie treasury had been taken to New York by Mr. Treasurer Drew. On learning this Fisk immediately got all of Drew's private funds, which were still in the Jersey bank, attached. No one unacquainted with the old gentleman's facial peculiarities can imagine the comic expression of mingled surprise and disappointment that marked his countenance when he returned from what he supposed a secret journey and found how completely his pupil had euchred him. He found he had been training up a power to be more than a match for him. The funds of the Erie treasury came back where James Fisk, Jr., could daily enjoy the sight of them. These secret visits told Vanderbilt that the position of things across the river was not pleasant and made him confident that no more Erie stock would be issued, which was his greatest danger, and he saw that he had only to hold things as they were to force his enemies to terms ultimately.

Despite all the efforts of his opponents, therefore, the star of Vanderbilt was still much in the ascendant and the moment anything was to be done at Albany the superiority of his position at once showed itself. He had been long familiar with the ways of the New York Legislature and the considerations most potent with lawmakers, and the Central, of which he was now master, had long had things quite its own way there. Consequently the bill introduced in the interest of the Drew party was promptly rejected on the 27th of March by the

decisive vote of 83 to 32, despite all the petitions that
had been sent in requesting its passage.

This overwhelming defeat taught the Fort Taylor
warriors that public sentiment was not exactly the harp
to play upon if they would charm the ear of legislators,
and that they could not successfully wield more potent
influences at such arm's-length while their antagonist was
on the battle field in *propria persona*. It was decided
that some one of the principals must be present at the
scene of action instead of longer trusting to mere agents
and telegraph and mail, and Jay Gould was detailed
from headquarters to go to Albany to remove the preju-
dices of the legislators and place things before them in a
clearer light, taking along half a million dollars for pocket
money and hotel expenses. He made his advent in
Albany March 30th, registered his name at the Delavan
House, took one of the finest suites of rooms, and had
just got nicely installed in them when he received a very
urgent invitation to visit New York, the invitation being
signed by Judge George G. Barnard and presented by a
gentleman so excessively polite in his attentions as to
insist that Mr. Gould should accept the invitation and
either go down with him immediately or give assurance
in the shape of half a million of dollars that he would
appear at the appointed place on the following Saturday.
There was important work on hand at Albany that
needed attending to immediately, therefore for this and
other reasons the required assurance was given in prefer-

ence to going with the officious gentleman, and Mr. Gould set earnestly about the business in hand.

The New York Legislature has for several years manifested unlimited faith in "investigating committees" as an invaluable adjunct to legislative machinery and as the most reliable and efficient mode of getting at the truth in many matters. Especially is this the favorite method of procedure if a large corporation is concerned or a question involving a large amount of money comes up for consideration. Either some standing committee is directed to inquire into the state of things generally and report its opinion for the information and guidance of the Legislature, or, in an extraordinary case, a special committee is appointed for the purpose. As the committee report, so the Legislature is pretty sure to decide, hence the committee often become men whom it is very important to persuade by all possible arguments to take a favorable view of matters. It is this circumstance that has rendered the Chairmanship of the Committee on Railways a position so very much sought after and the next most desirable place after the Speakership. The successful candidate for Speaker generally assuages the disappointment of his most prominent rival in his own party by appointing him Chairman of this committee, for then, though he has failed of the highest honors, he is pretty sure of returning home at the close of the session comfortably provided for for life. And in fact all the members of this committee, unless they have uncommonly poor luck, can rely upon returning to their constituents very much bettered in worldly condition.

Even prior to the last grand master-stroke of the Erie directors in Wall Street, the queer movements of the stock, the general rumors of corruption and unlawful acts and the extraordinary litigation instituted against the managers, had produced such a strong impression that there was something decidedly wrong that a special committee of five, to inquire into and report upon the condition of the Erie Railway, was appointed by the Legislature March 5th. This committee achieved great temporary celebrity and was known as the "Mattoon Committee," from the name of its most conspicuous member. Now, Mr. Mattoon was not one of your bigoted, prejudiced, opinionated men who prejudge a case and having formed a bias beforehand, shut their minds to the influence of all arguments and refuse to look at the matter in a new light or modify their opinion. He was one of those lofty natures whose minds are always open to conviction, who are not only willing but even eager to receive further light and be convinced that their views are erroneous and delight to admit their error and adopt the right position. Being of this peculiar mental cast, Mr. Mattoon very naturally deemed it indispensable to go straight to the fountain head for light immediately upon being appointed on the investigating committee. He visited the chiefs of the Drew faction to hear their side of the story and listen carefully to their arguments, and then he visited Mr. Vanderbilt to hear his cause and the opposing arguments. So intricate was the case and so difficult was it to get at the real merits that a single hearing seemed not to set the Mattoon mind and conscience at rest as to the right of the matter and his duty in the premises, and therefore he found it necessary to make several visits to each party in order that full justice might be done. Singularly enough, Mr. Mattoon seemed ever to incline to the views of the party that had his ear last, hence it became a matter of much more than usual importance who should have the last word. Some base spirits, judging from their own evil natures, insinuated that something more powerful than mere verbal arguments were brought to bear upon this mind ever so open to conviction, but it may be sufficient to satisfy a certain type of mind that these insinuations were only vile calumnies to state that there has never been produced in the matter any evidence that would constitute "legal proof." The investigation had been thus carried on for more than a month, during which time each party had several times thought the unbiased mind finally fixed in its favor, but only to find itself granted a further hearing. When at last the committee felt ready to report, it so happened that the other four members were equally divided, two desiring a favorable and two an unfavorable report upon the condition of the Erie Railway and its management. Mr. Mattoon finding himself thus holding the deciding vote, became suddenly impressed with the

gravity and responsibility of his position and the great
necessity of proceeding conscientiously in the matter and
requested a little further time to hear any further
argument that might be offered, reflect and make up his
mind. The report was still further delayed for his
accommodation, and the matter stood in this position
when Mr. Gould reached Albany. Being now on the
ground, he felt his chance for getting the important last
word, and so a favorable report, was much improved and
it was for this reason that he much preferred not to
accompany Judge Barnard's polite messenger to New
York immediately. He now applied himself vigorously
to bring the most cogent arguments to bear upon Mr.
Mattoon and remove the last cobwebs of doubt from the
mind of the conscientious Senator. And he finally parted
with him satisfied that he had had the last word, supplied
the dust that was to turn the scales, and that a favorable
report would be made so that further legislation favorable to Erie would be easily secured. The report was
made April 1st, and *it was unfavorable to Erie.* Mr.
Mattoon had placed his signature with the two whose
views were of the Vanderbilt hue. Gould expressed
himself " utterly astounded," when he heard how Mattoon had voted, but still he despaired not.

On Saturday morning Mr. Gould presented himself in
accordance with Judge Barnard's invitation, and after
much wrangling and some singular legal gymnastics he
was remanded to the charge of the sheriff. He, however,

speedily made his way back to Albany, taking the sheriff along as a travelling companion. When the time arrived for the sheriff to produce the body of Jay Gould in court in New York again, Mr. Gould did as some Sophomores do in college when they wish to get away from recitations for a short time—he fell suddenly ill and got a physician's certificate that he was under treatment and should be excused from attendance. With this instead of the body, the sheriff went back to New York and the magic certificate of the physician seemed to satisfy the mysteriously abating ire of the New York judge. And as the Sophomore finds that he is in no great danger soon after the physician has left a prescription, a certificate of ill health, and departed, but tears up the prescription, carefully preserves the certificate and goes off to visit some young lady cousin, so Mr. Gould found that he was not in too feeble a condition to devote himself earnestly to the difficult task of reversing the unfavorable votes that had been given and turning the tide in favor of Erie.

The defeat of the Erie bill March 27th and the unfavorable report of the committee April 1st, seemed to announce the entire triumph of Vanderbilt and the certain and speedy doom of Drew and his adherents. Their influence was very sensibly felt in the Stock Exchange, and Central, which had fallen from 132 to 109 in the three weeks of depression, instantly rallied again three or four per cent. and other stocks felt the influence. But Gould was not in the least disheartened. He surveyed

the position carefully and determined to win the smile of
the Legislature yet. His rooms at the Delavan House
became the favorite resort of many of the legislators.
They all departed with smiling faces, and Mr. Gould
soon had little left of his check book except the stumps.
On the 13th of April a bill of precisely the same import as
that rejected by the House March 27th, was introduced
into the Senate and the battle for its success now became
gigantic. One man was said to have come to Albany
furnished with $100,000 to work for Vanderbilt's interest
and to have been given $70,000 by Gould to run away
with Vanderbilt's $100,000. One Senator was openly
accused of receiving $15,000 from one side and $20,000
from the other. Many minor incidents of the struggle
were equally unique and interesting. It was a battle of
the giants and Erie must win this time or surrender at discretion. On the 18th the bill passed the Senate by a vote
of 17 to 12—Mr. Mattoon voting *for* the bill. The
result took the public by surprise and Wall Street felt a
little shudder. The bill was sent down to the House and
the members of the lower branch of the Legislature were
rubbing their hands with delight that it had now come
their turn to be tickled as the upper branch had been.
The lobby was out in full force in light drab overcoats,
diamond studs, large watch-chains and rubicund noses.
Every train from New York brought new recruits for the
battle. April 20th was the day for the grand final shock,
and the members took their seats of honor eager for

business to begin, each hoping his vote would be an object of Gould and Vanderbilt's rival bidding. The decisive moment approached and the bill was called up. In a few minutes a sickening shudder like that which was felt in Wall Street the day Fisk threw the last $5,000,000 of Erie stock upon the market ran through the Assembly. Hearts sank and hopes of fortune vanished. The news went round that Vanderbilt had tied up his purse strings and would not "bleed" another dollar. The wrath of the disappointed members was unbounded. The bill rejected three weeks before by a vote of 83 to 32, was now rushed through in the storm of rage by a vote of 101 to 6. Several other bills designed to injure the Central road and spite Vanderbilt were introduced at once for revenge. The bill went to the Governor and became a law by the signature of Ruben E. Fenton.

This bill Judge Barnard aptly described as "a bill to legalize counterfeit money." When its passage was made known at the Stock Exchange by telegraph, it was regarded as the defeat of Vanderbilt and the warning of a panic. The stocks with which Vanderbilt was known to be heavily loaded fell at once and large short sales were made in Central and Erie, when in another hour Central bounded from 112 to 120 and Erie from 66 to 71. Everybody was utterly astounded and puzzled at a movement so utterly at variance with the influence of the news. But it soon leaked out that Vanderbilt had not withdrawn his opposition at Albany without knowing

what he was about. He had indeed found men more
than a match for him in boldness at corrupting the Legislature and saw it could only be a battle of the lion and
the skunk. He could succeed only by spending more
money to corrupt men than Erie would bo worth and he
was now fully awake to the fact that he was dealing not
with Drew but with much more daring spirits, who would
hesitate at nothing to carry their point. Still, he released
his hold at Albany only when he was assured that the exiles would make a satisfactory settlement with him in order
to get back to their homes. Secret visits from across the
river had made him certain of this, and suggestions and
proposals for a settlement had been such that it was for
the interest of both parties to hold up the stocks. The
first rumors of this nature that reached the brokers were
confirmed by the appearance of Drew and some of the
other exiles on Wall Street the next day unmolested by
Barnard's sheriffs. April 25th arrangements for a settlement had proceeded so far that "Fort Taylor" was
abandoned and the exiles returned to their homes in
peace. The terms of this settlement were not made
known for some time, and then it proved to be quite in
keeping with the arrangement made by the same parties
six months before on the eve of election. The directors
took 50,000 shares of Erie stock off Vanderbilt's shoulders at 70, for which he received $2,500,000 in cash,
$1,250,000 in Boston Hartford & Erie bonds at 80.
He was also paid $1,000,000 cash for the "option" given

the directors of calling on him for 50,000 shares more of Erie at 70 any time within four months. And he was to name two new directors to be taken into the Erie board. This satisfied him, and for this he promised to have all the suits discontinued and let the fugitives return. The suits had all been brought, not in Vanderbilt's name, but in the names of men under his command, and to satisfy these men and the expenses of litigation, $429,250 cash was necessary. Mr. Eldridge received $4,000,000 of Erie acceptances for $5,000,000 of Boston, Hartford & Erie bonds at 80 and that satisfied him and his party. Mr. Drew was to retain all the money he had made by his numerous manipulations of Erie for the last two years, but was to pay into the Erie treasury $540,000 for a receipt in full for all claims the corporation might have against him and as a settlement of all their mutual accounts. This satisfied him. Fisk and Gould had not come in for any of the pecuniary spoil in this settlement and they opposed it strenuously till they found a majority in favor of it, so it was sure to pass in spite of them; and they were then induced to give their assent for the consideration that Eldridge, Drew and some others should resign their positions as directors and leave Fisk and Gould in full and sole possession of the Erie Railway.

Six months after this settlement a suit was commenced against Vanderbilt by Fisk and Gould in behalf of the Erie Railway to recover the money paid Vanderbilt at this settlement and make him take back the 50,000 shares of Erie stock, on the ground that the transaction was illegal. The testimony given by Mr. Fisk when on the stand as a witness in this case, is so unique in character and affords such a perfect picture of the man that some extracts from it are worth preserving and may form an acceptable close of this chapter. The suit was brought and conducted by Mr. David Dudley Field and his partners, his son and Thomas G. Shearman. The trial was held by Judge George G. Barnard, and the court room was crowded with distinguished lawyers and men who listened with the greatest interest. When Mr. Fisk was called he stepped upon the stand with most perfect self-assurance, evidently enjoying the situation, and in answer to questions testified :

I remember an interview with Commodore Vanderbilt in the summer of 1868. I don't remember just when the first interview was. It was after I returned from Jersey. I was absent in Jersey for a lapse of time (laughter) and on my return I made the Commodore a call (laughter). He said several of the directors were trying to make a trade with him and he would like to know who was the best man to trade with. I told him if the trade was a good one he had better trade with me (laughter). He said old man Drew was no better than a batter pudding (great laughter), Eldridge was completely demoralized and there was no head or tail to our concern (laughter). I said I thought so, too (great laughter). He said he had got his bloodhounds on us and would pursue us till we took his stock off his hands—he'd be d—d if he'd keep it. I said I'd be d—d if we'd take it back (sensation), that we would sell him stock as long as he'd stand up and take it (great laughter). Upon this he mellowed down (laughter) and said we must get together and arrange this matter. He said when we were in Jersey Drew used to slip over and see him whenever he could get out from under our eyes; that he had had a good deal of talk with him and wanted to know if a trade made with Drew and Eldridge could be slipped through our board, saying that if it could we should all be landed in the haven of peace and harmony. (Looking very determined.) I told him I would not submit to a robbery of the road under any circumstances and that I was dumbfounded that our directors—whom I had supposed respectable men—(great laughter) would have anything to do with such proceedings.

Counsel: Is that all that was said?

Mr. Fisk: I presume not. We had half an hour's conversation and I think I could say more than that in half an hour (laughter).

Counsel: Can you give anything more that was said?

Mr. Fisk: I don't remember what more was said. I remember the Commodore put on his other shoe (laughter). I remember that shoe on account of the buckle (laughter). You see, there were four buckles on that shoe. I hadn't ever seen any of that kind before, and I remember it passed through my mind that if such men wore that kind of shoe I must get me a pair (great laughter). This passed through my mind but I didn't speak of it to the Commodore. I was very civil to him (laughter).

Counsel: Where was Gould all this time?

Mr. Fisk: He was in the front room—I suppose. I left him there and found him there, but I don't know where he may have been in the meantime (laughter). The next interview was at the house of Mr. Pierrepoint. Gould and I had an appointment with Eldridge at the Fifth Avenue Hotel and as we did not find him there we went out to see if we could find him.

Counsel: Can you give the date of that meeting?—*A.* No, sir.

Q. Can you give the week?—*A.* No, sir.

Q. Can you give the month?—*A.* No, sir.

Q. Can you give the year?—*A.* No, sir! Not without reference.

Q. What reference do you want?—*A.* Well, I shall have to refer back to the various events of my life to see just where that day comes in, and the almighty robbery committed by this man Vanderbilt against the Erie Railway was the most impressive event in my life (laughter). The meeting at Pierrepoint's was a week or ten days after the first interview with Vanderbilt. Gould and I went there about nine o'clock. We stepped into the hall together. We asked if Mr. Pierrepoint was in. The servant said he would see. When the servant went into the drawing room I was very careful to keep on a line with the door so I could see in (laughter). Presently Mr. Pierrepoint stepped into the hall, resembling a man who wasn't in *much* (laughter). I asked him if our president was there. After some thoughtfulness on his part, he said he thought he was (laughter). During this time I had moved along towards the drawing room door, Mr. Pierrepoint having neglected to invite us in (laughter).

Q. Where was Gould?—*A.* O, he was just behind me; he's always right behind at such times (laughter), and while he entertained Pierrepoint I opened the door and stepped in (laughter), and found most of our directors there. I stepped up to Mr. Eldridge and told him we had been to the Fifth Avenue Hotel and did not find him. He said he knew he was not there (laughter). I asked what was going on and everybody seemed to wait for some one else to answer (laughter). Being better acquainted with Drew than any of the rest of them, though perhaps having less confidence in him (laughter), I asked him what under heavens was up. He said they were arranging the suits. I told him they ought to adopt a very different manner of doing it than being there in the night—that no settlement could be made without requiring the money of the corporation. He begun to picture his miseries to me, told me how he had suffered during his pilgrimage, saying he was worn and thrown away from his family and wanted to settle matters up;

that he had done everything he could and saw no other way out either for himself or the company. I told him I guessed he was more particular about himself than the company and he said, well, he was (laughter); that he was an old man and wanted to get out of the fight and his troubles; that they were much older in such affairs than we were—I was very glad to hear him say that—(laughter) and that it was no uncommon thing for great corporations to make arrangements of this sort. I told him if that was the case I thought our State Prison ought to be enlarged (laughter). Then Eldridge, he took hold of me. He talked about his great exertions, what he had done and consummated, that there were only two dissenting voices in the board—Gould and myself—and that if we came into the matter to-morrow the company would be free and clear of litigation and everything would be all right, as he had got the Commodore and Work and Schell to settle on a price. I told him I couldn't see it; I had fought that position for seven months night and day and ·for seven weeks in Jersey I had hardly taken off my clothes, fighting to keep the money of the company from being robbed; and I could see no reason why we should not fight it on still. He said he didn't want to go into it, but had tried to do the best he could with Gould and myself and could do nothing and now an arrangement had been made with Vanderbilt and it was all right and must go through that night. I said I did not believe it was legal; these lawyers were all on one side, and I wanted to see my lawyer. He said that was no good (laughter). Then Mr. Pierrepoint argued with me. He said he did not think there was any one present who was not going to derive benefit from it. Rapallo was writing at a table. Schell was buzzing around (laughter) interested in getting his share of the plunder. Work was sitting on a sofa. I had nothing to say to him (laughter) as we were not on very good terms. Gould and I had a conversation together and not till twelve o'clock at night did we give our consent. I told him I did not believe the proceedings were legal, that we had no lawyers, that the lawyers there were sold to Eldridge—hook, line and sinker (laughter). Gould said Eldridge had paid Evarts $10,000 for an opinion that it was all right and Eaton had been paid $15,000 for an opinion and said it was legal. I told him I thought it a queer way of classifying opinions (laughter). Gould consented first. He said he had made up his mind to do so as the best way to get out of the matter. I told him I would consent if he did. Drew came to me with tears in his eyes and asked me to consent and I consented. Then there was some paper drawn up and passed around for us to sign. I don't know what it contained. I didn't read it. I don't think I noticed a word of it. I don't know the contents and have always been glad I didn't (laughter). I have thought of it a thousand times. I don't know what other documents I signed—signed everything that was put before me (laughter). After the devil once got hold of me I kept on signing (laughter). Didn't read any of them and have no idea what they were. Don't know how many I signed—kept no account after the first. I went with the robbers then and have been with them ever since (laughter). After signing all the papers I took my hat and left at once in disgust (laughter). I don't know whether we sat down or not. I know we didn't have anything to eat (laughter).

Counsel: Didn't you have a glass of wine or something of that sort ?

Mr. Fisk: I don't remember.

Counsel: Wouldn't that have made an impression upon you ? (Laughter.)

Mr. Fisk: No, sir ! I never drink (laughter). I think I left at once as soon as I had done signing. As we went out I said to Gould we had sold our souls to the devil (laughter). He agreed to that and said he thought so, too (laughter). I remember Mr. White, the cashier, coming in with the check book under his arm and as he came in I said to him that he was bearing in the balance of the remains of our corporation to put into Vanderbilt's tomb (laughter).

The next interview with Vanderbilt was several days after.

Counsel: Was Gould with you ?

Mr. Fisk: Yes, Sir ! We never parted during that war (laughter). We went to his office one morning and found his man Friday in the front room (laughter). Don't know his name. It was the same man I had seen a hundred times before when I had been there with Drew. We found the Commodore in the back room. I asked him how he was getting on. He said "First rate" (laughter); that he had got the thing all arranged and the only question now was whether it could be slipped through our board. I told him that after what I had seen the other night I thought anything could be slipped through (laughter). He said we would have to manage it carefully. I told him I didn't think so—that they would be careful to go it blind (laughter). He said the trade had been consummated at Pierrepoint's house. I said I had no doubt of it. He said it ought not to have been carried out; that Schell had got the lion's share and some of the lawyers on the other side might have to go hungry (laughter). He asked if we were conversant with the rest of the trade. I said I had no doubt the whole thing had been cooked up in such a manner that it could be put through. He spoke about putting Banker and Stewart into our board and said it would help both him and us carry our stock, as people would say we had amalgamated, and Vanderbilt's men coming into the Erie board would strengthen the market. That was admitted, but it worked rather different from what we expected (laughter). I next saw him a day or two before the prosecution was closed up. Gould thought the Commodore's losses had not been so large as represented and asked to see his broker's account. The Commodore said he never showed anything and we must take his word. He reiterated his losses and said they were so large because when they had got him to give his order to sustain the market the skunks had run and sold out on him (laughter). As we were coming away he said, " Boys, you are young, and if you carry out this settlement there will be peace and harmony between the roads."

Previous to commencing this suit I made a tender of 50,000 shares of Erie stock to Vanderbilt. I went up to his house in company with T. G. Shearman. I received the certificates of shares from Gould and put them in a black satchel (laughter). It was a bad, stormy day, so we got into a carriage and I held the satchel tight between my legs (laughter) knowing they were valuable (laughter). I told Shearman not much reliance could be placed on him if we were attacked, he was such a little fellow (laughter, in which Mr. Shearman joined). We concurred in the opinion that it was dangerous property to travel with—(laughter)—might blow up (laughter). We rang the bell and went in. The gentleman came down and I said " Good morning, Commodore. I have come to tender you fifty thousand shares of Erie stock and demand back the securities and money." He said he had had no transactions with the Erie Railway Co. (laughter) and would have to consult his counsel. I told him I also demanded a million of dollars paid him for losses he purported to have sustained. He said he had nothing to do with it (laughter) and I bade him good morning (laughter).

I became director in the Erie Railway on the 13th of October, 1867.

Counsel: You remember that date?

Mr. Fisk: I do, well! It forms an episode in my life.

Counsel: What fixes it in your mind so well?

Mr. Fisk: I had no gray hairs then.

Counsel: You have gray hairs now?

Mr. Fisk: Plenty of them. And I saw more robbery during the next year than I had ever dreamed of as possible.

Counsel: You saw it, did you?

Mr. Fisk: I didn't see it, but I knew it was going on. I am now a director of the Erie Railway and its comptroller. My duty as comptroller is to audit all the bills; as director, to manage the affairs of the corporation—*honestly* (laughter).

I would like to make an apology to the Court. This is the first time I've been on the stand and I may overstep some of the rules (laughter). If I do, it is wholly in ignorance. It is new business to me and if I don't keep within the rules I ask my counsel to guide me, for I don't know when I may be imposed on (laughter).

Counsel: Your lawyer will look out for you.

Mr. Fisk: Oh, I'll look out for myself (laughter). Don't give yourself any trouble about that.

Counsel: You seem to be a very frank and outspoken witness (laughter).

Mr. Fisk: Well, I'm not much accustomed to you fellows (laughter). I was never on the stand but once before.

Counsel: When was that?

Mr. Fisk: That was when I was a boy, up in the country—in a cow case (great laughter).

CHAPTER VII.

Though the settlement of all the difficulties of the Vanderbilt-Erie war and the conclusion of peace was arrived at the last of April or early in May, it was not officially announced to the board of Erie directors till July 30th. On that day the president made the terms known to the board and after their adoption Mr. Eldridge resigned and retired to Massachusetts to devote his energies to the Boston, Hartford & Erie, which, after causing about as much scandal in the Massachusetts Legislature as Erie had done at Albany and swallowing several millions of the State funds, became bankrupt. Mr. Drew also retired from the board with several others, leaving Messrs. Fisk and Gould in undisputed sway. To most men the Erie Railway at the time these gentlemen came into full possessisn would have seemed no very goodly heritage. It had the appearance of a thoroughly sucked orange. But the new masters still saw signs of juice and felt it no mean windfall notwithstanding that its treasury had just been depleted of $9,000,000, that its affairs were in a very unfavorable condition and that the worst odor attached to its name. They addressed themselves earnestly to the difficult task of bringing order out chaos, infusing new life into the road and rescuing it from threatened bankruptcy. They took Wm. M. Tweed and Peter B. Sweeney into their board to fill the vacancies and with this accession of the masters of New York City and the State Legislature, Tammany Hall and the Erie ring were fused in interests and have since continued to serve each other faithfully. Messrs. Fisk and Gould concentrated all the power in their own hands, Gould becoming president and treasurer and Fisk comptroller, and they with Tweed and Lane constituting the executive committee. The new power had what is often a great element of strength and gives great advantages—they had nothing to lose, and could act with the boldness which that circumstance warrants.

The 50,000 shares of stock taken back from Vanderbilt was an elephant upon their hands. The disposition of this was the first thing to be attended to, and here they were eminently ingenious and successful. It was a season of the year when money was plenty and stocks naturally buoyant. Besides, for some inexplicable cause, English financiers commenced investing in Erie stock

COMMODORE VANDERBILT.

quite extensively about this time. The new board had purposely been made up in a way to create the impression that Vanderbilt had great influence in it, that his reputation might sustain the price of the stock. He still held several millions worth of it and therefore did not wish it to fall just yet. In addition to all these influences tending to keep the price up, the new masters resorted to a very shrewd piece of finessing for the same purpose. When operators are caught heavily short and feel confident the market will fall soon, instead of buying stock to meet contracts, they often borrow it of those who hold it, till they can buy at a lower price. The new direction now bethought themselves of making this custom serve them a good turn. They sold moderate quantities of Erie stock daily, but, instead of delivering the stock they had in their possession, they borrowed of any who held it and completed their sales by delivering this borrowed stock. This naturally gave the impression that there was a large short interest existing in the stock, hence many became bulls in the hope of pinching the supposed shorts and this tended to send up the price. At the expiration of the time for which the stock had been borrowed, it was of course repaid out of shares that had been in the Erie treasury all the time. By this means and under these various influences, all the 50,000 shares were soon disposed of at about 70 without loss, and thus the feeble condition of the treasury soon felt the healthy stimulus of some $3,000,000.. And finding that Erie went so well, Fisk and Gould saw no good reason why all who thirsted for it should not have their desire gratified, and therefore, profiting by their early instruction, they set the little mill going again and turned out stock in quantities to suit purchasers as long as they would take it. Moreover, it was a season of the year when the road did a heavy business and brought in a great deal of ready money. From all these sources the treasury was soon in a quite flourishing condition and the part that had fallen to Messrs. Fisk and Gould in the settlement proved to be something not so much like a sucked orange as at first appeared.

But Vanderbilt had not neglected an opportunity he saw when Erie was going readily at 70. By the settlement, he was under contract to deliver the directors 50,000 shares at 70 any time before the end of August, and they hoped he would not dare sell the stock he held for fear they would then run the price up and corner him. They also suspected he would make another attempt to control the election in October and would therefore continue to hold large quantities of stock for that purpose. Should he pursue this course they knew the market would remain buoyant till they got it so flooded with new stock that it would tumble at great strides all at once and Vanderbilt would again bleed freely for their benefit. But the Commodore was too wary to be caught in such a trap. He knew the men he had to deal with now. He soon became aware that they were putting upon the market all the stock they had taken back from him and knew they would manufacture a new supply for themselves if the price kept up. He knew they could not manipulate a corner on him with such a vast volume of the stock afloat, and he felt under no special obligation to sustain the market at 70 while his young friends amused themselves grinding out large quantities of new stock. He therefore availed himself of the demand for Erie at 70 to dispose quietly of the large amount of that valuable property still held by him and rid himself of all connection with it and the unscrupulous men now in control. The influence of these combined heavy sales soon began to be felt. Early in August Erie suddenly commenced to fall rapidly, and on the 19th went at 49. On that day the stockholders and public were taken by surprise by the announcement that the transfer books were closed to get ready for the election, which was not to occur till the 13th of October.

When stock is issued, the names of the parties to whom it is issued and their respective amounts, are entered in the stock register of the company. The entries thus made on their books are the sole evidence to the company as to who are owners of the stock, and from these entries is made up the list of those entitled to vote at elections. If any subsequent purchaser of the stock wishes to vote he must go to the office of the company and have the shares held by him transferred from the name of the man to whom they were issued, or to whose credit they now stand, to his own, else his name will not appear on the voting list made up from the books and some other man will have the right of voting on his stock. It is customary to close these transfer books—*i. e.*, suspend the privilege of having stock transferred from one name to another—after notice, a few days before an election, to give time to make out the voting list from them. Fisk and Gould had now suspended this right nearly *two months* before the election. The object was obvious. The 50,000 shares taken from Vanderbilt and all the new stock they had since issued now stood on the books in their own names or those of men in league with them, and by thus preventing their transfer they would be able to vote at the election upon vast amounts of stock owned by other people and so easily compass their own reëlection. Of course the proceeding was daringly illegal, and in any community where law has any force and a judge dare not openly be a scoundrel, they might have been compelled to make transfers till a reasonable time before election; but with recent experience as to the lengths these men were ready to go, and with Judge Barnard, who had driven them out of the State and made a great show of virtue by denouncing them in unsparing terms in March, now in closest friendship with them, no one cared to make the useless attempt. It had now got to the pass that these men openly defied the law, and it could not be enforced against them. How futile any such attempt would have been was proven two years later when, under similar circumstances, some English owners of 60,000 shares of the stock attempted to have it transferred to their names so they might vote on it at the approaching election. A motion for this purpose having been made, of course it was managed to have it come up before Judge Barnard and he coolly put it down for hearing *at a day subsequent to the election!* Application was then made to Judge Cardozo to remedy the outrage, but in vain. The counsel of the English stockholders was the Hon. Wm. M. Evarts, and all who are not familiar with the New York Courts would naturally think that a judge would be very slow to treat such a distinguished lawyer with wanton indignity, and that if such an outrage were perpetrated upon his clients a man of his great name, abilities and influence would raise a storm of public and professional indignation that would sweep the infamous men from the bench; but he was made the mere sport of the miserable ring-politician judges, driven back and forth like a shuttle-cock between Jew and Gentile, the rights of his clients were stolen from them, and all had to be submitted to, awakening no murmurs of surprise or resentment. This trick enabled Messrs. Fisk and Gould to vote upon vast quantities of stock owned by other men, and by the purchase of a sufficient number of proxies to give them control of a majority of votes on election day, they easily reëlected themselves, though they owned little or none of the stock—the stock of the men most anxious to turn them out having thus been made to secure their continuance in power.

Their reëlection having thus been made sure two months beforehand, they of course cared nothing more about the stock. However low it fell they would lose nothing as they owned none of it, so they not only continued to issue new stock and load it upon the market, but also deliberately entered upon a bear campaign to depress the price not only of Erie but of the whole list of stocks. The means adopted to accomplish this purpose was what is called a "lock up" of currency.

In the early autumn a large amount of currency is drawn from New York to the west and south to move the crops of the year. This makes money very scarce at the financial centre and in such demand that high rates of interest prevail and the whole stock market is depressed. The monetary stringency thus naturally produced was further increased this season by the fact that Mr. Mc-Culloch, Secretary of the Treasury at that time, favored the policy of contracting the volume of currency as a means of getting back to specie payment. A combination was formed by the Erie ring to take advantage of this state of circumstances. They had control of some fourteen millions of money, Daniel Drew engaging to supply four millions to the pool. The first step was to sell heavily short of all the leading stocks; then they suddenly withdrew from circulation all the money controlled by them, producing a critical stringency in money and a great fall in stocks, when they covered their short contracts at immense profits and the plot was an entire success. As soon as this scheme was well under way and stocks had fallen considerably and money readily commanded extortionate rates of interest, the timorous Drew became alarmed at the dizzy heights to which the young eagles were bent on soaring with him and looked anxiously about for a safe escape. Stocks had already fallen so that a handsome harvest could be gathered, and he was fain to be satisfied with this while his confederates had their hearts fixed on something much more grand. Among those who had already been forced into a very critical situation by the fall in stocks and the scarcity of money was Henry Keep, a former associate of Drew. He was now in the most pressing need of two millions of dollars to sustain himself and was willing to grant the most profitable terms to secure it, as he would fail and be ruined unless it was forthcoming. Faithful to his nature to do the best he can for himself always, regardless of associates, friends, and promises, Drew seized this fine opportunity of covering a safe retreat, loaned Keep the two millions, and withdrew his funds from the lock up. Fisk and Gould, however, continued to turn the screws and wring their victims without mercy, regarding the writhing and agony as rare sport and amusement.

The practices of the New York banks are such that a clique in command of such a large sum of money can often place Wall Street entirely at their mercy. The two customs of certifying checks and loaning money on speculative stocks are vulnerable points that may put the banks and all monetary interests in the power of such a band of conspirators. A check is "certified" by the cashier of the bank on which it is drawn writing "Good" across it and signing his name. Properly this means that the maker of the check has funds on deposit to meet it, and the certification is the same as the endorsement of a note, making the bank responsible, it being the cashier's duty to refuse to cash uncertified checks when the maker has in the bank only money enough to meet the checks that have been certified. In fact, however, many of the New York banks often certify checks of depositors in good credit for much larger sums than the maker has on deposit with them ; in other words, the bank endorses the notes of its depositors. As certified checks pass as readily as money, a man may command twice as much capital as he is really worth. Banks also loan money and take stocks for collateral security. It is in times of greatest stringency of course that depositors are most apt to have checks certified for much larger sums than they have on deposit and that money is borrowed by speculators on stock held by them. The banks thus become indirectly parties to the speculations and when a crisis comes they suddenly find themselves responsible for certified checks in much larger sums than the makers of the checks have on deposit, and they are themselves pressed for funds to meet the certified checks, yet dare not call in the demand loans they have made on stocks, for if they should the stocks would have to be sold in a depressed or falling market, thus increasing the depression and causing a financial crash. In this way the banks themselves are often drawn into a most critical position.

None of these opportunities for helping on their purpose were neglected by Fisk and Gould during their lock up. They continued to issue new stock and locked up all the money it brought. Between the time of their coming into absolute power in July and the 24th of October, 235,000 shares of new stock were secretly issued and put upon the market, increasing the capital stock from $34,265,300 to $57,766,300, or an increase of $23,501,000 in about three months. The first week in November was a most trying and critical one. Money commanded extraordinary rates of daily interest, all stocks were falling, several of the banks were greatly embarrassed, many firms were failing and a disastrous crash seemed imminent. Urgent appeals went from Wall Street to Washington for the Secretary of the Treasury to relieve the situation by re-issuing some of the currency that had been withdrawn from circulation under his policy of contraction, but he regarded it as a mere contest between speculators, in no wise affecting the business interests of the country and so refused to interfere or swerve from his course of contraction. Calumny even represented him as interested with the "lock up" clique, and of course the leading spirits eagerly encouraged this impression. Fisk and Gould now feeling Wall Street securely in their clutches gave the screws another remorseless turn.

Another fall in stocks followed, Erie going to 35, a fall of just 50 per cent. since the new management obtained control, and N. Y. Central fell to 114, or 23 per cent. since the commencement of the "lock up," a fall that told the making and losing of many a large fortune. Other stocks fell in like manner; more firms failed, the condition of the banks became more critical and renewed appeals were made to Secretary McCulloch and he was assured that unless relief was afforded there must result a financial crash that would involve not only New York but the business interests of the whole country. At length, finding the situation so serious, on Saturday morning, Nov. 7th, he telegraphed to New York that he would re-issue $50,000,000 of currency to relieve the situation if necessary. This gave assurance that the power of the clique was broken and so relieved apprehension, but as the currency was not issued the stock market did not react but dragged on through another week of depression. The combination taking the news from Washington as their warning, improved this week to cover all their shorts and prepare a new scheme. Of course stocks would react suddenly when the stringency was removed, so, after covering their shorts, they bought heavily and went long in all the leading stocks, preparatory to reaping another harvest from the coming rise. And now was discovered an opportunity for gratifying a little revenge.

When Drew deserted the "lock up," knowing that the

design of the managers was to depress the price of Erie and being aware of the large secret issue of new stock, he sold heavily short of Erie and waited for the fall. Fisk and Gould found out that he was short and resolved to make use of that circumstance not only to transfer large sums of money from his pockets to their own but also to wreak vengeance upon him for turning traitor to them in the "lock up" plot. Accordingly, while they made use of the week following the news from Washington to cover their own shorts most advantageously, they managed to keep Erie declining slightly so that Drew failed to cover his shorts. On Saturday, the 14th, all their plans being ripe, Erie sold for 35 during the regular business hour, but in the afternoon the managers of the "lock up" unlock their twelve millions of currency, and put it in circulation suddenly, making money very plenty and easy and under their new combination for a rise Erie quickly shot from 35 to 47—a rise of 12 per cent. in an hour or two. Drew was immediately filled with alarm and realized that he was caught in a trap. Great excitement prevailed late in the afternoon and through the evening, for it was now evident that new developments of an important character were at hand. The course of things for the last three months and the fall of 50 per cent. in Erie had dispelled the delusion which had led to such large foreign investments in that stock in July and August, and it was now discovered that New York agents of the foreign purchasers had been selling the stock and it was expected that large amounts of it would arrive from England .by the steamer due on Monday, the 23d. Those who had thus sold for their foreign customers when the stock was depressed now naturally desired with Drew that the price should not be suddenly run up again for speculative purposes. ·A consultation was held by the agents of the foreign stockholders and their sympathizers, and it was decided to resort to ·the Courts once more for protection. Accordingly Saturday night was employed by Drew in making the necessary affidavits, stating the course of the Erie managers in issuing new stock, for speculative purposes in violation of statutes, etc. These affidavits were to be used on Monday to procure the removal of Fisk and Gould from control of the Erie Railway and the appointment of a receiver to take charge of its affairs. Mr. August Belmont being the most prominent agent of the foreign stockholders and a gentleman of high standing and great influence, the suit was to be brought in his name. But Drew, true to his nature of pursuing no course vigorously more than a few hours at the most in a critical situation, and naturally having no very strong confidence in the efficacy of the Courts to relieve him in his present exigency, had no sooner sworn to the affidavits than he was ready to betray either party or both provided he could only get himself out of the difficulty. · Accordingly after spending ·Saturday night in conference with those united with him to oppose Fisk and Gould, and in making affidavits to be used by Mr. Belmont in legal proceedings against those gentlemen on Monday morning, he made it his first business on Sunday to call on Fisk and endeavor to secure pardon and relief for himself by disclosing the situation and betraying the designs of his friends in council the previous night. He made a perfect confidant of his whilom *protégé* and pupil, revealing to him without reserve all the details and dangers of the position in which his victims were placed by the sudden rise, telling him of the legal proceedings that would be instituted against him on the morrow, and then, in return for all this confidence, frankness and treachery, meekly requested that some small hole be opened through which he himself might escape. Fisk listened attentively till he had drawn from his informant full knowledge of every detail of the circumstances and designs of his opponents and then to the request with which the narrative ended he returned a sardonic laugh and said, "Ah! ha! old fellow, I've got you just where I want you now! By this revelation of the situation you are all placed wholly in my power. You're in and you can't get out, bellow as much as you may!"

The "old man eloquent" in tears plead and besought to be relieved and expressed an entire willingness to retract the affidavits on which the suit was to be instituted and help to harrass all the rest in every possible way if he were only assisted to provide for "them shorts" on easy terms. But Fisk was inexorable. He knew

how much a promise of Drew's was worth, he knew that
Drew could now help him to nothing which he could not
do better. alone, he knew that Drew was his choicest
piece of game, the man from whom most money could be
wrung in the present situation, and he prized as do few
men, fortunately, the fine opportunity of gratifying revenge. He therefore turned a deaf ear to all the mournful entreaties, told Drew he was "the last man that ought
to whine over any position he placed himself in with
regard to Erie," and finally got so impatient of the
continued appeals that he informed him he could listen to
him no longer. After hours of self-humiliation and
abject cringing, the wily veteran of two-and-seventy years
suddenly composed his countenance as a child dries its
tears on finding they are useless, and, acting upon Fisk's
polite request to leave, heaping coals of fire on his
enemy's head with an urbanity that Chesterfield might
have envied, though it must have fallen much like a pun
at a funeral, he mildly said " I'll bid you good evening "
and bowed himself out.

The situation now called for immediate action on the
part of Fisk and Gould and not a moment was to be lost.
As soon as Drew had retired Fisk summoned a council of
his confederates to listen to the information he had gained
and decide upon the course to pursue. The tactics
speedily adopted stamped them as men of no common
mould and as possessed of no common power. It was
decided to forestall the coming Belmont suit by commenc-

ing a suit first. Affidavits were at once made alleging that certain parties were conspiring to injure the Erie Railway by interfering with the directors, that there was danger of injunctions that would be of great injury to the interests of the road, the stockholders and the public, etc., etc., and therefore the appointment of a receiver to take charge of the road was prayed for. And now to whom should they go to get this legal farce and bare-faced fraud carried out? What judge, in the light of this nineteenth century and in this land of boasted liberty and law, would disgrace the bench by performing such a monstrous parody on the very name of law? Who would dream of their going to the very judge whom they had declared corrupt in a former affidavit, who had chased them out of the State only eight months before, taken the lead in denouncing them as villains, and pronounced the bill they had bribed through the Legislature to be "a bill legalizing counterfeit money?" Yet this was what they did. George G. Barnard was the judge selected to authorize this fraud. Nor did they wait for him to appear in his Court. They surprised him on Monday morning before his toilet was completed, and such was the strange transformation that had come over the mental, moral and legal nature of this man since the spring months that he extended a cordial greeting to these men he then so vehemently anathematized, and soon the outrage was legalized by the same signature that was attached to the writs which had driven the suitors into exile on the 11th of the preceding March. This infamous step taken, the details were in perfect keeping. The request for a receiver having been granted, who was a proper person for such a responsible trust? The man whom this upright judge deemed it most appropriate to appoint was none other than Jay Gould! And as the receiver of such a responsible trust must give heavy and most undoubted bonds, who would be his bondsman? The one bondsman in every way satisfactory to the distinguished Court was James Fisk, Jr.! With this monstrous proceeding thus sanctioned by the Supreme Court, the surprise party withdrew and left Judge Barnard to complete his toilet at leisure.

When the Courts opened at ten o'clock, Mr. Belmont's lawyers appeared before Judge Sutherland and commenced proceedings in the regular way, obtaining an injunction and getting Mr. Davies, an ex-judge of the Court of Appeals, appointed receiver. When they had been through with all their trouble and felt themselves now secure, the Drew-Belmont party were somewhat surprised to learn that "the regular way" was altogether too slow a coach to travel by if they would head off Messrs. Fisk and Gould and were astonished not a little to find that a receiver had already been appointed in the interest of Messrs. Fisk and Gould while Judge Sutherland was still enjoying his last slumbers in the morning, and that that receiver was Jay Gould, with James Fisk, Jr., for bondsman. Under the influence of this news in Wall

Street that day, Erie fluctuated wildly from 50 up to 61 and then back to 48. It seemed as though the utmost length of iniquity to which a judge would dare go had been reached by Judge Barnard in this day's proceedings, but on Wednesday morning he followed it up by an order which made the one of Monday, black as it was, seem "pure as the driven snow." Fisk and Gould wanted to use the funds of the Erie treasury in manipulating their "corner," but there is a statute expressly forbidding any railroad to speculate in its own stock and they felt it worth while to clothe their steps with some small show of legality. To compass their purpose, affidavits were made stating that some doubts existed as to the legality of a recent issue of two or three hundred thousand shares of stock, wherefore Mr. Receiver Gould petitioned the Court for instruction and authority to use the funds of the Erie treasury to buy back this stock of doubtful legality at any price less than par, that it might be cancelled. In other words, Jay Gould, as president of the Erie Railway, had issued two or three hundred thousand shares of stock, in direct violation of a statute forbidding an increase of capital stock, and disposed of it at about 40 to depress the market and help on the "lock up," and after this course had sent the stock to 35, Jay Gould, as receiver, alleging the illegality of his act as president, now asked for authority in direct conflict with another statute forbidding any railroad to speculate in its own stock, to use the funds of the treasury to buy back *at par* this very stock recently sold by him at about 40. And this authority Judge Barnard promptly granted!

Drew had no time to ejaculate over the enormity of this order. Whatever its nature, he knew it meant "business" for him. He saw that there was now no possible escape for him and that he must face the music and buy Erie on the best terms he could to cover his shorts before a corner could be closed on him. Fisk and Gould, with the whole Erie treasury at their disposal by order of Judge Barnard, now also set to buying with all their might, determined to corner their early instructor. Drew was 70,000 shares short and the fight was a desperate one. He knew it meant a heavy loss to him, but a corner meant a still heavier one, and he fought against it accordingly. The battle raged all day long on Wednesday and at night Erie stood at 57. Still the contest was not decided. Drew had not secured enough to cover his contracts, Fisk and Gould had not secured enough to perfect the corner. The next morning the battle was renewed, both parties knowing that the decisive hour would be past and victory decided before that day closed. The books of the company show pretty accurately where all the stock is—how much in Europe and how much in Wall Street, so Fisk and Gould could tell very nearly how much they had to control to secure their corner. On Thursday the battle raged with a fierceness and violence that quite eclipsed that on the 10th of March.

Collisions and blows were not infrequent in the excitement. As it approached two o'clock Erie stood at 62 and the scales seemed turning against Drew. So desperate was the struggle that there was a difference of 10 per cent. between stock delivered immediately and that to be delivered at a quarter to three. As the strife was only for the corner, which must culminate that day, and it was certain the stock would fall again when the crisis was over, and especially after the steamer arrived on Monday bringing back from Europe a large amount of the stock, there was a difference of 16 per cent. between stock to be delivered that day and that to be delivered in three days. It is two o'clock and in fifteen minutes more the battle will be over. . Fisk and Gould are now confident and Drew's heart is sinking as he feels himself falling into their pitiless clutches. The noise of conflict has extended much further than usual from Wall Street, and an unwonted number of lookers-on have gathered around. Every man holding a share of the stock that has been so fickle deems this his most favorable time to sell and every available share is now thrown upon the market. Suddenly large quantities of stock supposed to be in Europe make their appearance. This makes matters seem very dangerous for the side that has almost won. A hasty investigation shows that some hundred thousand shares issued in certificates of ten shares each, intended for circulation in Europe only, had been laid away by small purchasers in New York and were now being brought out.

This is a damaging blow to Fisk and Gould and a heavy
reinforcement of their opponent at the very turning point
of the battle. However, there must be no wavering or
the day is lost. The stock must be absorbed at all
hazards and as but ten minutes more remain they throw
themselves into the breech with all the vehemence and
nerve for which Fisk is noted, undaunted by the untoward event. They are gathering in the unexpected
stock by the hundred shares per minute, when their
bank becomes suddenly alarmed at the amount of checks
that flow in for certification to meet this last grand charge
and refuse to certify their checks for any further sums,
and dealers refuse to accept their checks unless certified.
The blow is vexatious, but Fisk is still undaunted and
rallies to the new emergency with the energy of a man
borne on by the most determined will and desperation
combined. Arrangements are instantly made to have
their checks certified at another bank and they return for
the last desperate charge that is to win the day. But five
minutes have been lost in making the new arrangement
for having their checks certified and they are the five last,
decisive moments of the struggle. Drew improved them
while his enemies were crippled. His shorts were covered
and the corner was defeated. Erie dropped at once to 42.
It had been a battle of giants in which both parties had
suffered severely, each inflicting heavy and damaging
blows upon the other and neither gaining a triumph.
Drew had escaped the ruinous grip of a corner, but had

been forced to cover at about 58 his contracts for 70,000 shares of which he went short at about 38, and the day had cost him about a million and a half dollars. Fisk and Gould had gratified revenge upon Drew, but as they had bought enormous quantities of stock at the high prices and had failed to get their corner on Drew to relieve them of their burdens and the stock had now fallen on their hands, the revenge had cost them, or the Erie Railway, heavily, and the day had probably more than cancelled all their profits from the preceding "lock up" and bear campaign.

With this day's battle Daniel Drew retired from all active part in Wall Street affairs. A long career of constant strifes and battles closed with a severe and bitter blow, but it left him still possessed of millions. He saw the spirit of young America was getting far too strong for his aged nerves and retired to his native town to devote himself entirely to building and endowing Methodist churches, Methodist seminaries and attending Methodist prayer-meetings. He is seen "on the street" no more except at rare intervals, when he comes down to look on with an expression of mute, child-like wonder on his countenance and his arms folded behind him as he watches how deftly his young pupils now stack the cards and throw the dice; but to all invitations to take a hand in the game once more he mournfully shakes his head.

Through the week following the culmination of the struggle between Drew and Fisk the utmost confusion prevailed in regard to Erie matters, several new suits being instituted on the one side and the other, opposing receivers contending for possession, and the wildest reports circulated as to the designs of Messrs. Fisk and Gould. For a day or two it was fully believed that they intended to abscond to Canada or Europe, taking with them all the funds of the Erie treasury. They barricaded themselves in the Erie offices and it was found impossible to get to them to serve upon them any papers in the suits that had been instituted. Officers were stationed around the building and at all the ferries and depots to catch them in case they attempted to escape. After this situation had lasted for a week, late on Sunday night several of the party emerged from the office and started for the ferry. Fisk was immediately approached and served with some legal papers, whereupon he returned to the office to ascertain their nature. Knowing now that he was closely watched and that he might be served with numberless other legal documents and even be arrested if he made another open attempt to cross the ferry, he prepared himself as if for a masquerade. In this guise, with his identity concealed, he once more emerged from the office and approaching a carriage that stood in waiting, instructed the driver, in a loud disguised voice, to drive to the Fifth Avenue Hotel, and then entered the carriage. The driver drove rapidly up the street a few blocks and then in obedience to previous secret instructions disobeyed the loud direction given out as a blind, drove to the Courtlandt Street ferry, and by this circuitous passage landed his precious freight safely in New Jersey. Some officers, suspecting such a move, had crossed over the ferry to the Erie depot in Jersey City. Here they found a director's car and an engine ready for a start, though they were informed no train was going out. Waiting to watch developments, they soon heard an unusual whistle up the road towards the Bergen tunnel. At sound of this the track-master feigned much excitement at the position of the director's car, told the engineer he had no business on that track and ordered him to start up and back down upon another track. The engineer started up but, instead of backing down as directed, kept increasing his speed and passed off up the road, leaving the officers standing alone. These circumstances were put together and it was now considered as a certainty that Fisk and Gould had run away and carried all the money of the Erie Railway with them, and announcements to that effect were made in all the papers next morning. When Fisk got the morning papers from New York and read the news, he telegraphed back an indignant denial and his card was published in the same papers next morning. He declared he had only gone to Binghampton on matters connected with the business of the road, and such proved to be the fact. Mr. Fisk regarded the articles published about him as gross libels and on returning to the city he immediately commenced suits for libel against all the leading papers, laying the damages in each case at $100,000. He, however, subsequently so

far controlled his indignation as to think it not worth his
while to bring any of these suits to trial.   Everybody now
seeming to feel satisfied that it was useless to attempt to do
anything to bring the managing spirits to justice or rescue
the property of the Erie stockholders from these men, and
that there was no way but to let them run their course, a
calm succeeded in Erie affairs, and all attacks and efforts
ceased.   This seemed to give Mr. Fisk the impression that
he held the world in a sling and he now commenced legal
proceedings against nearly everybody on a most magnificent scale.   December 10th he commenced a suit against
Vanderbilt for $3,500,000, alleging that the settlement of
July was illegal, and seeking to recover the money paid
Vanderbilt on that occasion.   A suit was commenced
against Work and Schell on the same transaction in the
sum of $429,250.   August Belmont was sued for injuring
the Erie Railway by commencing a suit against its directors and the damages were placed at a million of dollars.
An examination of the records of the Erie office showed
that some years before when Drew was director he had
bought certain steamboats of the company, used them in
the company's business on Lake Erie, charged the company for said service and finally resold the steamers to
the company.   This proceeding was alleged to be fraudulent from beginning to end, and a suit therefor was
commenced against Drew for the sum of a million of
dollars.   It is impossible to predict how far similar proceedings might have been kept up had not some other

business of a diverting nature required a little attention from Mr. Fisk and afforded him a new amusement.

The Legislature was soon to meet at Albany and Messrs. Fisk and Gould naturally apprehended that trouble might come to them from that quarter and that investigating committees might be showered down upon them to inquire into their conduct and the condition of the Erie Railway. Hostile legislation was expected in the matter of their enormous issue of new stock. But Vanderbilt had declared a stock dividend of 80 per cent. on the capital of the N. Y. Central Dec. 19th, and this was an increase of capital or a watering of the stock about the legality of which there was some doubt also as well as about the Erie issue. Here was an excellent opportunity for log rolling. A bill legalizing Vanderbilt's stock dividend was passed through the Legislature without any difficulty and the affairs of Erie were permitted to rest in peace. But now Vanderbilt wanted to get through a bill to consolidate the Hudson River and Central roads. Fisk and Gould, apprehending that their election from year to year would be a matter involving them in a severe contest and many unpleasant circumstances, wanted to avoid the necessity of an annual battle to prevent the stockholders from turning them out of office. They therefore had a bill prepared providing that after the next annual election the Erie directors should be classified so that only one fifth of them should be elected annually. They were to be divided into classes, the first to hold office for six

years, the second for five and so on, the last class holding
for one year only, but all future elections to be for six
years. Either this bill or Vanderbilt's consolidation bill
would, alone, meet with a bitter opposition and require
vast sums of money to put them in a favorable light before the legislators. The Legislature was Republican,
though the Governor was Democratic (a circumstance
explained by the ingenious system of "repeating" in
New York city), and the man engineering the Erie classification bill was Wm. M. Tweed, "boss" of the Demo-
crats and also himself an Erie director. The wishes of
Vanderbilt and the Erie ring not being antagonistic, and
knowing how much harm they could do each other by
opposition, the two parties now joined in another little
"pool," this time to operate not in stocks but in the votes
of the worthy law-makers and guardians of the public
weal in the great Empire State. They knew how many
votes must be bought and what was their price under
various circumstances. They could unite and carry both
bills through for a much less sum than each would cost
if the other opposed. Hence a truce was made to their
enmities, the two bills went speedily through without
difficulty and the same day the suit of Belmont (in which
Vanderbilt was supposed to be influential) against the Erie
Railway was discontinued. This classification bill, though
its avowed purpose and immediate consequence were well
known, and though there was no doubt but that it was
bribed through the Legislature, received the signature of

Governor John T. Hoffman.   At the next annual election
Fisk and Gould carried everything their own way by arts
similar to those practised the previous year, and then proceeded to "draw lots" to determine who should have the
long terms and who the short ones under the classification
bill. · Of course Fisk and Gould both drew the longest
term, and thus by the act of a bribed Legislature and tho
signature of John T. Hoffman the Erie Railway was
placed in the absolute control of James Fisk, Jr., and Jay
Gould for six years beyond the reach of the wishes and
voice of the stockholders.   Of the directors chosen at this
election, five were salaried clerks in the employ of Fisk
and Gould and were of course their obedient tools, mere
holders of places like so many wooden men, with no voice
whatever in the management, thus giving these two men
absolute control of a majority of the board of directors.
Some six or seven of the other directors were men of much
higher character, but they were merely put in as respectable figure-heads, and had all signed a pledge to support
Gould's policy or resign.   And, in fact, even the formality
of calling an occasional meeting of the board of directors
was long ago dispensed with and everything is managed
by the executive committee, Fisk, Gould, Lane and Tweed,
without ever thinking of taking a vote of the others.
Indeed Messrs. Fisk and Gould have probably forgotten
that there is such a thing as a board of directors of the
Erie Railway, and practically there is nono.   In this
manner have things gone on now for three years with

hardly an effort from any quarter to oppose them. One
public-spirited citizen purchased some of the stock and
commenced legal proceedings with a design of bringing
Fisk and Gould to account. The result was that his suit
was taken out of the district in which he brought it,
dragged before Judge Barnard in New York city, who
issued an injunction forbidding him from taking any further proceedings, fined him $5,000 for contempt of court
in violating this injunction by making preparations for the
trial, then he was forced to trial without any preparation
and before this same judge, and, when he objected to
going to trial before Barnard, judgment was entered
against him by default. This experiment was not encouraging for any one else to attempt to interfere with
Messrs. Fisk and Gould in their management. A bill
was introduced into the last Legislature to repeal the Erie
classification bill, but after slumbering in the hands of the
committee for several weeks, a majority reported against
the repeal, having been convinced of its propriety. Probably the committee on railroads for many years to come
will need to have their minds convinced annually on this
subject by the arguments Messrs. Gould and Fisk are
adepts at applying, and after considering the matter carefully, *à la* Mattoon, will report against the repeal.

The issue of new stock and the tricks of the management in the fall of 1868 became so outrageous that the
Stock Board at length resolved to shield itself from such
frauds. On the 27th of October a committee of the

board waited upon Jay Gould to make inquiries as to the amount of new stock that had been issued and the probabilities as to more new issues. The president of Erie was very bland and affable to the committee, his nervous black eye twinkling with an unwonted sparkle as he talked at much length upon every question asked him. The committee were quite dazzled by the grandeur of his notions and ideas, and with their eyes thus loaded with dust they returned to report progress. When the knowledge they had gathered was submitted to the crucible of the board and stripped of Jay Gould's verbiage, it was found that new stock had been issued to the extent of ten millions of dollars and there was no telling how long the process would be kept up. This much-enduring body, unable to restrain their indignation and impatience any longer, passed a resolution :

"That on and after January 31st, 1869, this board will not call or deal in any active speculative stock of any company a registry of whose stock is not kept in some responsible bank or trust company or other satisfactory agency, and which shall not give public notice at the time of establishing such registry of the number of shares so entrusted to be registered and shall not give at least thirty days' notice through the newspapers and in writing to the president of this board of any intended increase of the number of shares, either direct or through an issue of convertible bonds, and which shall not at the same time give notice of the object for which such issue of stock or bonds is about to be made."

This was a most reasonable and appropriate regulation and one to which no honest board of directors could .make the least objection; but when the appointed 31st of January, 1869, arrived Erie had not registered in compliance with this resolution and it was consequently stricken from the list of stocks called at the Stock Board. Fisk and Gould, with an utter indifference and even contempt for this disgrace of their road and stock, stepped just across Broad Street from the Stock Exchange, engaged a suitable room, organized a new board of their own, called the National Board, wherein Erie and all the other stocks were called and dealt in as though nothing had happened. It was not till a year and a half later that Erie was finally registered and resumed its place on the list at the Stock Board.

Between the time that these men came into power and September 30th, 1869, the capital stock of the road was increased $53,425,700. The amount expended in equipping and improving the road during the same time was $6,297,067, leaving $49,128,633 wholly unaccounted for. No dividend was declared on any of the stock after the advent of Fisk and Gould; the debts of the corporation were largely increased, so that all the profits earned by the road, as well as the many millions received for new stock, remained unaccounted for. No one but Fisk and Gould knew anything about it, and what they knew they were sagely inclined to keep to themselves. The same policy and style of management was kept up to the end, the deeds constantly deepening in darkness of hue, as a course of crime ever does—the stock fluctuating between twenty and thirty per cent. of its par value.

CHAPTER VIII.

Mr. Fisk closed the first year of his prominence in New
York by an act betraying the worst and most dangerous
trait of his character—a trait much more dangerous to
himself than to its victims—a delight in spiteful, wanton,
bootless revenge. On the morning of December 23d the
citizens of New York were startled by an item of news in
the morning papers that sounded more like an echo of
the days of *lettres de cachet* and the French Bastile than
the nineteenth century and the land that boasts of being
in the van of liberty and personal security. A distinguished and highly respected gentleman had been
suddenly seized the previous night and whipped into
prison without being informed of the cause, handled in
the roughest manner, and all friends were refused
admittance to see him till morning.

About nine o'clock on the night of December 22d,
while the New England Society in New York were

around the "festive board" commemorating the landing of tho Pilgrims on Plymouth Rock, and the Sachems of Tammany Hall were in like manner celebrating the election of A. Oakey Hall as Mayor, Samuel Bowles, Esq., the well-known editor of the Springfield *Republican*, was standing in the main hall of the Fifth Avenue Hotel, talking with some friends, when two men came in, one of whom passed behind him then turned suddenly, seized him by the arms, and rushed him along towards the street while the other held a crumpled paper in his face saying it was an order for his arrest and helping push him out of the house. When they reached the sidewalk a carriage was in waiting into which Mr. Bowles was hurriedly forced and then driven rapidly away to Ludlow Street jail. The movement was so sudden, and the spectators were taken so completely by surprise, that no interference could be made on his behalf. When securely behind the bars of the jail, Mr. Bowles was permitted to read the legal document in virtue of which he had thus been seized and incarcerated. The foundation of the proceeding proved to be as follows:

SUPERIOR COURT, CITY OF NEW YORK.

JAMES FISK, JR.,
vs.
SAMUEL BOWLES and others, composing the firm of Samuel Bowles & Co.

CITY AND COUNTY OF NEW YORK, *ss.*:

James Fisk, Jr., being duly sworn, deposes and says

that he is the plaintiff in the above entitled action; that on the 28th day of November, 1868, the defendant, Samuel Bowles, being the principal editor or editor in chief of certain newspapers published by the said Samuel Bowles & Co., in the City of Springfield and State of Massachusetts, known and described as "The Daily Springfield *Republican*" and "The Semi-Weekly Springfield *Republican*," did compose and publish of and concerning this deponent, plaintiff aforesaid, the following false, malicious scandalous and defamatory matter, to wit: "But Fisk has probably destroyed the credit of the railroad (meaning the Erie Railway Co.), while piling up a fortune for himself. The multiplication of its stock has been fearful. From thirty millions of nominal capital a year ago it has been raised to sixty or seventy millions and what there is to show for the difference beyond some worthless securities of the Hartford & Erie Railroad, and a million or two of real estate it is now impossible to say. The issue of new shares seems to have been wanton, and to no purpose in great part but to gamble in Wall Street with. Nothing so audacious, nothing more gigantic in the way of swindling has ever been perpetrated in this country, and yet it may be that Mr. Fisk and his associates have done nothing that they cannot legally justify, at least in the New York Courts, several of which they (meaning deponent Fisk and others) seem wholly to own. Fisk's operations are said to be under the legal guidance of both David Dudley Field and Charles O'Connor, and now both Judge Barnard of the State and Judge Blatchford of the United States Court, back up and help on his proceedings. . . . . . Many even of his friends predict for him the state prison or the lunatic asylum."

Deponent further says that the same matter as last above recited as having been published in the said "Daily and Semi-Weekly Springfield *Republican*," was republished in "The Weekly Springfield *Republican*," also published by the above named defendants, on the 5th day of December, A. D. 1868. Deponent further says that an action was commenced in this Court by this deponent on the 21st day of December, 1868, for libel for the above recited false, malicious, scandalous and defamatory matter, as above stated, published by the defendants against the above named plaintiff, claiming damages in the sum of $50,000.

Deponent further says that the said newspapers, published by the defendants, have a wide and extensive circulation in the City and County of New York and elsewhere, and that by reason of said publication this deponent has been damaged and injured in his character and reputation and his usefulness and efficiency as a director and manager of the vast interests intrusted to his care as managing director of the Erie Railway Company seriously and wantonly injured and damaged—this as well for the stockholders in said company at large as for this deponent.

JAMES FISK, JR.

To accommodate Mr. Fisk, Judge McCunn held a special evening session of his Court, so urgent were the needs of justice in this case deemed, and upon the above affidavit granted an order for the arrest of Mr. Bowles. Sheriff James O'Brien being then on very intimate terms with Fisk and often detailing deputies to serve him, was also easily found on this occasion and deemed the matter

so important that he went to give his personal superin-
tendence (a rare favor) to the arrest of Mr. Bowles.   But
the moment the arrest was effected, none of the faithful
guardians and depositaries of the law could be found any
where.   Every one with power to accept bail and release
Mr. Bowles had disappeared for the night and he was
consigned to the jail till morning.   Several of Mr. Bowles's
friends called to see him soon after his incarceration, but
the jailor seemed to be a friend of Fisk's also, for they
were refused permission to see the prisoner.   Mr. Dudley Field was greatly scandalized at this act of his
distinguished client, and as Mr. Bowles was then an
intimate friend of the Field family, he rode about
town till the early morning hours in search of Mr.
Fisk to obtain the release of the friend of his family, but
in vain.   All attempts to find a magistrate to accept bail
being of no avail and the efforts of his friends to obtain
his release before morning proving fruitless, Mr. Bowles
prepared to spend the night in Ludlow Street jail.   It
was not a fate that disturbed his nerves in the least and
he would have cared nothing about it except for his wife.
She was in very feeble health, and he feared the news of
the outrage coming so suddenly upon her might affect
her quite injuriously.   He did manage to obtain from the
jailor the great favor of sending her a letter, humorously
describing his prospective lodgings for the night and then
passed the night without any of the agony or mortification
which Mr. Fisk would doubtless have felt in the same

situation, and therefore supposed another would feel. Ethics was not included in the small curriculum of Mr. Fisk's education and he was never a frequenter of Sabbath schools in his youth, so he has never attained to such a high moral perception as to understand that it is not the fact of being in jail, but the *cause* of being there, that constitutes the disgrace, if disgrace there be. To him the mere circumstance of being behind grates and iron doors is disgrace and mortification, and so long as that cannot be said of a man he is honorable no matter what his acts, but with the jailor's key once turned on him he must bow his head in shame forever. He seems to be imbued with the Greek morals and philosophy, which placed the disgrace not in stealing the fox but in getting caught.

The next morning of course Mr. Bowles was immediately bailed and released, the bail being put at the moderate sum of $50,000. He rather enjoyed the episode than otherwise, and nothing else that Mr. Fisk could possibly have done would have been such a benefit to Mr. Bowles. Every honest man in the country saw the principle of his own liberty rudely struck at in the person of the Springfield editor and felt that if such imperial outrages as this were possible under the machinations of the greatest scapegraces outside of Sing Sing, and with the connivance of courts and sheriffs, personal freedom and safety were at an end and the time for a vigilance committee had arrived. The whole press of the country teemed with denunciations of the outrage and indignation and sympathy for the victim. Letters flowed in upon Mr. Bowles by tho bushel and tho most distinguished citizens of Boston offered him tho compliment of a public reception and dinner, which was modestly declined. Tho act which Mr. Fisk intended should disgrace and mortify Mr. Bowles raised him instantly to an honored fame and prominence which he would probably otherwise never havo achieved. But Mr. Fisk evidently felt he had dono a very "smart" thing and gloried so much in tho *éclat* of this climax to his first year of conspicuous position beforo tho public that he went into print on tho subject as follows:

AT HOME, BOSTON, MASS.,
Christmas Day.

On tho 28th of November last "Samuel Bowles, Esq., of Springfield, Mass.," published an editorial headed "Tho New Hero of Wall Street." It was dovoted to a bitter, abusive, untruthful and unprovoked attack on my origin, vocation, habits, personal appearance, and family afflictions. For example, with a reckless disregard of truth and railroad possibilities, "Samuel Bowles, Esq., of Springfield, Mass.," said: "But Fisk has probably destroyed tho credit of tho railroad whilo piling up a fortuno for himself. Tho multiplication of its stock has been fearful. From thirty millions of nominal capital a year ago it has been raised to sixty or seventy millions, and what thero is to show for tho difference beyond somo worthless securities of tho Hartford & Erio Railroad and a million or two of real estato it is now impossiblo to say." Were it not inconsistent with my well-known good nature and forgiving disposition, I should unhesitatingly pronounce "Samuel Bowles, Esq., of Springfield, Mass.," an abandoned falsifier and a fool on that single statement. Further on, the Springfield *Republican* has asserted its capacity for wholesale slander by the following astounding calumny on the Bench and Bar of New York: "Nothing so audacious, nothing more gigantic in the way of swindling has ever been perpetrated in this country and yet it may be that Mr. Fisk and his associates have done nothing that they cannot legally justify, at least in the New York Courts, several of which they seem wholly to own. Fisk's operations are said to be under the legal guidance of both David Dudley Field and Charles O'Connor, and now both Judge Barnard of the State and Judge Blatchford of the United States Court back up and help on his proceedings."

The alleged indifference of the New York city authorities to the incarceration of "Samuel Bowles, Esq., of Springfield, Mass.," was not, you will see, entirely unjustifiable. Culpable as I am in selling "silks, poplins and velvets by the yard," the generous nature of "Samuel Bowles, Esq., of Springfield, Mass.," is not finally and utterly turned against me until he has ascertained that I am guilty of having a father who is unhappily an inmate of a lunatic asylum. This sours all the milk of human kindness in the breast of the Springfield journalist, and he prophetically consigns me to a "mad house or state prison." Under the circumstances, Messrs. Editors, don't you think I had cause to feel vexed with "Samuel Bowles, Esq., of Springfield, Mass."? In order to protect my rights I appealed to the law, which is the highest expression of human wisdom for the good government of mankind. If any error has been committed, those who made the law committed it. I regret that the wife of "Samuel Bowles, Esq., of Springfield, Mass." was disturbed or even annoyed by her husband's temporary absence. As for the sympathy of the sycophantic horde of office seekers and small-beer editors, who clamored around the jail gates for their comrade's release, their abuse I expected and am indifferent to. Mr. Bowles proposed the game himself and I bowled him over the first innings. I think it will be generally conceded that I have as much right to defend my personal character as *any* newspaper has to attack it. At all events I shall do so with the most unflinching determination until it is proven to the contrary. Mr. Bowles need not fear but that I will bring him to trial before a judicial tribunal, and then "let justice be done though the heavens fall," and these are a few of the reasons, Messrs. Editors, why I arrested and locked up "Samuel Bowles, Esq., of Springfield, Mass."

Your obedient servant,

JAMES FISK, JR.

This letter needs no comment. The peculiar notions which the writer entertains as to the duty of "New York city officials," his interpretation and application of "law," as well as some of the things which give him pleasure and which he thinks very "smart," are perfectly apparent. The letter is a faithful photograph of the man. It is evident from his own words that he was stung, not by what he quotes in his affidavits and makes the ground of his complaint, and that he cared not a straw for its effect upon his railroad, but that the personalities inflicted the wound and that Mr. Fisk sought not "justice" at the hands of "the law," but revenge. When he had kept Mr. Bowles in jail over night he was quite satisfied, felt his "personal character" amply defended, and despite the braggart conclusion of his letter nothing more ever came of the suit. He had previously commenced a suit for libel against Mr. Bowles in the Massachusetts Courts, putting the damage at $50,000. The sudden discontinuance of this suit and the instantaneous bringing another in New York and spiriting Mr. Bowles into jail makes his real purpose manifest and shows how little he cared to "let justice be done."

The article in the *Republican* was written in the cheap sensational style which has largely characterized the columns of that paper, and, in parts at least, was utterly reckless of the truth and of private feelings and disgustingly coarse and vulgar. The paragraph which undoubtedly did most to excite Mr. Fisk's desire for revenge, and justly, was that running:

"The appellation of ' fat, fair and forty,' so often applied to well preserved women, belongs peculiarly to him. He is almost as broad as he is high, and so round that he rolls rather than walks. But his nervous energy is stimulated rather than deadened by his fat which gives indeed a momentum to his mental movement and his personal influence."

This is grossly and scurrilously false, in the first place, and in the second, were it true, it would be none the less unjustifiable, mean, coarse and unworthy a place in any paper making the slightest claim to decency. Again it proceeds: "Yankee of course, and Vermonter at that, and a peddler to boot, do we not tell the whole secret of his life?" A sneer at the people probably constituting nineteen-twentieths of the *Republican's* patrons, a special fling at Vermonters as of eminence in the contemptible, the climax capped with the sneer "a peddler to boot," and yet Mr. Bowles says, "there is nothing in it that ridiculed Mr. Fisk's previous occupation." But Mr. Bowles has shown the worth of his opinion on the subject by giving two of an almost exactly opposite character.

In one place he has said "there is a rollicking impudence in the style of the article; but how could the subject be treated sympathetically in any other way? You might as well paint a red rose with white coloring as to portray Mr. Fisk's character in any other than the style used." In another place he has said it was "*a friendly warning* . . . to husband the resources of his health . . . and to dedicate his energies to better and more legitimate purposes."

The journalist that prostitutes his position and panders to the morbid taste for sensation in order to secure a large circulation for his paper, deserves to be ranked with the publisher of obscene literature. He is even meaner, for he does more to corrupt public taste and makes a pretence to decency while engaged in the filthiest work for gain. The extent to which private rights and feelings are outraged in this country, in order that papers, claiming, like the *Republican*, to be decent, may make their columns " racy," has grown to be almost insufferable, and had Mr. Fisk pushed his suit for libel in a proper way and succeeded in mulcting Mr. Bowles in a heavy sum, as he richly deserved, nearly every one would have rejoiced and thanked him for doing a good service to the public. But proceeding by an outrage upon the law, abandoning all punishment and seeming satisfied after securing the offender in jail a few hours by means of a conspiracy, was too sudden a passage from the sublime to the ridiculous and for the moment stamped as a hero and martyr a man whose legal incarceration would have been well deserved.

CHAPTER IX

Having achieved all the notoriety possible in railroad
management by the close of 1868, Mr. Fisk suddenly
blossomed into an entirely new *rôle* before the New York
public with the opening of 1869, becoming all at once the
Mæcenas of the stage. It has been a favorite pastime of
royalty in all ages to dally with the children of Melpom-
ene, Thalia or Terpsichore, according to taste and temperament. Mr. Fisk's financial resources being now quite
royal, he became a patron of histrionic art as a means of
using a portion of his revenue in a good cause at the same
time that it yielded him much amusement and recreation.
And this he did on a scale quite worthy the most illustri-
ous of his royal prototypes and in a style of grandeur that
many a prince might envy. First he purchased Piko's
Opera House, a grand new marble palace at the corner of
23d Street and 8th Avenue, the name being at once
changed to "The Grand Opera House" on his coming
into possession. He next almost entirely rebuilt what is

now the Fifth Avenue Theatre, in 23d Street, making it one of the most elegant little theatres in the world. In May he leased the Academy of Music, in 14th Street, and was thus operating all at one time, the three finest places of amusement in New York. He prepared entertainments at each of the three establishments without the slightest regard to expense, determined on having every detail and appointment perfect. Thirty thousand dollars and more was said to have been expended in preparing one piece alone for the stage. But he soon became conscious of the quicksands upon which all *impressarios* seem.fated to stand in this country. The public did not sustain him in his unsparing outlay for their entertainment and he soon found himself losing heavily at each of his three theatres. When he came into possession of Pike's Opera House, French Comic Opera was on the boards there, and had been a very unprofitable venture for his predecessor. This he continued for a time, but finding it could not be made to pay, he closed the establishment for some changes and to prepare for the presentation of Shakspeare's grand play of "The Tempest." Elaborate preparations were made for the revival of this piece which had been long absent from the New York boards, and when the curtain again rose upon an audience in the Grand Opera House they were dazzled with the new splendors and beautiful decorations and frescoes which had completely transformed the appearance of the place And the change behind the scenes had been no less complete, every appointment being now of the most perfect style. But this play, too, failed to meet the reward which the efforts expended in its presentation merited and was withdrawn after a brief unprosperous season.

The little "Boudoir Theatre" in 24th Street, had been built for Mr. John Brougham, the well-known actor and playwright and was called after him "Brougham's Theatre." But he had not been installed in his elegant house long ere Mr. Fisk's hearty and generous admiration for him waned and then changed into an irreconcilable unpleasantness. Mr. Brougham's management failed of the anticipated success, and after two unsuccessful months he was turned out of his beautiful possession rather unceremoniously, and its name was changed to the "Fifth Avenue Theatre." The French Opera which had been withdrawn from the Grand Opera House was given another trial here, but with a success equally lacking in encouragement for its long continuance.

At the Academy of Music the celebrated Opera of "Lurline" was presented after the most expensive preparations, being rendered in English and Italian on alternate nights. But the result was so discouraging that after a run of two weeks it had to be withdrawn and the doors closed, about $20,000 having been lost in the enterprise.

His first season of theatrical experience had been one of expensive schooling and amusement to him. But disastrous as each venture had been pecuniarily, he was not discouraged or crippled. Though any other manager would most likely have been ruined financially by the losses incurred at either of the places, Mr. Fisk stood up under them all without a nerve shaken and whiffed his cigar as calmly as though all had gone prosperously. He, however, did not care to go over the same ground again the following season. The lease of the Academy of Music was not renewed, and the Fifth Avenue Theatre was leased and passed out of Mr. Fisk's personal supervision. But he still retained control of the Grand Opera House, and concentrated all his attention in the theatrical line to this one place. It is very doubtful if his fortune does not still continue to grow worse rather than better from this enterprise. One piece alone has had any lasting success and long run with him. "The Twelve Temptations" was brought out the second winter of his management and had a long run to crowded houses and must have been a fine pecuniary success. It was a piece in the spectacular, "Black Crook" style, depending largely upon the *ballet* and the exhibition of the charms of the female form for its attraction. New attractions were added from time to time, and to keep up the interest at the close a corps of beautiful blondes alternated with one of ravishing brunettes from night to night.

But Mr. Fisk has shown his strongest admiration for theatrical amusement to be in Opera Bouffe. This seems to be his ideal of fun and fine music combined and he has manifested the most unflinching determination to bring the public to his taste and way of thinking. It has formed the continuous programme at his Grand Opera House the past season and has been given, as is everything that he presents, with all the attractions that an unstinted expenditure of money could produce. He sent Max Maretzek, the most experienced opera manager in the country, to Europe as his special agent to import a first-class company for his theatre, and left nothing undone to present French Opera to the citizens of New York in its most attractive guise. To lend variety and increase the charms, three different leading artists were introduced to sustain a single part, each carrying it through one act. Almost without regard to pecuniary results, he has manifested the most persistent determination to give Opera Bouffe a firm hold upon New Yorkers as it had upon Parisians. The effort has not been so far successful that any other manager could present it in New York without speedily becoming bankrupt.

Mr. Fisk started in his theatrical career by securing the ablest and most experienced managers in the country to direct his establishments, and this would seem to be the course of wisdom and prudence; but somehow his relations soon proved unpleasant and incompatible with all of them. Brougham, Bergfeldt, Tayleure, and Maretzek, all eminently first class men in their lines, came and passed in quick succession in the management of his various enterprises on the stage. It is almost an axiom that two first class men can never work advantageously together in the head management of any enterprise, a truth that has been well illustrated here. All these men employed by Mr. Fisk were men of marked ability, excellent judgment and taste and high culture in their calling, and of. a mental cast and self-respect that could yield no servile or sycophantic deference to the notions of Mr. Fisk in matters pertaining to their profession, while he is a man whose individuality is so marked and positive as to make harmony impossible unless he is yielded to, hence irreconcilable differences soon arose, and, under the law that obtains in this age and country, the taste, judgment and preference of the man holding the purse strings prevailed over the men of culture and education and the latter retired leaving Mr. Fisk to carry out his own peculiar notions. The treatment of Mr. Brougham was such as might well have provoked a personal encounter had that gentlemen been as impulsive and as indifferent to a "scene" as Mr. Fisk, but being a man with the passions trained into a better control and knowing the quietest way was the best in such circumstances, their connection ended without blows. But the more irascible Maretzek was destined to a bellicose close of relations with his impulsive and blunt patron. The Opera Bouffe company that had been imported from Europe for the Grand Opera House were in rehearsal for their first appearance at the same time that Nilsson arrived. The company was in charge of Maretzek at the rehearsals, and as he had been sent abroad to select it, the tacit understanding was that he would be the conductor at the Grand Opera House for the season; but Mr. Fisk had failed to enter into any written agreement in the matter and held Maretzek entirely at the mercy of his pleasure and caprice—an insecurity which the veteran *impressario* did not at all relish. Feeling that nothing was secure as to his position with Mr. Fisk, ho was naturally disinclined to neglect any other opportunity that he might have and therefore accepted a proposition to act as conductor at the first Nilsson concert. Now, Mr. Fisk looked upon the Nilsson company as an " opposition show " to his and was for that reason somewhat jealous of it, and hearing that his man Max was to conduct on the occasion of the first appearance of the Swedish songstress he wrote a note ordering him not to do so. Mr. Fisk was present on the opening night of the " opposition show " and his temper was somewhat ruffled when the grand *entrée* revealed to his sight his man Max coming forward in full dress, baton in hand and making his bow as conductor in defiance of the imperial note of warning. Despite the purifying influence of the sublime emotions awakened by the echo of another world that sounded in the unearthly strains of the wonderful songstress and the elevation far above all things earthly to which she lifted her auditors, the displeasure of Mr. Fisk excited by the act of disobedience was softened only for the moment, if at all. On reaching the Grand Opera House the next morning he gave orders that if Maretzek came to conduct the rehearsal that day, word should be brought him immediately. Maretzek came and his arrival was announced as directed. Mr. Fisk hastened down into the theatre and approached the conductor's stand with an expression that meant "business" on his countenance. He proceeded at once to call Max to account for disobeying the note and conducting an "opposition show." Max attempted to explain, but Mr. Fisk knew the whole story, refused to be appeased and instead of waiting to hear the explanation, proceeded to pronounce Maretzek a "swindler," "thief," "liar," and other kindred epithets. This was more than Max could endure and he immediately descended from his stand and levelled a powerful blow at Mr. Fisk's nose. The latter parried and dodged in such a way that the blow did no serious damage, and then the two closed in a fierce struggle and soon went down, Fisk coming on top. The shrieks and fright of the assembled *corps de ballet* and *prime donne* would have won them great credit at an evening performance, and in fact it is doubtful if the whole scene would not have excelled in interest anything that has ever been put upon the Grand Opera House boards, could it have taken place before an audience in the evening. When some of the bystanders recovered sufficient presence of mind to separate the combatants it was found that no great damage had been done beyond a serious soiling of Mr. Fisk's tidy toilet and attire and the making of a slightly black eye for Maretzek. Beyond affording a racy topic for the newspapers for two or three days, and a suit commenced or threatened by each of the parties, but of which nothing ever came, the matter died away like its many predecessors and Mr. Fisk's connection with the last of his distinguished managers ended.

With his Opera Bouffe *prime donne*, too, Mr. Fisk seems not to get on at all well. At the beginning of the season M'lles. Montaland and Silly, the two leading characters whom Maretzek had brought out, seemed to please Mr. Fisk not a little, and they in turn seemed dazzled by the grandeur of the great *impressario*, and all went "merry as a marriage bell" for a time. Ere long, however, disagreements and unpleasant relations grew up, Montaland and Silly disappeared from the Grand Opera House boards and Aimée was summoned from London by telegram. She at once became a great favorite with the frequenters of Opera Bouffe and everything went smoothly till the close of the season at the Grand Opera House. When the company started on a summer tour, however, Aimée became indignant at some treatment of her in the matter of her salary, and the difficulty grew so great that she suddenly refused to sing any more in the performances going on in Boston and left the company in disgust.

Perhaps Mr. Fisk would have been obliged to close his last theatre and withdraw from theatrical business altogether were it not that the Grand Opera House has been otherwise turned to such good account that he is not entailed with much if any expense for the rent of the theatre. He paid $820,000 for the edifice. In the summer of 1869 the second floor was most sumptuously fitted up and became the offices of the Erie Railway. It is unequalled in elegance by any building in the world used for a similar purpose. The doors are of massive, elegantly carved black walnut, all the offices are fitted up and furnished in black walnut and the most expensive glass, and over the door of each office is a silver plate sign indicating the department. On the opposite side from the main entrance door is an ante-room where stand several ushers preventing further admission without first sending in your card or stating your business in advance and getting permission. Behind the door opening from the ante-room into the presence-chamber stands a large screen, so that when the door opens nothing but a red curtain can be seen. Should your card or business be looked upon favorably and obtain you permission to enter, the usher will bow you through the door, past the screen, and there, behind a richly carved black walnut desk of mammoth size, in a luxurious chair, sits James Fisk, Jr., on his throne. About him are numerous clerks, messengers and lackeys doing his bidding and laughing at his humor, which he keeps constantly flowing in the midst of all his business. Within his reach are springs sending signals to all parts of the building, so that every *employé* in the establishment can be summoned to him instantly in case of necessity. All the ceilings are richly frescoed, that in the main room being an elegant symbolic design having at the four sides the words New York, San Francisco, Chicago, St. Louis. On the floor above is a grand banqueting room fitted up in the same style of splendor, where sumptuous entertainments are occasionally given. The Erie Railway pays $75,000 rent for the apartments occupied for its offices, and in addition to this is the rent of the stores on the ground floor and some other property included in the purchase—the whole making the investment a very profitable one aside from the theatre and the apartments appropriated to the owner's private use. Mr. Fisk's residence is in the immediate vicinity on 23d Street, which makes all his arrangements very complete. Here, surrounded by all the luxury which his taste and wealth can devise he leads a much more lordly and imperial life than many a modern Prince, and in his sumptuous halls may well be called "Prince Erie."

CHAPTER X.

A LION AGAIN—METAMORPHOSIS—AT THE BOSTON PEACE JUBI-
LEE—A FLOATING PALACE—SUNDAY TRIPS UP THE HUDSON
—THE ADMIRAL.

Through all the varied phases of his life since leaving
his peddling business at Brattleboro Mr. Fisk had never
held any position which compelled people to look at him
daily in all his splendors with anything like the attention
he attracted in that first stage of his career. But he had
now achieved a notoriety so great that the gay throng of
the city would gaze at him as the country people once had
done, were opportunity offered. The summer of 1869 gave
the opportunity and he enjoyed all the gratification in this
respect that could be desired. The Narraganset Steamship Company was formed this season. Mr. Fisk became
its president and thereby came into control of the finest
line of steamers running on Long Island Sound. The two
boats, Providence and Bristol, were thoroughly over-
hauled, renovated, fitted up in the most luxuriant style,
refurnished with elegant carpets, upholstering, bronzes
and general fixtures. The dining rooms were conducted
on the *à la carte*, or European, plan and supplied all the

accommodations and luxuries of a first-class hotel. To add to the pleasure of the lovely ride up the Sound, a fine band of music accompanies each steamer and delights the passengers with sweet strains of choice music through the first four hours of the trip. This novel feature adds much to the enjoyment of the journey and is highly appreciated by the public. It is to be regretted that the famous North River line has not followed the innovation. Everything objectionable under the former management disappeared and this became one of the most delightful and wholly enjoyable trips to be had anywhere in the world.

It was in these steamers that Mr. Fisk seemed to take his special pride that summer, as he justly might. Each afternoon, a half hour or so before it was time for the steamer to start, he came upon the pier, in a " nobby " citizen's suit, disappeared in some of the company's offices and soon emerged again in a full Admiral's uniform of the finest make. In this attire, which was quite becoming to him, he took his place at the gangway, where he must be seen by all who entered. His appearance the first few evenings created a grand sensation. The gay company that were promenading the decks and saloons, admiring the rich gilding, furniture, bronzes and mirrors, and listening to the music, suddenly turned all their attention upon the man who had achieved so much notoriety, who had furnished the pleasures they were then enjoying and who dictated orders to the noble steamer and the crew. All

crowded around to get a view of the man they had heard
so much about of late. Young ladies whispered to each
other and turned to gaze at him after they passed in;
fathers pointed him out to their wives and children, and
no one wished to miss a sight of him. There, in his elegant uniform, with the huge diamond sparkling in his
shirt bosom, stood the man who had trapped both Vanderbilt and Drew, who had been the shield and sword of
the Erie exiles in "Fort Taylor," who had made all Wall
Street howl under his manipulations, who had purchased
the Grand Opera House, built the Fifth Avenue Theatre
and leased the Academy of Music—all within one short
year. He was now the cynosure of all eyes and created
the same sensation among the gaily dressed denizens of the
city as he had formerly done among rustic villagers. The
situation was one which he evidently enjoyed to the full,
though he seemed sublimely unconscious of the curiosity
directed to him, and issued his orders and directions as
rapidly and imperatively as though he were wholly absorbed in his duties. Precisely on the moment announced
for starting, he gave the command and the elegant
steamer put out into the stream with her heavy load of
passengers crowding her decks, music playing, flags
flying, all her crew in uniform, each man having a badge
on his cap showing his office and duty. It was a moment
that was a full renewal of the feeling of pride which the
young peddler felt on the morning when he first mounted
his brilliant new cart and dashed out of Brattleboro with

his four-in-hand and followers. The Admiral remained on board till the steamer was well out in the bay or hauled round into the East River. Here he was met by a small tug boat that came out to bear him back to the city. As he parted from the steamer that was now his pride, the company crowded around for another glimpse of him and the officers gave their commander a parting salute.

The sensation and dramatic effect of Mr. Fisk's arrival upon the pier and casting off from the steamer upon the tug, was greatly intensified the first few evenings by his being accompanied by his female favorite of the hour, attired like himself in naval style—a jacket of navy blue with gilt buttons and epaulettes, a hat in the sailor style, and decked out in all matters of detail in a manner evidently indicating a careful consultation of the Admiral's taste.

The custom of going out into the stream with the departing steamer was not continued long. It necessitated a stop and some inconvenience, and was therefore discontinued as soon as the novelty and glory of the ceremony had worn away. Thereafter Mr. Fisk contented himself with giving and receiving the parting salute as the steamer put out from the pier. This formality over, he again disappeared in the offices of the company and soon came out metamorphosed in a surprisingly short time from a full-blown Admiral into a private citizen dressed in the extreme of fashion.

It was in June of this year that the great Peace Jubilee took place in Boston. President Grant went on to attend and when he arrived in New York the best accommodations of Mr. Fisk's steamers were placed at his disposal and accepted. The Admiral improved this opportunity to have a little familiar conversation with the President. Jay Gould and several others of this *genus* were also passengers that night and sought to make themselves as intimate as might be with the chief magistrate of the nation. The Admiral, in full uniform, even accompanied the President to the Coliseum, the place in which the jubilee was held, and for simple sensation his presence on that occasion quite surpassed that of General Grant. It was this episode that won for him the title of " Jim Jubilee."

This line of steamers was his plaything for the season of 1869, but of course it grew stale, lacking in novelty and excitement, by the end of the summer, and something now must be had. When the season of 1870 opened he completely eclipsed all his previous achievements in the steamboat line by adding the " Plymouth Rock " to his flotilla. This new steamer is 345 feet long and of upwards of 5,000 tuns burden. She had been almost completely rebuilt to his order during the winter. She contains thirty-two suites of apartments that rival New York's finest hotel for elegance and comfort. The restaurant dining-room is equally marvellous for the character of its supplies and *cuisine*. The bar-room is of a

size and elegance rarely equalled in any establishment on
terra firma, being extensively finished in white marble,
with large mirrors and all the usual appurtenances in the
most improved style.   Nothing so gorgeous and extensive
was ever before attempted in the way of a steamer.   The
furniture throughout is of the richest and most elegant
style, the gilding, embellishments, bronzes, etc., surpassing in profusion and luxuriance anything to be met with
by a traveller anywhere else in the world.   While walk-
ing through its saloons and cabins it is almost impossible
to avoid the delusion that you are in some grand hotel
furnished with oriental splendor.   In fact the steamer
was intended for a sort of floating hotel.   She was specially designed to accommodate the summer travel to
Long Branch—of late the most famous of our seaside
watering .places. She runs from New York to Sandy
Hook, and was designed to afford first-class accommodations for those who might wish to go on board in the
afternoon, use a suite of apartments for dressing, take
dinner on board, drive to the hotels to any ball or entertainment in the evening, return to their apartments on the
steamer to sleep, and wake up in New York next
morning.

This grand floating palace was Mr. Fisk's new sensation for the season of 1870.   On Sundays he often used
her for a pleasure excursion up the Hudson.   On these
occasions she was crowded by people seeking a day of
leisure enjoyment, and it is difficult to imagine a greater

combination of delightful influences and pleasures than that afforded by this palatial steamer gliding up the lovely Hudson on a beautiful summer's morning, amid scenery unsurpassed in grandeur by any in the world, replete with the historic interest that clings around Washington, Benedict Arnold; and André, the Palisades and Highlands echoing the strains of sweet music from the band on board. The trip was to Poughkeepsie, 75 miles, and back. On these excursions Mr. Fisk was present in his Admiral's uniform, smiling blandly upon everybody and playing the host with the proverbial good nature and affability of the man who "knows how to keep a hotel."

In the summer of 1869, when the Erie offices were moved to the Grand Opera House, Mr. Fisk also established a new ferry from the Erie depot in Jersy City to 23d Street, and a free line of omnibuses from the ferry, past the Grand Opera House, to the Fifth Avenue Hotel. The two boats placed upon this ferry of course surpassed in elegance everything used on any of the other ferries. They are named "James Fisk, Jr.," and "Jay Gould" and are in entire keeping with the rest of Admiral Fisk's flotilla.

CHAPTER XL

ALBANY & SUSQUEHANNA RAILROAD WAR—MR. FISK COM-
MENCES HIS TWENTY-SIXTH RAID AND GETS HUSTLED DOWN
STAIRS—OPPOSING RECEIVERS AND OPPOSING JUDGES—THE
TWO PARTIES IN COLLISION—A RIOT—THE MILITIA CALLED
OUT—THE GOVERNOR INTERFERES—FLIGHT TO NEW YORK—
ERIE BEATEN.

After seventeen years of desperate struggle for existence, through repeated discouragements and many sus-
pensions of work upon its construction, the Albany &
Susquehanna Railroad was finally completed in January,
1869. The one man who had stood by it and worked
unceasingly for it from the beginning, whose faith and
courage had not faltered under the seventeen years of
trial nor slackened in the least while all the rest of its
original friends and many new relays had fallen by the
way and abandoned the project, the man who had pushed
it through all its discouragements to final completion, was
Joseph H. Ramsey. It is not too much to say that but
for his energy, determination and perseverance, the road
would not be in existence to-day. He was now its

president. The road runs diagonally across the State of New York from Albany on the Hudson to Binghamton on the Susquehanna, in Broome County. Here it meets the Erie. The road had been projected and built as a purely local enterprise to benefit the towns through which it ran, and for this reason it had received some aid from the State and the towns along the line had subscribed for some of the stock. In its later stages the Governor had vetoed all bills for giving it further assistance. Many of those who had originally subscribed for the stock, after paying in a certain per cent. of their subscription, had failed to pay the remainder and in consequence of this failure their stock was declared forfeited to the company. The subscribers consented to this forfeiture and seemed glad to get rid of the stock in that way. It was by using this forfeited stock as collateral security for a loan that Mr. Ramsey had obtained funds to complete the last section of the road. It was against the law to issue stock at less than par, but this being stock that had been already issued and forfeited, it was deemed legal to re-issue it for less than par.

But as soon as all the difficulties were surmounted and the road was finished, it was found to be of great value for more than local use. If run in connection with the Erie road it formed the necessary connecting link to render that road a rival of the New York Central for the through business between New England and the West; but it was of still greater value in affording the great anthracite coal regions of Northeastern Pennsylvania a more direct communication with New England and the country north from Albany, and as such was destined to destroy a very profitable part of tho business of the branch of the Erie road running to Newburgh.

As is always the case when an energetic, determined, persevering man pushes a great enterprise through to success, Mr. Ramsey had made some opponents, not to say enemies, during the seventeen years of determined perseverance, and now, during tho first year of its through operation, he found nearly one half of tho board of directors sullenly opposed to him. Ho is not a man of half-way measures or entangling compromises and has no taste for a house divided against itself; it was therefore distinctly understood that at the next election either ho or his opponents must go out and an entirely harmonious board be elected. Mr. Ramsey's opponents well know what the result of such a contest would bo if they did not secure tho assistance of some outside power much stronger than themselves, and therefore invited tho Erie road, or Messrs. Fisk and Gould, to undertako tho battlo for them. As these gentlemen woro already coveting this road as a great prize to possess in connection with Erie, they eagerly accepted tho invitation, and Mr. Ramsey suddenly found himself confronted by tho men who had beaten Vanderbilt and Drew, had had everything their own way in the Courts and Legislature for a year, and who now had all the resources of Erie and Tammany Hall behind them.

The control of the election necessitated a control of a majority of stock, and herein Mr. Ramsey felt reasonably secure, despite all the resources and power of his new antagonists. He knew he could command a majority of the floating stock and he felt quite as secure about the stock held by the towns along the road. This stock the towns were not permitted to sell for less than par, cash down. As the nominal value of the stock was only 20 cents on the dollar, there seemed no likelihood of the towns getting par for their stock and there was no doubt that if they held the stock they would vote on it for Mr. Ramsey against the men whose principles had been made manifest in connection with Erie the past year. Under the purchases made by the Erie party to get control, the small amount of floating stock rose quickly from 20 to 40, 50 and 65. Still Mr. Ramsey felt secure of a majority till he heard that agents of his opponents were out among the towns on the road offering par in cash for the stock held by the towns. In one or two instances the extraordinary offer proved too tempting and was accepted. Under the competition thus excited the stock held by towns suddenly rose to a premium. But Messrs. Fisk and Gould did not care to spend so much money as would be required to obtain a majority of the stock at prices above par when they knew it must fall back to 20 or near it immediately after election, and consequently bethought themselves of means to compass their purpose without the use of capital. The officers of some of the towns owning the stock were invited down to New York and entertained most hospitably and an arrangement very nice for Messrs. Fisk and Gould was made on the heads-I-win-tails-you-lose plan. An agreement was made that the stock should be taken of the towns at par *after* the election, provided that *at* the election the officers would vote as Mr. Fisk wished. For the fulfilment of this agreement the town officers had the private bond of Messrs. Fisk and Gould. The latter gentlemen probably were well aware that, as the town officers had no power to sell except for cash down, this agreement was wholly illegal and could not be enforced against them after they had secured the votes in their favor.

On the 3d of August considerable of the stock held by the towns was presented for transfer. The treasurer at once transferred all stock which he thought had been actually purchased and paid for, whether by the Erie or Ramsey party; but he refused to transfer such stock as he suspected had been bought only by bargain, under the convenient arrangement patched up in New York. The next day a war of injunctions commenced. The Erie party got an injunction from Judge Barnard in New York forbidding any vote to be cast on the forfeited stock that had been re-issued and was held as collateral security for a loan to the company. On the same day Mr. Ramsey got an injunction from Judge Parker at Owego forbidding the transfer of stock held by the towns of Oneonta and Worcester. The next day, August 5th, Mr. Shearman, the lawyer of the Erie party, went to Owego and got the injunction obtained by Mr. Ramsey removed and then elsewhere obtained an order commanding the transfer that had been forbidden the day before. Encouraged by so much success, a bolder step was taken. An order was obtained restraining Mr. Ramsey from acting as an officer of the road. With Mr. Ramsey in the board, it was equally divided; his removal therefore placed his opponents in the majority and as the vice-president was in the interest of the Erie party this move gave them a great advantage, putting them in possession of the transfer books and enabling them to make the transfers to their own liking. But Mr. Ramsey did not surrender quietly. An angry assertion of conflicting rights prevailed all day at the offices of the company in Albany, and became so serious that the police had to be called in to preserve order and prevent the two parties from coming to a trial of muscular strength to determine which should hold possession. Night put an end to this angry growl, but Mr. Ramsey knew the opponents he had to deal with and that immediate, decisive measures were necessary to foil them. Therefore he improved the evening. It was felt on both sides that possession of the transfer books greatly increased the chances of success for the party holding them, as they were to be closed on the 7th and it was now the evening of the 5th. Accordingly Mr. Ramsey had the books removed from the office that night and when his enemies came in next morning the prize they most coveted in getting possession was not to be found. Many were the wild goose chases made to regain possession of these books. They were heard of, now in Pittsfield, out of the State, now in Troy only six miles away, then in Schenectedy; but on the arrival of officers at the place where rumor had last placed them, they were found to be quite as far off in some other direction and the pursuit was like seeking the gold at the end of the rainbow. A great point was attempted to be made against Mr. Ramsey for the abstraction of the books in this manner, his opponents crying out against the dishonesty, violation of power and rights, and dread of justice, implied in the act. And another step served them still better to the same effect. The night the books were removed, Mr. Ramsey got several of his friends to subscribe for considerable sums of the stock of the company which had not yet been taken up, he promising to provide for the 10 per cent. of the price which was to be paid in immediately in order to enable them to have the stock entered in their names. This of course was not a *bona fide* subscription, but was resorted to as a means of controling the election. As such it made Mr. Ramsey obnoxious to the charge of unfair and lawless acts, and he made his position in this respect still weaker by the means taken to secure the necessary 10 per cent. of the subscription money. He took the equipment bonds of the company and pledged them as collateral security for a loan. This was exceeding any power that he ever could have had, and his enemies were not slow to seize the handle thus afforded them. So immeasurably superior to his opponents was the strength of Mr. Ramsey's position in the matter of personal character, business and social standing, that charges from them against his integrity fell like peas pelted at the Rocky Mountains; but in the excitement of the hour they tended somewhat to damage and weaken his position.

But the Erie party were not left to exercise their power long, though the books, the most valuable part of the corporation for their immediate purpose, had been removed beyond their reach. The next morning, the 6th, just as they were getting ready to exercise their newly acquired functions, an injunction was obtained and served upon them by the Ramsey party, restraining them from acting as officers of the corporation. The road was thus left without a head or management. This new move was immediately telegraphed to the Grand Opera House in New York. Mr. Shearman was there at Mr. Fisk's side and immediately saw the legal aspect of the situation. The corporation being left without officers, an order must be obtained appointing a receiver to take charge of the road. Mr. Shearman immediately set about preparing the papers necessary to obtain the desired order. A judge must be had to grant the order. There were three judges of the First District in the city, while the fourth was absent in Poughkeepsie, at the bedside of his dying mother. There were judges of the Second District to be found in Brooklyn in case of need.   But there seemed some magic virtue in the orders of the one absent judge, consequently he was summoned from his dying mother by telegraph and came down to New York.   This was Judge George G. Barnard.   The papers were not ready till ten o'clock at night.   At that hour the judge who had come down from Poughkeepsie for the purpose was so near at hand and was so quick to perceive the merits of the case that fifteen minutes or thereabouts sufficed for the whole process of taking the papers to him, obtaining a hearing and securing his signature to the document.   The receivers appointed for this important trust were James Fisk, Jr.! and Mr. Courter.

Equipped with Judge Barnard's order, Mr. Fisk and party left for Albany by the eleven o'clock P. M. train to assume the delicate responsibility; but on arriving there in the morning they found the Ramsey party had been as quick as themselves to understand the situation and had had the Hon. R. H. Pruyn appointed receiver a few minutes earlier than Mr. Fisk received his authority. When Judge Barnard's receivers went to the offices to take possession they found them already held by the opposing receiver's representatives, with Mr. Van Vaulkenburg in command.   Mr. Fisk introduced himself to Mr. Van Vaulkenburg and announced his mission.   The gentleman in possession intimated that he did not propose to surrender the trust of which he had been put in charge.   Thereupon Mr. Fisk turned to the choice band of supporters he had brought up from New York with him and said, "Come on, boys!" Then, addressing himself to Mr. Van Vaulkenburg, he continued, "this is my twenty-sixth raid and I'm going to take you fellows if it costs a million dollars." With these words he and his "boys" proceeded to take possession and oust the occupants by force; but this attempt took a very unexpected turn and Mr. Fisk and his "boys" got hustled down stairs with a haste that paid no regard to ceremony, Mr. Van Vaulkenburg proving to be a man of such muscular activity that Mr. Fisk instead of "taking you fellows," suddenly brought up on the sidewalk with his spruce attire and toilet in a rather disordered condition. He had hardly had time to adjust his hat properly, when a fussy little man stepped up and marched him off to the station house for creating a disturbance. On reaching police headquarters Mr. Fisk was released and found that the little man who had marched him off so promptly was not a policeman at all, but an *employé* of the railroad and a supporter of Mr. Ramsey.

Such an ignominious and ludicrous result of the first move in his twenty-sixth raid might well have afflicted Mr. Fisk with a little chagrin and disturbed his temper; but he seemed to appreciate the comic element of the proceeding quite as fully as any one, so lively is his sense of the ridiculous and humorous, and on being set free at the station house he immediately returned to the offices from which he had been so summarily ejected and actually led his opponents in venting humor at his own expense over the episode in which he came out at the little end of the horn.	To Mr. Van Vaulkenburg who had so kindly assisted in his hasty exit he was especially pleasant and facetious and saluted him in the poetic spirit,

> "Perhaps it was right to dissemble your love,
> But why did you kick me down stairs ?"

He seated himself upon a table, swinging his feet beneath after the manner of the evening gathering in a country variety store, and in that situation he manifested his high admiration for manly strength of character and muscle by complimenting Mr. Van Vaulkenburg, saying he had never before met a man who dared face him and do his duty in that way and that he wanted just such a man in his employ.	He further proposed that, instead of any more fuss of this kind, himself and Mr. Ramsey should play a game of "seven up" to determine which should have possession of the road.

When Mr. Fisk got back to the scene of his rout he found that Mr. Pruyn had arrived and was now in possession in *propria persona*, so the two opposing receivers met face to face and each claimed to be in possession. The news of the affair of the morning was immediately telegraphed to New York and upon the strength of the telegram Mr. Shearman made a new affidavit and obtained from Judge Barnard a new injunction forbidding everybody from interfering with receivers Fisk and Courter and also granting an absolute "writ of assistance" empowering the sheriff to impress the whole *posse comitatus* into his service to execute this last injunction. This new injunction and writ were *telegraphed* to Albany and about three o'clock P. M. the sheriff actually attempted to proceed upon authority purporting to have been obtained from New York, based upon acts that had occurred in Albany only five hours previous. The authority was contemptuously disregarded. A counterblast was fired in the shape of an order for the arrest of Mr. Fisk for contempt of Court in interfering with its officer, Receiver Pruyn. This closed the active hostilities of the day and it being now evident that no crisis or decision could be reached, a truce till nine o'clock Monday morning was agreed upon and the two opposing chiefs withdrew, each leaving deputies behind to maintain the situation *in statu quo* till the hour appointed.

Mr. Fisk left immediately for New York to receive instructions from his legal guides and get the original copy of Judge Barnard's last injunction and the writ of assistance. With these and a retinue of a dozen or fifteen "boys" he departed for the front again Sunday evening, determined on a brilliant *coup de grace* in his first charge on the morrow. He presented himself at the scene of action Monday morning but was completely surprised by his adversary's crying "check!" before he had made a single move. During his sojourn at the Grand Opera House, the Ramsey party had obtained a new injunction restraining everybody from interfering with Receiver Pruyn and expressly enjoining sheriffs from proceeding to any

measures on the authority of the writ of assistance. A
train with forty or fifty Ramsey men and Mr. Smith as
legal adviser, was early started from Albany, serving this
injunction on sheriffs and installing deputies of Receiver
Pruyn as they went.   Mr. Fisk thus found himself effectually foiled and the situation looked very unfavorable for
his prospects.   But a consultation was held with his
lawyers and advisers, and a brilliant device was hit upon
for bringing matters to a dead lock and the road to a
stand still.   As his enemies were now in possession of the
Albany end of the road beyond the power of removal
except by actual force, he determined to get possession of
as much of the other end as possible, so that while his
opponents governed the head he might hang on by the
tail.   There was but one way of accomplishing this now
most desirable object.   The power of his opponent was
extending toward Binghamton as fast as steam could take
it and nothing but electricity could get there ahead of it.
Accordingly, he telegraphed his orders, injunctions and
writs of assistance to Binghamton, where Erie is much
more of a power than at Albany, and there he met with
better success than where he was personally present.
Men were found ready and eager to do his bidding and
under his telegraphed orders and documents the Binghamton end of the road was immediately taken possession
of in his name as receiver.   An Erie superintendent was
placed in charge.   A train standing at the station ready
to start was not permitted to proceed till an Erie engine

had been substituted, an Erie conductor placed in charge, and an Erie sheriff was on board to distribute Erie injunctions and writs of assistance and replace all *employés* by Erie sympathizers, wherever the train stopped.   There were four Albany and Susquehanna engines at Binghamton.   The sheriff of Erie got possession of three of them and was riding down the track on one of those he had captured to secure the fourth, when the engineer of the latter suddenly moved a switch in such a way as to send the sheriff and the engine bearing him off the track, then jumped quickly upon his own, let on the steam and made good time towards Albany.

The doings of the Erie men at Binghamton had been telegraphed to Albany and Mr. Van Vaulkenburg was at length fully roused and determined on the most decisive measures.   Mr. Fisk had not been permitted to enter the Albany & Susquehanna offices at all that day, but his deputy and brother receiver, Mr. Courter, had remained since Saturday to assert possession for the Fisk party. When news of the proceedings at Binghamton arrived and fired Mr. Van Vaulkenburg's will, he immediately notified Mr. Courter that the farce of his pretended possession had gone far enough and that he must leave the premises at once.   The experience of Saturday morning being fresh in Mr. Courter's memory, he deemed it best to go without assistance and retired, though under protest.   Mr. Van Vaulkenburg then telegraphed along the road ordering his trains to stop where they were.

The train that left Albany in the morning had reached Harpersville, twenty-five miles from Binghamton, when, hearing of the situation at the latter place, they decided not to proceed and fell back to Bainbridge, thirty-six miles from Binghamton and there waited further developments.

The afternoon train from Binghamton, thoroughly transformed into an Erie establishment, proceeded on its way, sheriff aboard, and put the road into Erie hands as it went. When they reached Afton, thirty miles from Binghamton, they were met by a telegram from Mr. Van Vaulkenburg warning them that any further advance would be at their peril. They therefore halted and telegraphed for further instructions from Mr. Fisk at Albany. They received a peremptory order to proceed and accordingly started again. It was now late in the night and they advanced with much caution, feeling their way as they went, to see that no bridge had been destroyed or rails torn up by their adversaries. The Ramsey party had with them a patent "frog," designed to get displaced cars on to the track, but it now occurred to some one that it was equally well adapted to throwing them off. This they fixed to a rail and then took up a position on a side track to await the enemy's approach. The Erie party came in sight of the Bainbridge station and, all dangerous places being passed, they moved on more boldly and unsuspiciously when, just before reaching the station, they suddenly became conscious of something irregular and found themselves off the track. The Ramsey train now immediately moved up on to the main track behind them and they were prisoners. The Ramsey party gallantly helped them out of their car, and finding themselves captured they quietly surrendered.

Emboldened by success, the Ramsey party now resolved to advance and started once more towards Binghamton early Tuesday morning. They removed the Erie men placed in charge the previous day and restored the former *employés*. All went smoothly till they reached a spot known as "the Tunnel," about fifteen miles from Binghamton. The tunnel is some two hundred feet long, on the brow of a hill, and is approached from either side by a steep up grade and over a sharply curving track. On reaching this point at about 10 A. M. they received news of a new Erie train that had come up from Binghamton with several hundred men to give them battle. At this intelligence they halted and the two hostile bands stood on the opposite sides of the tunnel all day reconnoitering and preparing, neither party apparently daring to attack. The Fisk party was composed of *employés* of the Erie road and work-shops and was increased during the day by the arrival of new trains bringing up men and provisions, till their forces numbered about eight hundred. But their very numbers told against them. Without discipline, organization or conscious purpose, with no acknowledged commanders, they were a

mere unwieldy mob, to whom fifty men with an acknowledged leader would have been infinitely superior.
The Ramsey company was also reinforced during the day
by the arrival of another train from Albany and by the
gathering of sympathizers from the vicinity and now
numbered about four hundred, or one half the party on
the other side of the tunnel. Besides being fewer in
number, which in this case was doubtless an advantage,
the men directing their movements were gentlemen of
such personal force and character as to establish something like organization among them, and, still more, they
were all inspired by a definite principle and strong feeling, a unifying and strengthening element in which their
opponents were entirely lacking. At last, after such
feeble preparation as was possible under the circumstances, and under imperative orders by telegraph from
commander Fisk at Albany to commence offensive operations, the Erie party decided to advance and took the
initiative about seven o'clock in the evening. Their chief
reliance seems to have been upon the amount of *momentum* they could get up, and this was undoubtedly the one
point in which they were strongest; but since Cæzar's day
mere *momentum* as a determining element in warfare has
dwindled in importance as against scientific manœuvring
much more than these improvised warriors seem to have
been conscious of. However, as this was their best if not
their only weapon, it was probably the part of wisdom to
adopt it since they were under peremptory commands to

advance. Their philosophy seems to have been to load a train as heavily as possible and set it going, trusting to luck for all the rest. They put together the heaviest train they could make up, filled it with men (though for what purpose does not appear, unless for their weight and to dispose of them *somehow*) and started it through the long tunnel. With hearts trembling in trepidation, more from the darkness and the utter indefiniteness of purpose than from any apprehended harm, these crusaders moved cautiously through the tunnel, emerged upon the Albany side and halted to take breath. They found a single rail removed by their opponents. This was replaced and once more they moved forward, having now a down grade. The Ramsey men had been warned of the approach and were not afraid even to try *momentum* as the first move, probably conscious that this could determine nothing and only serve as a signal for further operations depending much more upon skill, organization, and commanders, in which they felt superior. Accordingly when the rail was replaced and the attacking train was advancing again, the Ramsey train started, too, puffing up the hill most determinedly, bent on mischief. The Erie train moving slowly down the hill, turned a sharp corner and suddenly became aware of the approach of their enemy under full headway with the manifest intention of a collision. Perhaps the Erie men had "sogered" under McClellan, for they had evidently expected to go through this war without hurting anybody. The sudden prospect of danger therefore took them wholly by surprise and threw them into the greatest consternation. The conductor swung his hat and gesticulated frantically to induce the Ramsey train to stop. The engineer instantly whistled "down brakes!" then whistled the signal of danger and reversed his engine. The Ramsey engineer merely whistled "get out of the way!" steamed ahead with his full strength, and smash! went the two engines into each other. The shock and panic to Erie was complete. The men leaped from the train and without stopping to see what had happened "skedaddled" for the Binghamton side of the tunnel with their utmost speed, some running through the tunnel, others over the hill above it, each going like an Olympian runner, as if life depended upon reaching the other end, affording one of the most unique and amusing foot races ever witnessed. Their engine and train participated in the hasty retreat, and backed up to the home side of the tunnel. The Ramsey men, having intended the collision, were not in the least disturbed or demoralized, but were perfectly self-possessed and set upon the Erie men with shouts, and sticks and stones as they jumped from their cars in a panic, and pursued them a short distance in their flight.

As the Erie train was moving slowly, reversed the engine and put on the brakes the moment danger was foreseen, and as the grade was too heavy for the Ramsey train to get up much speed, the collision did little damage beyond smashing the cow-catcher and headlights and throwing the Ramsey engine partially off the track. The power of locomotion was not destroyed in either. The Ramsey men set immediately to work to replace their engine upon the track and then, resolving to follow up their success, pushed on through the tunnel. But on emerging they found the time spent in getting their engine upon the track had sufficed to arrest the course of the fugitives, allay their panic, and gather them into a more disorganized mob than ever. They stood crowded together ready in turn to dispute any further advance. The Ramsey train therefore halted and the two parties stood facing each other at a safe distance apart. The scene was now much like that often presented by the boys of two cities on opposite sides of a river meeting on the ice for a championship fight. Each party stood, as it were, with a chip on its shoulder and bravely dared the other to come and knock it off. The war was hardly more than one of words, but in this respect it perhaps stands unequalled. Many of the Erie men had indulged quite freely in "fire water" to get up some "Dutch courage" and the vollies of profanity and coarse denunciation poured in upon their adversaries was revolting in the extreme. As in the boy fights, some of the more bold and venturesome characters on either side stepped out a few paces in front of the rest and indulged in a little skirmishing. Sticks and stones were thrown, a few hand to hand fights occurred, and a few random pistol shots were fired. The Ramsey party were much the most exasperated and in earnest, so the Erie men sustained nearly all the injuries and rested all their laurels on the capture of one prisoner. One of the Ramsey men advanced so boldly that he suddenly found himself separated from his comrades and his retreat cut off. He ran behind a freight car for refuge and was there surrounded by a large party who now heroically captured him, kicked and cuffed him, and proposed to kill him. At length he was recognized as an acquaintance by one of the captors, who proposed to make him a prisoner instead of killing him and the suggestion was adopted. He was placed under a strong guard but the watch over him gradually grew careless and at half past eleven he succeeded in making his escape from durance vile, but only to wander about all night in a vain effort to rejoin his comrades.

Matters had assumed such a serious aspect in the afternoon that the civil authorities of Broome County had despaired of being able to maintain order and called upon the military for assistance. In obedience to this request the 44th regiment was called out and reached the scene of disorder about eight o'clock, when the shouting and oaths had grown hideous in the night and the riot was growing quite serious. At the sound of its drums the Ramsey men retreated through the tunnel with their train, left a freight car off the track inside the tunnel, tore up a few rails, and then fell back to Harpersville for the night, firing a few bridges as they went.

Only two of the Erie men had been hit by pistol shots and only a few more had been hurt at all seriously, while the report of the Ramsey party was, "nobody hurt." Thus ended a riot combining so many of the worst elements of a mob as to make it a great wonder that it proved so harmless.

Excitement over the riot and the whole situation had now spread throughout the State, was all absorbing along the line of the road, and culminated at Albany, the headquarters of both parties. The Governor had been summoned from a pleasure sojourn at the Catskills to take action upon the situation, a feeling of insecurity existed everywhere between Albany and Binghamton, and marked public demonstrations were everywhere made. When the engine that dodged the sheriff at Binghamton and the train that was captured at Bainbridge, arrived in Albany they were received with the most enthusiastic demonstrations by a large crowd of citizens; wherever Erie men or sympathizers appeared in the neighborhood of the riot they were treated to a shower of opprobrious epithets by the women and children and requested to "clear out;" and everywhere the feeling seemed unanimous in favor of Mr. Ramsey and decidedly bitter against Erie. To all this Mr. Fisk manifested characteristic indifference and on Tuesday afternoon there appeared in the papers a letter from him in which he said:

"Quick sharp work and so much to be done on a stamping ground new to me, left me only to feel that the

great majority of the good people of Albany were
running away with a wrong idea of our side of the
question and overlooked the great benefits and advantages we were bringing to their doors. . . I should
suppose the people of this good city would welcome us
with open arms. Look at the past. Has not everything
been done by the Central line to make you a mere local
station, to ruin your shipping and wipe out your instruments of business and leave you with nothing on hand
but pleasure all the time, which is very tiresome—or
rather to leave you a Rip Van Winkle sleep? . . . Mr.
Ramsey and myself have long been friends and nothing
but the welfare of the great interests involved would
have brought me in collision with him. I have the
highest regard for him, barring my opinion of him as a
railroad manager. I am sorry that he stands to-day
between the interests of the people and our corporation.
There can be but one result, and that will be free
admission to us in Albany. For all we ask we give you
four-fold in return. The star of the Albany & Susquehanna road, as a mere local road, has set. It must now
be part of the great thoroughfare from the Atlantic to the
Pacific. . . It is evident the hostility to our interests
is stimulated by those in the interest of the Central. . .
The interest of the Erie is to run it; the interest of the
Central is to discontinue it. . . It is not a question of
to-day but of the future, and I think my holding out
powers will last with those who are opposed to me. I
ask no advantage to which my case does not entitle me.
Give Mr. Ramsey the advantages of every doubt and
what is left will waft us on to victory."

The evening after this letter appeared in print a large

public meeting was held in Albany at which speeches were made by Mr. Ramsey and several other eminent citizens, and nowhere (save in one suite of rooms at the Delavan House) was there anything but the strongest feeling in favor of the Ramsey side.

During the day which culminated in the riot at Tunnel Station, the usual programme had been repeated at Albany. The morning brought a new injunction and a new writ of assistance from Judge Barnard, designed to disarm the proceedings of Judge Peckham of the day before. Matters had now, however, got to such a pass that these documents were of little consequence except as a sort of feminine contest to see which should have the last word. Nevertheless, being devoid of any other amusement, Messrs. Fisk and Courter approached the Albany & Susquehanna offices in a carriage that afternoon and demanded possession. Of course Mr. Van Vaulkenburg regarded the demand as a very good joke and answered it simply with a smile that showed an appreciation of the comic element in Mr. Fisk's character. The Barnard receivers had so little confidence of the success of their mission that they did not deem it worth while to get out of their carriage. Mr. Fisk merely pointed to a bundle of papers sticking out of his pocket as he lay back in his barouche and looking up to the windows with a cigar in his mouth said, "Here's an order and writ of assistance from friend Barnard, fresh up from New York, and it tells me to take possession." Mr. Van Vaulkenburg merely

looked down from the window and smiled at the humorous
man.   There was no more of the "I'm going to take you
fellows if it costs a million dollars" style or tone in this
last demand.   All that was gone and Mr. Fisk seemed to
have come direct from "kissing the blarney stone."   He
lay there at ease in his carriage and looked up at Mr.
Van Vaulkenburg as Romeo looks up at Juliet in the
balcony scene, and in tones as soft as a lover's assured
Mr. Van Vaulkenburg that if he would only yield obeis-
ence to "them documents" from Judge Barnard he
should be splendidly fixed for life and have a high seat
beside the divinities that preside over the Grand Opera
House, the Erie treasury, the Narraganset Steamship
Company or Tammany Hall.   While the kind-hearted
man was thus cooing in the *suaviter in modo* style and
harmlessly amusing "you fellows" with a most humorous
scene, he was suddenly set upon by the police, who
arrested him on a warrant from Judge Clute for a conspiracy against the public peace and order in attempting
to take possession of the Albany & Susquehanna railroad offices by force.   He turned his eyes from Mr. Van
Vaulkenburg to the police with a most comical expression
on his countenance, looked at them a moment in a puzzled way, then said, "All right!   Git in here!" took the
policemen who had arrested him into his carriage and
said, "Proceed, driver!   Good-bye, Van Vaulkenburg.
Come and see me if you git a chance and bring along
something good to eat."   Thus the afternoon's drive and

entertainment of his rivals with a little amusement ended in being ignominiously marched off under arrest and taken into the presence of Judge Clute as a culprit. He immediately gave bail, however, and was released from custody and returned to the Delavan House to tell the outrages and indignities that had been perpetrated upon him and make himself a great hero by giving his minions and retainers a graphic description of a most dastardly attempt to assassinate him. This last story was founded upon a rumor that as he approached the Albany & Susquehanna offices in the afternoon, so great had grown the exasperation against him that two men stood on a balcony armed with pistols determined to shoot him and were only prevented from doing so by the dissuasion of one of their friends. With these recitals Mr. Fisk still maintained the air of a hero despite the decidedly unfavorable current of the day's events for his cause.

Immediately upon acquainting himself with the condition of affairs on Tuesday, the Governor notified all sheriffs and other officers to take no further proceedings in favor of either side, but to maintain matters just as they now stood, treating the party in actual possession as being there of right, till the Courts should decide between the contestants. Each party being now in actual possession of one end of the road, of course this order must bring its business to a stand still. But the next morning brought the details of the riot at the tunnel and the Governor now determined on more decisive measures.

He at once gave the opposing receivers notice that their proceedings must cease and they must come to some agreement in the matter, or else he should declare the district though which the road ran to be in a state of insurrection to the State and take possession of the road as a military measure and run it as a military road till the dispute was settled. The parties held a consultation but could come to no agreement and therefore the opposing receivers united in a written request to the Governor to take possession of the road and run it in the name of the State till the legal complications were decided. This he consented to do. General James McQuade and Col. Robert Lenox Banks were detailed from his staff to take possession and conduct the affairs of the road. They entered at once upon their new duties and in a day or two had all the bridges and rails replaced and the road in regular operation again.

Wednesday morning was Judge Peckham's turn again to issue a new order setting aside Barnard's of the day before. The Albanians had now come to expect a fresh injunction from one or other of the parties every morning as being as much a matter of course as their breakfast. In this they were not disappointed by the judge upon whom they had conferred so many and varied honors. He opened the morning in the usual way, staying proceedings under the orders from New York the previous day and attempting to tie up Mr. Fisk's hands in various ways. These matters and the arrangement with the

Governor occupied Mr. Fisk's attention till some new papers could be obtained from New York. These appeared and were ready for use in the afternoon. They were non-bailable writs for the arrest of Messrs Pruyn, Ramsey and Van Vaulkenburg for contempt of Judge Barnard's Court. These gentlemen were all arrested while in the Executive Chamber at the Capitol that afternoon and the design was to spirit them away to New York and give them an inside view of Ludlow Street jail before their friends could rally to their rescue. The first part of the programme was successfully accomplished, but the parties were a little too far from New York city for such an easy execution of the second step. A private steamer, the "Erastus Corning, Jr.," was chartered for the especial purpose or carrying the prisoners to New York, where Mr. Fisk would undoubtedly be on much better vantage ground for treating them entirely to his pleasure than he was in Albany. But before they could be got aboard the steamer provided for their accommodation at an expense of $500, Judge Clute came to the rescue with a writ of *habeas corpus*. On this they were carried before him and he decided to take till the next morning to consider the case, but meanwhile they were set free from the sheriff in whose hands Judge Barnard's order had placed them. This new attempt to spirit distinguished citizens into jail therefore proved abortive and the trick now returned to plague the author. For while Mr. Fisk was eating his dinner at the Delavan House that evening, still vividly portraying the narrow escapes his life had passed through in the last two days, a rumor was brought in to him that an order similar to Judge Barnard's had been issued for his own arrest, and that the officers were already on their way to secure him. On hearing this he jumped up from the table, leaving a most tempting piece of steak unfinished, hurried down stairs, jumped into a hack and was driven to the bridge, whence he boarded the "Erastus Corning, Jr.," and had her put under headway for New York at once, thus being forced to make good his escape in the vessel hired as a sort of prison ship for his enemies and being obliged to take the romantic trip down the Hudson as a fugitive instead of as triumphant guard over his fallen foe. On reaching New York he immediately betook himself to the recesses of the Grand Opera House, where his "holding out powers" could be exhibited under much more favorable circumstances than at Albany, and kept very close quarters for a day or two, his ushers being instructed to be doubly precautious about admitting any one to his presence without special permission. Thus ended the first campaign of Mr. Fisk's twenty-sixth raid.

The fire from the Barnard guns was still kept up for a time, however. He was at first very much enraged that Judge Clute, having a jurisdiction inferior to his own, should presume to interfere with the execution of one of his orders and threatened to arrest Judge Clute himself. His ire on this point calmed gradually, as it is wont to do, and Judge Clute was not disturbed in the exercise of his judicial functions. But the men whom ho had rescued by the offensive *habeas corpus* felt their position so insecure that they betook themselves out of the State for safety. Now, however, set in one of those periods of peace and good will which is wont to follow when a sufficient number of injunctions has been issued to appease the love for the exercise and make it impossible for the judge himself to keep track of them or bring any of them to an issue. By some of the influences knowledge whereof constitutes an occult science, Judge Barnard became suddenly mollified, declared there was no malice in his heart, and the Albany fugitives returned to their homes and were permitted to enjoy them in peace. Only one further order of consequence was granted by the judge. This was an order appointing Wm. J. A. Fuller receiver of the stock which was alleged to have been illegally re-issued by Mr. Ramsey and others. Under this order, supplemented by the resurrected writ of assistance, Mr. Fuller obtained possession of some three thousand shares of the said illegal stock.

In this situation the opposing forces now rested on their arms to await the annual election of stockholders, which was to occur on September 7th, each being confident of victory on that day. The requisites for this election, as established by the by-laws of the corporation, were: that the polls should be open one hour, from 12 to 1, on the day of election; no stock to be transferred during the 30 days preceding the election; the inspectors of the election should be chosen annually by the stockholders and must themselves be owners of stock; and the stock books of the company must be present for the use of the inspectors on the day of election. The abstraction of the books had left the Erie party very much in the dark as to their relative strength in the amount of stock actually held, and feeling far from confident of success by fair means a most artful *coup de main* was planned, which is probably without a parallel for a daring outrage in a free, civilized country.

It was discovered that the inspectors who had been chosen for this year were not stockholders, as required by the by-laws, and so were incompetent to act. An order restraining them from acting was therefore perfectly proper, and was obtained from Judge Clerke. The chosen inspectors being removed, all the plans were laid for selecting to act in their places inspectors wholly favorable to the Erie party. To further this purpose as well as others, it was desirable to have Mr. Ramsey and all his leading supporters out of the way. To compass this end a suit was instituted against Messrs. Ramsey, Van Vaulkenburg, Phelps and Smith (their counsel) for abstracting the books of the company, and orders for their arrest, with bail fixed at a large sum, were asked for. This request being on the face of it of a most monstrous character, the petitioners took it before Judge Barnard, who of course granted it without hesitation. These orders were obtained on *ex parte* representations, without notice to the parties against whom they applied, and were kept a dead secret till the moment for which they were specially designed, the whole success of the plot depending upon its being sprung as a surprise at the proper moment. Not satisfied with these legal documents, Mr. Fisk, retaining a vivid memory of Mr. Van Vaulkenburg's muscular powers, thought it prudent to take up to the election what he, after all, deemed much more potent than the law, and what might be much needed to make Barnard's orders respected so far from home and at the same time guard him from another ungraceful hustling down stairs and hasty flight to New York by special private conveyance. Accordingly some fifty New York roughs of the worst type, chosen for their especial fitness for the occasion, were secured to go to Albany to stand behind Judge Barnard's law and Mr. Fisk's dignity and protect the sanctity of the Albany & Susquehanna ballot-box.

Thus armed and equipped with legal documents and "tools to do it with," Mr. Fisk with a small army of legal advisers, clerks, boon companions, and lackeys, departed for "the front" once more the day before the election, that he might be on the "stamping ground" in time to arrange carefully all the details for the last grand charge in his "twenty-sixth raid." In his suite of rooms at the Delavan House on the night of the 6th and the morning of the 7th of September, the whole plan was arranged with such precision of detail as to "work like a clock," and was carefully kept from all knowledge of the enemy. The hardy men of muscle, carefully selected from the eminent social element that rules New York city, supplies forces for the State establishment at Sing Sing and elects the like of Barnard to the bench of the Supreme Court, were left to follow by a later train and reached Albany on the morning of the 7th, the day of the election. The *personnel* of this unique company of New York's masters on appearing in Albany has been graphically pictured by Mr. Charles Francis Adams, Jr.:

"A breakfast was negotiated for them at the saloon in the station, and there they stood and fed, as rough a set of patriots as ever stuffed a ballot-box or hit from the shoulder. Some of them had coats and some had not; their clothes were in various stages of dilapidation, as also were their countenances; open shirts displayed muscular breasts and rolled up trousers stockingless feet; one man saved himself the trouble of rolling up both legs of his trousers by having only one . . a class subsequently described as men with scarred faces and noses and black eyes. Under the circumstances it was little to be wondered at that while they indulged a 'square meal' the keeper of the saloon gave directions to have his silver counted."

After being fed, these choice spirits were each supplied with a few proxies of Albany & Susquehanna stock, which entitled them to enter the offices of the company as stockholders. Of course Mr. Fisk could have voted himself just as well on his own stock, but it was deemed especially desirable that these delegates from the slums of New York should be present out of respect to Mr. Van Vaulkenburg's much-admired-muscular powers, and this was the best and only sure means of securing their peaceable admission to the room.

As the hour of noon approached it was time to set the ball in motion. All the actors were required to set their watches exactly together and each was instructed as to the precise second at which he should speak his piece and play his part. Mr. Thomas G. Shearman, of the eminent law firm of Field & Shearman, acted as master of ceremonies on the occasion. The improvised stockholders were marched from the depôt to the poll in due season and, proxies in hand, were admitted to the room by the police on guard. The inspectors were waylaid on their way to the offices a few moments only before the time for them to enter upon the discharge of their duties and were served with the order forbidding them to act. This was a complete surprise, as it was planned to be, and of course threw the Ramsey men into a little confusion. At a quarter before twelve, master of ceremonies Shearman gave the nod which was the signal for actor No. 1 to move the organization of a meeting of stockholders to elect inspectors in the place of those removed. The move was seconded and carried, the fifty roughs with whom the room was packed giving a lusty "aye" when they caught the signal "this is the place to laugh." The meeting organized, the vote proceed. in like manner and resulted in the election of inspectors in every respect satisfactory to Mr. Fisk. The preliminaries thus all successfully carried in their favor, at a few seconds past twelve, the hour prescribed by the by-laws, the newly chosen inspectors entered upon their duty, the ballot box (which consisted of a straw hat) was placed in position and the voting commenced. But with everything thus nicely started entirely in his favor, Mr. Shearman, like all masters of ceremonies upon important occasions, was still a little anxious lest something should happen to mar the smooth flow before the entertainment was over. Messrs. Ramsey, Van Vaulkenburg, Phelps and Smith were in the adjoining room and were looked upon as a possible disturbing element. The polls would be closed in an hour, and if these gents could only be tied up and prevented from action for that little length of time, all would be over and well. And a little string, especially designed for this very emergency, had been brought along and was now produced to do the desired tieing up. The order granted by Judge Barnard for the arrest of these gentlemen for the abstraction of the books and which had been carefully held back from all publicity, was now produced and at about the same moment that the newly-organized polls were opened the sheriff arrested them. This was the final blow and if successful—if an hour could be occupied in marching the arrested gentlemen before a magistrate and getting bondsmen to give the outra-

geously large bail ($25,000) demanded—entire success of
the *coup de main* and complete triumph for Mr. Fisk
seemed beyond a peradventure. But, alas for human
devices! this move did not work so successfully as was
hoped. Either Mr. Shearman and the sheriff differed as
to the proper manner for the latter to proceed in the
discharge of his duty or else the sheriff's courage failed
him at the vital moment through a consciousness of the
outrageous character of the proceeding. The sheriff did
not deem it indispensable that his prisoners should be
taken from the building and carried before a magistrate.
He obligingly consented to have the formalities of giving
the required bail gone through with there in the room
where they were and was guilty of the (in Erie oyes)
unpardonable breach of duty and sin of having blank
bail bonds in his pockets and furnishing them for the
occasion instead of requiring time to be spent in sending
to a stationer's. With these kindnesses Mr. Ramsey
immediately set about furnishing satisfactory bondsmen,
not in the least disconcerted by the surprise sprung upon
him—doubly outrageous in its nature and the manner
of its execution. Any number of most unquestionable
men stood ready to give the bail demanded, and, interpose
every captious, technical, pettifogging, frivolous objection
that he could in "sparring for wind" and the passage of
the hour, Mr. Shearman was unable to consume more
than a few minutes of time in the ceremony of bail
giving. Before this ceremony was over, however, and

H

the move thus blocked, Mr. Smith, by direction of Mr.
Ramsey, had gone into the entry of the building, there
organized another meeting, chosen another set of inspectors, opened another poll, and proceeded to hold their
own election. A few minutes after twelve therefore,
there were two polls open and two elections going on.

But Mr. Ramsey, despite the traps sprung upon him
and the numerous troublesome irons he had in the fire,
still found time to cope with his enemies in wielding the
now much enfeebled weapon of injunctions. Just as the
Fisk poll was about to open, its inspectors were served
with an injunction forbidding them to hold an election
unless they allowed votes to be cast upon the twenty-four
hundred shares of stock which had been placed in the
hands of a receiver on the ground that it was illegal and
could not be voted on. Of course it was intended by this
order to give the men from whom this stock had been
taken the privilege of voting upon it, they clearly being
the only persons that could by any possibility have any
right to vote upon it. But Mr. Shearman, eminent
lawyer, as he was, managed to make this order serve
exactly the opposite purpose from that for which he
knew it was designed. Mr. Fuller, the receiver, being
present was directed to vote upon the stock, and he
proceeded to do so and voted directly against the wishes
of the men who owned the stock and to whom the order
was expressly intended to give the right of voting thereon.
Thus twenty-four hundred votes were given to Fisk on

stock owned by his most active opponents. Some fifteen minutes later a second injunction was served on the Fisk inspectors enjoining them absolutely from holding an election ; but the delegation from the Five Points, partly perhaps from their eagerness to exercise the dignity of their novel and very ephemeral character as stockholders, and partly from Mr. Shearman's desire to work as rapidly as possible for fear of interference, had voted early, as they were accustomed to do when "repeating" in New York, and nearly all the votes of the Fisk party had been safely deposited in the straw hat before the last injunction came, so it was necessary to violate it only a little to receive the few that remained to be cast.

So well was the programme matured and rehearsed beforehand and such was the presence of mind displayed by the accomplished master of ceremonies that only a single desired detail in the performance had been omitted, but this little oversight was an important one. In their haste to organize and get their poll open first, the new Fisk inspectors had omitted to take the oath prescribed by the by-laws before entering upon the discharge of their duties. The books, which the by-laws required should be present for inspection on election day, had been secretly replaced by Mr. Ramsey the night before, and so the proceedings of his inspectors had been every way regular, and in accordance with the by-laws, and Mr. Shearman's sole claim to have his poll treated as the legal one rested upon the circumstance of its having been organized a few minutes before the rival poll. Neither party voted at the other's poll, so of course each elected its own ticket without one opposing vote. At the Fisk poll 13,400 votes were cast and the inspectors declared their ticket elected. At the Ramsey poll 10,742 votes were cast and the inspectors declared their ticket elected.

Thus the election was over and matters stood just as before—with two opposing sets of officers claiming the road. The Fisk party had sought to win a little moral support, add an air of respectability to their ticket and gain an advantage, by electing General McQuade and Colonel Banks among their directors. These gentlemen being already in possession of the road and running it in the name of the State, by their election on the Fisk ticket the road was already in the possession of the Erie party— nine points gained. But these gentlemen resigned immediately on hearing of their election, which had been without their consent or knowledge, and thus Mr. Fisk was left no better off than on the morning when Mr. Van Vaulkenburg hustled him down stairs a month before. He was obliged to return to New York with his "boys," more empty handed than he came, while the Governor still retained possession of the road and directed the Court to decide which election was valid and which set of directors was entitled to have possession.

It was nearly three months before the issue came on for trial and even then Mr. Fisk's lawyers made a strenuous effort to obtain further delay, but in vain. The question was tried before Judge E. Darwin Smith at Rochester. After a most thorough trial and a careful consideration of the points raised the substance of Judge Smith's decision was that the proceeding of the Fisk party, purporting to be an election, was a fraud, conspiracy and outrage from beginning to end, a great disgrace to every one concerned in it, a scandal to the State, and utterly null and void. The Ramsey directors were declared legally elected and entitled to possession of the road. When the news of this decision reached New York, Mr. Fisk's lawyers obtained an order to prevent the judgment being entered, but that formality had been already gone through with when this New York order reached Rochester, so this was a waste of powder. Foiled in this move they immediately got another order staying all proceedings under the judgment and served it upon Messrs. McQuade and Banks to prevent possession being given to the Ramsey directors. Judge Peckham again came to the rescue, set aside this last order and directed possession to be given to the directors that had been declared legally elected. This order of Judge Peckham's was acted upon and the possession transferred as directed before any new order from New York could come to check it, and thus Mr. Ramsey at last again came into possession of his road. He was not long in transferring it beyond the reach of any further interference from Mr. Fisk or Judge Barnard. The Erie party finding themselves utterly discomfited in their effort to get the road by a raid, now made overtures for leasing it and offered very advantageous terms; but Mr. Ramsey soon found that the bond of Messrs. Fisk and Gould was all the guarantee they proposed to give for the fulfilment of the contract and thereupon immediately discontinued negotiations with them and leased the road to the Delaware & Hudson Canal Co. for a long term of years upon very favorable conditions.

Judge Smith allowed extra costs to the Ramsey party for all the annoyance and expense to which they had been subjected, and Hon. Samuel L. Selden, an ex-judge of the Court of Appeals, was appointed to determine the amount of extra costs that would be just and he decided that ninety-two thousand dollars was no more than a proper sum for the Erie party to pay to indemnify Mr. Ramsey and the road. Of course Judge Smith's opinion was appealed from; but the General Term sustained his judgment as to the total illegality of the election of the Fisk board and the entire legality of that of the Ramsey board, though overruling (not on its merits but upon technical grounds) the allowance of extra costs. And thus was a final *quietus* put upon Mr. Fisk's twenty-sixth raid.

CHAPTER XII.

Towards the close of summer, 1869, a feeling seemed to prevail that speculating in gold, which had been so extensively engaged in and been the making and breaking of many fine fortunes since the outbreak of the war in 1861, was drawing rapidly to a close, and that the country would soon return to specie payments. August 21st gold was selling for about 131, and so general was the feeling that it was destined to make steady progress towards par that many large operators sold heavily short to profit by the anticipated fall.

In the spring gold fell to 131, at which price Jay Gould bought several millions and then, inducing various newspapers to magnify the probabilities of difficulties from the Alabama claims, a European war, the Cuban insurrection, and various other matters that really had about as much influence upon gold as upon the moon, he pushed the price up to 145 and gathered a rich harvest. It was under reaction from this "bull" movement that the price had again dropped to 131 and created a feeling that it would quickly touch 120. Contrary to all expectation, however, it suddenly turned again at 131 and was pushed gradually back to 137, at which price it sold during the forenoon of Wednesday, September 22d. The bears and those who had sold short had been fighting this rise vigorously and confidently believed it would now fall again, when in the early afternoon it went strongly up 2 *per. cent.* more, and later in the afternoon touched 141—a firm advance of 4 *per cent.* in one day, in the face of all opposition and against all natural causes. The movement puzzled everybody and ruined all the small "bears." The Gold Room again witnessed scenes of excitement to which it had been a stranger since the critical war days. Stocks always sympathize with a marked change in gold, moving in the opposite direction, and on this day the excitement and fluctuations in the stock market were even more surprising than the advance in gold. New York Central fell 22 per cent. in about as many minutes, and then fluctuated wildly over a range of 8 or 10 *per cent.* through the remainder of the day. Hudson River fell 13 *per cent.* and other stocks sympathized in the heavy fall. These movements placed dealers in great straits. Brokers called on their customers to increase their margins, which the day had wiped out. Money became very tight and brokers had to pay high rates to get their balances carried over to the next day. The vicinity of the Stock Exchange and Gold Room was crowded till a much later hour than usual, and a throng gathered at the Fifth Avenue Hotel in the evening to discuss the events of the day, compare views, and to buy and sell on their belief as to what the morning would develop. The day had revealed the existence of a clique, small in numbers but very powerful and unscrupulous, in conspiracy for a "corner" in gold. Inquiry had shown the "short" contracts to be many times as large as all the obtainable gold in New York, and those who thus found themselves caught well know the character of their opponents. Appeals had been made to the Secretary of the Treasury to relieve the situation by ordering a sale of Government gold; but he regarded it as a struggle between gamblers and refused to interfere. But the shorts believed a corner in gold too gigantic a move to be successful and still held out. When the dealings of Thursday morning opened it was at once made evident that the clique was in the ascendant, for gold still continued to advance. The margins that had been increased with the greatest difficulty the night before were again swept away and there was a new call for their increase. This was beyond the power of all but the very strongest dealers. All the small and medium operators were either stranded or settled their obligations on the best terms they could, fell out of the ranks and became observers merely.   In this way the clique gathered rich profits this day.   They laid aside their masks entirely now and appeared boldly in the most intimidating attitude.   The Gold Room was crowded, not as usual, mostly with clerks and mere boys, but the principals themselves of all the great firms appeared in the arena as they had rarely done before.   To cap the climax of the unusual, James Fisk, Jr., personally appeared in the Gold Room and struck terror into the bears and encouraged the bulls to push forward by offering to bet any part of $50,000 that gold would go to 200, and finding no one to take the offer. Everywhere that day the clique bulled gold in the same braggadocio way, insinuating that the Government officials were interested with them and would sell no Government gold (the only hope of the "bears") and informing the "shorts" that they had better settle up or higher rates would be demanded.   The wealthy firms only still defied the clique.   This was a day of excitement and running, of alternating hope and fear, such as had rarely if ever been witnessed, even in the times of the war, and yet night closed upon the scene with the agony wholly unrelieved, with gold standing at 144, leaving the contending parties to another midnight session at the Fifth Avenue Hotel and a night of most anxious suspense.

Friday, September 24th, 1869, the sun rose bright and beautiful over New York, and its rays seemed to fill the air with a quietude and calm as if in mockery of bustling, greedy men.   But those whose treasure was concerned in the course of things in Wall Street that day rose with no heart for the poetic but were wholly absorbed with thoughts of what the day would bring forth in the matter of their fortune and hurried to the battle field to be ready for all opportunities. The region of the Stock Exchange and Gold Room was astir at a much earlier hour than usual. The boards open at ten o'clock, but long before that hour on this day all the small dealers and commission brokers were on the scene, ready and anxious to improve any opportunity that might occur for outside operations. At a much earlier hour than usual, too, came the young "bloods" who drive down grandly in their dogcarts with liveried footmen, and the dignified gents of more mature years in their *coupés*. That the scene might not be lacking in any of its proprieties, James Fisk, Jr., came driving down and turned into Broad Street in company with two richly attired actresses, one of them chiefly known to fame through her charms as displayed in "Mazeppa" and "The French Spy." Long before the regular business hour the greatest excitement prevailed, for the clique had already displayed unbroken nerve and power and turned on the screws another relentless stage, and many men riding down in their carriages were met far up Broadway by their clerks who had run to tell them the exciting news that gold was going at 152! But all outside dealings and quotations are apocryphal and brokers base all their demands for margins upon the quotations at the regular board; so, wildly as the price might fluctuate, no panic could come till the board opened at ten o'clock. When this hour arrived, New Street and every passage leading to the Gold Room was completely blocked up by one dense mass of humanity, all under the greatest state of excitement. Inside on the floor were gathered all the great dealers, or as many as could be packed within the limited circle, and the gallery was equally crowded with men all of whose worldly fortunes now hung tremblingly in the balance. At length the hour of ten arrived, the hammer fell and the board opened. The yell that immediately went up in the contending bids rent the air till it seemed the very roof must be lifted, and in the din, so far surpassing all that had ever been heard there before, even the trained ears could hardly distinguish a word. In a moment, however, the presiding officer caught and recorded the price 150!—six per cent. advance on the highest price of the day before! A howl went up from the crowd inside as their eyes caught upon the indicator and was promptly taken up and echoed by the greater crowd outside. Such a manifestation of strength and determination on the part of the clique surprised even those who knew they were powerful. A livid pallor spread to nearly every face and a large portion of the crowd instantly bolted from the room, the brokers to demand a renewal of margins, the operators to provide for the demand or settle on the best terms they could obtain, many of both classes knowing tho quotation meant their entiro ruin.

Tho cliquo and their agents stood ready to tako advantago of tho panic. "Settlo up!" they cried, "or a higher rato will bo demanded at onco. The Government is with us and wo havo you wholly in our power." It was now well known that tho short interest was about $250,000,000 and that tho clique themselves held in gold and contracts for delivery something liko $120,000,000, whilo all tho current gold in Now York could bo scarcely moro than $20,000,000. Tho situation, therefore, looked very much as though tho corner was perfected and a success. Tho Government alone could break it by the salo of gold held in tho sub-treasury, but tho deaf car which had been turned to all appeals to Washington, if they did not confirm the boast of tho cliquo that the Washington authorities wero interested with them, at least destroyed all hope of relief from that quarter. Under theso circumstances, many who could do so without failing settled up, and many moro cither from choice or necessity failed to settlo or increaso their margins and failed. The cliquo having gathered all they could from their first assault, and many still holding out and bidding them defianco, they gavo the screws another merciless turn, and at about 11 o'clock gold mado another bound upward, and the indicator marked 155 ! Another fierco yell went up inside tho Gold Room, and ran through the surging mass of human-

ity now packing the streets outside. Men! Could these be
rational men? Faces marked with an unearthly pallor
and expression, eyes glaring wildly, hands and arms
gesticulating frantically, voices screeching to the utmost
power of the lungs and hoarse from continued exertion,
it was a spectacle that beggars all description and cannot
be even faintly imagined by those who have never witnessed the doings of this class of men. No boys or mere
clerks were there to-day. They had disappeared two
days before, their space being wanted by the older men
and the heads of the great firms. Prominent in the circle
around the fountain, to-day, was Albert Speyers, a German Jew, a large man now past the middle of life, with a
long record as a prominent and wealthy dealer in both
stocks and gold. He was now the leader of the bull
clique, bidding the price up to the highest point every
moment, and buying in untold quantities, and acting like
a mad man. William Heath, the head of an old, wealthy
and most respectable firm, was also there, acting with the
bulls and bidding in person. The great house of Brown
Brothers was also represented by one of the firm in person,
and the room was now filled with only the members of
the wealthiest and most powerful firms. When the price
went to 155, "Settle up!" cried Fisk and the rest of the
clique. "Never! do your worst!" was the defiant
response of the great firms who were still able to hold
out and did not believe a corner in gold possible. "Up
she goes, then!" threatened Fisk, and at half-past eleven

the indicator jumped to 160 ! It rested there but a moment and then pushed up to 162, and for a moment touched 164 ! Speyers was buying by the million at a bid, always bidding the highest price, and William Heath bid for a million at 160. The men in the room and on the street, had already reached the highest possible state of excitement and confusion under the previous advances, and this last upward movement served only to keep them up to that degree of nervous tension which cannot be long maintained without new stimulant. All were now rushing wildly about in apparent desperation, and the braggart declaration of Fisk the day before that gold would go to 200 seemed likely to be made good. Loud imprecations against the clique were now rife upon the street, and had any of them appeared they would not unlikely have answered with their lives. But they were conscious of their danger, carefully avoided the crowd and were strongly guarded from any attack that might be made upon them.

In the midst of the greatest excitement, when gold was vibrating between 160 and 164, a messenger arrived in the Gold Room with the news " *the Government is selling gold !*" "How much?" was quickly inquired. "*Fifteen millions !*" was the prompt reply, and instantly the bears bounded as an army bounds when a mine is exploded beneath it. A thrill spread as if by an electric current and in less than one minute gold fell to 135 ! Albert Speyers attempted to fill the breach and maintain an unbroken front by boldly bidding for a million at 160. The offer was instantly snatched at by a hundred bears, and the foolish effort was vain. Gold had gone down like a plummet dropped in the ocean—30 per cent. in a minute and could not be rallied. Speyers fell back in the crowd in entire nervous exhaustion. The wand of the clique was hopelessly broken, the most daring gold plot the world has ever known was defeated, and the great crisis was at an end.

But relief from the death grip of the clique and the shock of active battle only gave the first opportunity to survey the field and realize how wide-spread and disastrous the conflict had been. The agony and heart sickness was increased rather than diminished by the cessation of the excitement of the Gold Room, for it seemed that disaster and ruin had gone everywhere, or at least no one was sure how he should stand when the day's score was settled. Numerous failures were reported and it was certain others would speedily follow. Everywhere around Broad, Wall and New Streets, and Exchange Place, crowds were gathered discussing incidents and reporting news ; faces were ashy pale, eyes were wild with excitement, countenances vividly portrayed the greatest anxiety, and frequent resorts to Delmonico's was the only means by which many sustained the severe draft upon their nerves. The spectacle was one such as Dante might have seen in Inferno and was more wretched than any he has described. Those whose dealings had been on the winning side felt but little safer or more contented than those who had lost, for those to whom they had sold gold might fail and be unable to take it and then it would entail loss where there had seemed to be gain. In not a few cases men who had bought gold at something above 140 sold at about 160 and, had the dealings been cleared in the ordinary way, would have made a very handsome fortune; but the parties to whom they sold failed and could not take the gold, so it came back upon their hands when they could only get 133 for it. So large had been the dealings that the Gold Exchange had not yet been able to foot up and settle Thursday's transactions, so all was doubt and uncertainty and the shadow of disaster brooded over all Wall Street and its ramifications.

Affairs were in this unsettled and nerve-disturbing state when the afternoon hour arrived and it was time to think of home. That thought brought to many their first full realization of the day's disaster. Home! How many could not bear think of home now! How many now first fully realized what they had staked upon the fortunes of the day. Many who had left happy homes, and not a few who had been lordly owners of the most elegant residences on the Hudson or the Sound in the morning, must now return at evening to meet wife and children, feeling that those homes were no longer theirs, ruin and penury staring them in the face. The disaster which the clique had spread was now fully felt and so great was the indignation against them that they secured safety only by concealment. Early in the day Fisk had fled the scene and was securely barricaded in the Grand Opera House. The doors of Jay Gould's office were guarded by a strong force of police and no one could gain admission. The day closed upon such a scene as was never before witnessed in Wall Street and probably may never be again. Its *habitués* lingered in its haunts much later than usual, as if unable to face home, and in the evening gas-lights were detected in many offices where they had never been seen before, so eager were men to balance their accounts and, if possible, gain some idea how they stood. The spectacle of agonized hearts and countenances was continued in the evening at the Fifth Avenue Hotel and surpassed anything that had ever been witnessed there. Threats against Fisk and his fellow conspirators were frequent, and a spectacle of men suffering greater mental torment could not be.

When the Wall Street men gathered in their places Saturday morning a calmer feeling prevailed, but the utter wretchedness of the situation was still more clearly depicted in their faces. It was like surveying the ruins the next morning after a great fire has swept across a whole region and left only charred remains and crumbled walls where yesterday stood stately buildings. The Gold Exchange Bank had been unable to get the figures even of Thursday's business arranged as yet, so no clearance of the gold dealings could be hoped for and no one could determine how his affairs stood. New failures were reported and the gloom thickened. The Gold Board met but without doing any business adjourned till Monday to give the Gold Exchange time to arrange the accounts and effect the clearances, and this produced a more contented feeling.

The Gold Exchange Bank increased its force of clerks and kept them all busily at work through the night and as constantly as their physical powers would permit; yet Monday morning came and found the bank unprepared to discharge its duties or give any relief to the situation, not even Thursday's accounts having been straightened. Men had gone to their homes on Saturday in the full confidence that when they returned again the bank would be ready to effect the clearances and the situation would then be fully known at least and men would be able to know how they were coming out. The disappointment was therefore very bitter and rumors began to prevail that the bank itself was involved. The situation seemed helpless under the circumstances and no one knew what to do. Several meetings of the Gold Board were held, and numerous propositions were made, but they finally adjourned to give the bank one more opportunity of clearing the obstruction, thus entailing one more night of anxious suspense upon those whose operations were bound up by the delay in the clearing house. Tuesday morning found things in no better condition at the Gold Exchange Bank, and those whose action was fettered by this blockup were now almost desperate. The murmurs against the bank and the imputations upon its solvency and good faith, were now loud and numerous. The Gold Board met and it was now felt that something must be done independent of the Gold Exchange to settle the balances for Friday's dealings, as that institution had proved its inability to do so. Various plans were suggested but none of them seemed practicable or satisfactory till it was announced that the Bank of New York would undertake to act as a clearing house for Friday's transactions. This announcement was hailed with joy and promised relief at last. The brokers immediately made out their statements and handed them in to the bank, and early in the afternoon clerks began to gather at the bank to get the balances of their firms settled. The line formed and grew rapidly till it extended out of the building into the street and then far up the sidewalk on Wall Street. The bank officers and clerks had been busily at work but the business was new to them and when they realized the vast volume of work to be done they became discouraged at once and saw they had undertaken a task they could not perform. Great as was the mortification and disastrous as they know the consequence would be upon the Street, they therefore, at half past two, announced their utter inability to effect the clearances and discontinued the work. The instant effect of this announcement was a new panic. Distrust now spread everywhere. New York Central dropped at once to 145, completing a fall of 73 per cent. in a few days. A great universal crash seemed imminent. A new meeting of the Gold Board was held and after many propositions, a committee of twenty was appointed to settle Friday's business. New hope caught upon this move and it looked as though the end of the agony would now soon be reached. Tho apartments of the banking house of Jay Cooko & Co., corner of Wall and Nassau Streets, wero placed at the servico of the committee, and they went immediately to their work. Brokers handed in their statements and went home confident that tho committce would straighten matters and afford relief by morning. All night long tho committee and their clerks workod busily and niade excellent progross in offecting the balances. Only ono difficulty hampered them—ono or two firms had failed to hand in their statemonts. In the early part of the evening these firms had promised to have their statements in by ten o'clock, but this they failed to do, making a now promiso that they should certainly be in early in tho morning. With this the committeo were contented and pushod forword with tho other statements. Morning came, but one of tho statements still lingered. The hour for tho meeting of tho Gold Board camo and one of tho committeo went down to roport progress. He represented that they woro very much encouraged, had nearly completed all tho accounts, and as soon as they had one more statement, which they wero promised soon, all the details would bo arranged and tho settlements could go forward. This producod a favorablo offect and tho members scattered, feeling that thoir difficulties would be relieved before the day was over. At two o'clock the Gold Board met again and the member of the committee came in to make a further report. He was evidently very deeply moved and he was listened to in impressive silence as he announced that the one dilatory statement had not been handed in, that the committee were satisfied the firm did not intend to hand it in, and that without it they could not go on or effect any relief of the situation. He announced the delinquent firm to be Jay Gould's. The members were almost frantic at this announcement of the conduct of that firm, and shouted "Hang them! Lynch them!" It was felt the firm were prolonging the troubles perposely to profit by the situation. But nothing could be done. The committee was discharged and the board thrown back upon its wits to get out of the difficulty. The Gold Exchange Bank had now been placed in the hands of a receiver and the situation had become sadly complicated.

Tho gloom of this day was greatly deepened by the announcement of the failure of the great firm of Lockwood & Co. It was a firm of thirty years' standing and with many millions of capital. They were largely loaded with western railroad stocks and the great sudden decline had swamped them.

By a rule of the board, if a member fails, his gold, if he has any with the bank, may be sold and applied to his accounts, and if he is indebted, a purchase is made for forms' sake to meet his account, and the loss adjusted among his creditors.   Under this rule it was now proposed to sell out the account of Jay Gould's firm and then settle the other accounts.   To block this move an injunction was obtained by the firm forbidding any such sale, and the board was once more at a stand still. It was now decided that each dealer must settle his Friday's dealings by himself in the mercantile way, without any reference to a clearing house or dealing by balances. Injunctions against this mode of settlement were issued against all the firms with which Jay Gould's firm had had any dealings ; and as the Stock Exchange had voted to deal in gold and had a regulation similar to the Gold Board about selling out the accounts of delinquents, an injunction was also served upon the Stock Exchange forbidding their selling out the accounts of delinquents. And in this manner matters were now tied up. But the brokers went forward settling their own accounts with each other. Soon Jay Gould showed a willingness to fall in with the arrangement, and thus, after about ten days, matters were restored to their usual state, the injunctions were removed, and business went on.

The great gold plot was ended and though it had made skeletons thicker in Wall Street than any other event had ever done yet it had been substantially a failure even for its originators. The arch conspirator, the originator of the plot, was Jay Gould. He commenced plotting the scheme early in the summer, and at first boldly designed and attempted to get the Government implicated with him,

or at least committed to a non-interference with his plot.
The evening Gen. Grant was a passenger on the Fisk line
of steamers on his way to the Boston Peace Jubilee, in
June, he was surrounded by Gould, Fisk and several
of their friends and the conversation was turned to the
financial policy of the Government. Gould, Fisk and
others earnestly maintained that the policy of the Government ought to be to keep gold high during the fall, while
the crops were being moved, that the farmers and pro-
ducers might get a good price for their crops and the
business of the country generally be kept in a flourishing
condition. And for this purpose, it was argued, the
Government should cease its monthly sales of gold, announce that it would appear no more as a seller of coin,
and pursue a policy looking to a rise. The specious rea-
soning was listened to carefully, but the President in no
wise committed himself. A letter advocating the same
views, written by Mr. James McHenry, was extensively
circulated and went the rounds of the press under Mr.
Gould's manipulations. The 'first' attempt to get some
reliable impression as to what the policy of the President
would be having entirely failed, it was resolved to ask
him the question directly. To perform this brazen office
of course Gould selected Mr. Fisk. A few weeks later
when the President was on his way to Long Branch on
one occasion, Mr. Fisk went down to the boat, approached
the President and boldly told him that he and Mr. Gould
would like a little private information as to the future

intention of the Government in the matter of gold. Gen. Grant quietly asked Mr. Fisk if he thought it right that they should be furnished with such private information. Mr. Fisk is very quick to read men, and seeing from the President's manner and the nature of his interrogative answer that the desired information could not be had, he made a virtue of necessity, admitting that it would not be fair, and gracefully retired. •

Foiled in these direct attempts upon the very fountain-head of authority, Mr. Gould resolved to work indirectly and get information at second hand—any way to get the President committed and secure the desired point. For this purpose recourse was now had to Abel R. Corbin, General Grant's brother-in-law. He seems to have been an exceedingly weak, superannuated man, and he fell in with Mr. Gould's plans and wishes altogether too readily for a hopeful subject. He was eager to join the gold plot, was sure it could be carried out successfully, and represented that he was privy to all the plans of the President and could find out all they wished to know, even if he could not himself control the policy of the Government on the gold question through his great influence over General Grant. Though a little suspicious of such ready eagerness and such grand claims to influence, Gould made use of this tool as the best to be had under the circumstances. In his frequent passages through New York, of course the President was several times at the house of his brother-in-law during the summer, and Corbin represented that he

had got the President all right in the matter of favoring.
the plan of keeping gold high while the crops were
moving and that Government would not interfere with
their plans or break their ring by selling gold. A new.
Assistant Secretary of the Treasury had to be appointed.
for New York, and the securing of this place for General,
Butterfield seemed partially to confirm Corbin's representations as to influence and assure Gould that his tool.
was worthy of some reliance. Under these circumstances
Gould with W. S. Woodard and Arthur Kimber, who
were with him in the plot for a corner, made their first
heavy purchases of gold. The Government made the
usual monthly sales of gold in August and September.
This greatly weakened Gould's reliance upon Corbin,
still Gen. Butterfield, the new assistant treasurer, was
speculating in gold, looking to an advance, and the
chances were that the Government would not interfere
with the plot by ordering an extra sale to break a corner.
The purchases were pushed forward, and after falling
from 137 (near which the clique had made some heavy
purchases), to 131, it rallied, and went up to 141, Wednesday, Sept. 22d. At this point Woodard and Kimber,
having lost faith in the success of the more daring scheme
of a perfect corner, sold out their gold and retired from
the clique. Fisk had not thus far had much to do with
the matter, but Gould being now alarmed by the deser-
tion of his confederates and having but little faith in
Corbin, was in desperate need of some man of tremen-

dous nerve and boldness to come to his rescue, and Fisk came in to fill the breach and made his public appearance in the Gold Room on Thursday. Fisk's own characteristic and poetic description of his advent in the affair was: "When Gould found himself loaded down to the gunwales and likely to go under, the cussed fellow never said a word. He's too proud for that. But I saw him tearing up bits of paper, and when Gould snips off corners of newspapers and tears 'em up in bits, I knew there was trouble. Then I came in to help. He knows I'd go my bottom dollar on him, and I said to him, Look here, old fellow! When I was a boy on a farm in Vermont, I've seen the old man go out to yoke up Buck and Brindle; he'd lift the heavy yoke on to Brindle's neck, key the bow and then, holding up the other end, motion to old Buck to come under, and old Buck would back off and off, and sometimes before he could persuade him under, the yoke would get too heavy for dad. And Gould, old fellow, Wall Street won't be persuaded and the yoke is getting heavy, and here I am to give you a lift."

It was determined to push boldly forward in the attempt at a corner and at the same time guard this move by resorting to another trick so that even if the Government should sell gold to break the corner the clique could yet save themselves. This supplementary trick was for two or three dealers of little means but good credit to buy heavily and keep forcing the price up, while other members of the clique would sell heavily at the high prices thus created; then if the corner failed. and a panic sent the price down, those of the clique who had bought the enormous sums would fail and be unable to keep their contracts and so lose little or nothing, while those who had sold to responsible men at the high rates would make enormous sums, and the clique could then divide the spoil among the members. This is the explanation of Albert Speyers and Belden buying at 160 or above when Gould was selling at about 150. Speyers failed on contracts for $47,000,000 and Belden on contracts for $50,000,000.

After the collapse Fisk repudiated large numbers of purchases made on his account at the high prices, saying they were unauthorized, but insisted on the execution of all sales made for him. Many suits for large sums were brought against him to enforce the contract of purchases made by his brokers and the Grand Opera House property was attached in the proceedings. The suits have been worried through a year and a half of delay and no decision or trial has yet been obtained by the plaintiffs.

For quite a time after the panic Mr. Fisk remained closely barricaded in the Grand Opera House, at first because of the threats against him, afterwards to avoid being served with papers in the suits commenced against him. During this time the whole region of the Opera House was kept under complete *espionage*. If any one was seen standing about near there with no apparent business, or looking up at the Opera House windows and doors, he was immediately approached by a small squad of Mr. Fisk's minions and warned to take the next car up or down town or quit the vicinity at once—a warning which the recipient invariably deemed it wise to heed. In this way the service of legal documents was eluded for a long time.

Soon after the collapse and when his part in the affair leaked out, Mr. Corbin was suddenly *non est*, and was rumored to have gone to Kentucky. Some allusion to his whereabouts being made in Mr. Fisk's presence, he made the characteristic remark that enjoyed a nine days' celebrity—"He's gone where the woodbine twineth."

The most persistent and scandalous efforts were made to implicate the President in the gold speculation. All the haberdasher bills and private notes of Mrs. Grant for the months preceeding were pried into to give coloring to the insinuation, but all in vain. Congress appointed a committee to investigate the charge and it was proven to be utterly baseless. Fisk, Gould and Corbin were examined by the committee. Corbin said that when he went to the Opera House, after the panic, Fisk said to him; "O, Gould has sunk right down under it. You won't see anything left of him but a pair of eyes and a suit of clothes."

CHAPTER XIII.

In the latter part of March, 1870, rumors began to circulate in New York that the many-sided Mr. Fisk was about to create another new sensation and appear in still another entirely new *rôle*—that of Colonel of the Ninth Regiment National Guard State of New York. At first the journalists treated the rumor as a jest and ridiculed the idea as they ridiculed the idea of the Boston Peace Jubilee a year before. And the members of the National Guard especially scouted the story as too absurd for anything but a laugh, deeming it impossible that a regiment with such an excellent war record would be guilty of such a breach of *esprit de corps* as to go outside of its own organization and select a civilian, and one of Mr. Fisk's character, for its commander. But confirmation followed upon rumor so speedily that the news soon ceased to be regarded as a jest and on the 7th of April all doubts in the matter were put at rest by his election.

The regiment was not in a flourishing condition, either in numbers or financially, and the rank and file were very desirous of adopting some means of filling their ranks and their treasury and securing for their organization a prominent standing in the National Guard. The readiest and easiest means of accomplishing this purpose seemed to be to capture Admiral Fisk and transfer him from the navy to the land forces as their Colonel. The Admiral did not at all object to being thus captured, but on the contrary seemed on what, at a Methodist prayer-meeting, would be called the " anxious seat."

Lieut.-Colonel Braine, a most excellent officer who had served with the regiment through the war, was first elected to fill the vacant Colonelcy. He was by every consideration entitled to the place and in every way worthy of it. The commissioned officers felt this and could not disregard his claims, but his election seemed a great disappointment to the privates. They loved and honored him, but they had set their hearts upon the Prince of Erie as the one man who could speedily lift them over all their difficulties into a flourishing condition and give them the most good times. In deference to what was thus known to be the desire of his men, Colonel Braine immediately resigned his new office, was reëlected Lieutenant-Colonel, and Admiral Fisk was elected Colonel.

The event created no little surprise in military circles

and was variously commented on by the press. Many surmises were indulged as to the remote designs and consequences of this new move, some affecting to see in it a scheme of dark portent and a determination to have a band of reliable men ready at command in the event of another affair like the Albany & Susquehanna railroad war. To be the subject of such absurd suspicion is the price Mr. Fisk has to pay for the character he has achieved. In seeking the Colonelcy of the Ninth he merely had the same ambition that any other man would have and sought it for the opportunity it gave him of gratifying the desire of being conspicuous and making a sensation which he had already manifested in so many other ways.

Though he had never had any experience in military matters, not even to play soldier with broomstick and paper *chapeau* when a boy, he assumed his new charge with an unhesitating confidence, thinking there was not much in its requirements beyond a uniform and a sword. At his first meeting with his command he freely ventilated his ideas on the military art and the needs of the regiment and at once announced his intentions and will in an imperious tone. The regiment mustered something less than two hundred and fifty men when they first assembled to receive their new Colonel. Feeling that money was the great motive power here as elsewhere, he immediately offered a prize of $500 for the company that would secure the greatest number of recruits by the 1st of July. There was one letter in the regiment wholly vacant. A new company was immediately organized to fill this vacant letter and constituted the special Fisk Guard. Recruiting went briskly forward and so many of the Colonel's retainers in the various departments of Erie enrolled themselves under the banners of the Ninth that the lonesome appearance of its thin ranks quickly disappeared and the lines lengthened rapidly. On the 14th of April the Ninth marched out for its first moonlight parade under its new commander. The event had been looked forward to with the peculiar interest that now attaches to everything that Mr. Fisk does. It was a lovely moonlight evening and the Colonel led his regiment past the Fifth Avenue Hotel, Delmonico's and the numerous club houses on Fifth Avenue. He was gazed at everywhere with the usual curiosity and interest and the spectacle excited a significant smile and many sallies of wit from the contemptuous grandees who looked down from club-room windows. During the whole of this march he acted (what he really is to the regiment), only as a figure-head, all the orders being given by the Lieutenant-Colonel.

The next grand show of the Ninth was May 13th, when they were taken to the Grand Opera House to witness "The Twelve Temptations." Owing to the elaborate toilet of the Colonel for the occasion he was nearly an hour behind time and the audience were kept waiting in their seats till near nine o'clock before the curtain rose. Then the Manager-Colonel came marching in with his command and his ballet commenced dancing to amuse his soldier boys. As he stood at the grand entrance, drinking deeply of the glory of the occasion, his warriors filing past him to their choice seats, a constable stepped up and served a summons and complaint upon him. He glanced at the legal document and found a grocer had sued him for a butter bill of $41.25. He became exceedingly irate and indignant when he found out the nature of the document, stamped it under his feet and stalked off to his private box with a most lordly 36-inch stride, declaring it a trick patched up by some one to insult him in the presence of his men. The soldiers saw that something had been done to offend their Colonel's dignity and deported themselves in such a way that the constable serving the papers found it advisable to get out of the Grand Opera House as soon as possible. The soothing strains of the orchestra, the lively and graceful *pas* of his favorite *danseuse*, the bewildering mazes of the ravishing ballet, the wonderful gyrations of Herr Von Ajax, the grand transformation scene at the close, all delighted his brave men wonderfully, but their influence could not recall the Colonel to his wonted spirits and make him forget that little incident of the butter bill. After the performance he entertained his officers and some of his chief *danseuses* at a sumptuous entertainment in his elegant banqueting hall.

Recruiting progressed quite successfully and by the first of July the regiment numbered about seven hundred men and the subject of a summer encampment began to be considered. Long Branch is now the gayest of our seaside watering places; at Long Branch Mr. Fisk has his summer residence; to Long Branch runs Mr. Fisk's floating palace, the "Plymouth Rock;" and to Long Branch it was decided to go for the summer encampment. They were to go into camp for ten days—for instruction, the Colonel informed them, and not for fun. The strictest military regulations of camp life were to be observed and the men were notified beforehand not to ask for leaves of absence during the time, as none would be granted. Saturday, August 20th, was fixed upon for the day of departure. The morning dawned bright and beautiful and the boys of the gallant Ninth were seen gathering from every direction for the grand event. The regiment was ordered to be in line at eight o'clock, but the usual delays incident to such occasions were experienced and it was nine o'clock before the line was formed. The Colonel appeared mounted upon a grand chestnut charger and wore an elegant uniform said to have cost two thousand dollars. As he took his place at the head of the column he made a much better figure than had been generally anticipated. He had now learned enough of the commands to start and halt his regiment, so he was now able to put them in motion without being prompted by Colonel Braine. As they marched down Broadway the sidewalks and windows were crowded on either side. The regiment made a fine appearance and marched well, but the Colonel was the chief object of interest and the centre of all the curiosity. They were late in reaching the wharf and the Plymouth Rock had to wait half an hour or so beyond her appointed time for starting. As she put out into the stream some vessel in the bay fired a salute which she returned and then steamed on her way and made up her lost time before reaching Sandy Hook.

When the end of the journey was reached and the Adjutant had formed his regiment in line preparatory to marching to the camp ground, a most ludicrous scene occurred. The Colonel wished to make a little preliminary display and straighten out the muscles that had been cramped during the ride; but he knew not the commands which it now devolved upon him to give, so his Lieutenant-Colonel was placed close behind to prompt him in an undertone. The Colonel quickly repeated the first order to his men without making the proper pause between the warning and order. This naturally caused an awkward execution of the order by the men. As soon as he had repeated the first order, Colonel Braine prompted him on the next that he might have it ready when the proper time came; but without waiting at all he repeated it to the men as soon as he caught it himself, without observing whether they were ready for it or not, and in the same unmilitary-like way in which he had given the first. The consequence was a still more awkward exhibition on the part of the men and a laugh. This slightly disconcerted the gallant Colonel and his only thought now was to catch and repeat the commands. He deemed it wholly the regiment's business and none of his how they were executed if he only got them out. With all his attention turned behind him to hear his prompter, he forgot his men entirely. They had but half finished "Shoulder arms!" when "Right shoulder shift arms!" came upon them and they were thrown into utter confusion. If the Colonel did not understand the prompter exactly he blurted out something sounding as nearly like it as possible, like the boy in the Sunday school. The result was that every one set up a great laugh at his Highness, which he turned in the best way by joining in it himself, and turned over the regiment to the orders of the Adjutant and rode off to the camp at its head. The march of course lead it by all the large hotels and here as in the city the regiment, or the Colonel, created a great sensation.

The camp was very elegantly laid out and was christened "Camp Gould" in compliment to the one single man who shares every secret of Mr. Fisk's breast, who has been his one trusted, inseparable companion and confederate through all his noted career, and on whom he says he would "go his bottom dollar." It was in the midst of the almost unprecedentedly hot period of that summer that they reached their camp. The first thing the Colonel did on reaching his grand tent was to doff all his fine feathers instantly and make himself as comforable as possible. His elegant new uniform had absorbed an immense quantity of perspiration from him that day and he realized that "sogering" was not all fun. He felt with Sidney Smith that it would be very comfortable to take off his flesh and sit in his bones for a time. Having reduced himself to a condition of entire *dishabille*, he proceeded on a tour of inspection round the camp to acquaint himself with the condition and wants of his men. They were very much amused to see their commander so greatly changed, the peacock stripped of all his gaudy plumage, and this tour of inspection made the camp jolly in the extreme. This, however, was only the beginning of the humors of the day. As the Colonel approached his marquee on completing the circuit of the camp, he was met by almost all the band men, who were Germans, and respectfully petitioned him that they be supplied with lager for a beverage. But the Colonel was determined on military rigor while in camp and answered "Oh, no! we brought you down hear to play music, not to drink lager beer. You can't play that on me!" But the Teutons pleaded that their throats were parched from blowing so much on their instruments, and finally the kind-hearted Colonel relaxed so far as to let them have some lager. This delegation had hardly retired when another son of the Fatherland appeared, saluted the Colonel, and said, "I vants to go out." "You can't have a pass from me," was the reply. "Den me goes midout it! I bet you ten dollar me goes out ven I pleazhe!" ejaculated the insubordinate Teuton, and the Colonel was looking very much puzzled what to do with such a troublesome customer when the Adjutant came to his rescue by putting the man under arrest and marching him off towards the guard-house. As soon as the Colonel divined the nature of this act of discipline he shouted "Adjutant, put that man in the guard-house." In his new and close quarters the German was soon joined by two other men who had been caught attempting to break bounds. After the party had been kept in confinement for an hour or two they became penitent and asked to be taken to the Colonel to obtain his pardon. As they came up in front of the marquee the Colonel fixing a determined eye on the obstreperous Teuton said " Well, old boy ! don't you think you'd 've lost your ten dollars if you'd made that bet ? I guess you would !" Then addressing himself to all the numerous applicants around him for passes to go out and those who had been caught attempting to run out, he continued, " Now look a-here, no chap is going to leave without a pass from me. This camp ought to be like a country grave-yard—no one who is outside should want to come in and no one who is inside can get out." With this he dismissed them to their tents. But as soon as the darkness set in nearly half the men were trying to steal out of camp to see what was going on among the gay world of fashion. The Colonel had been suspicious of this and so was on the look-out. He joined personally in pursuit of deserters and chasing them afforded him great fun for a time, but the novelty of it soon wore off as in his other pleasures. He was, however, determined to establish a system of thorough discipline, and so spent the greater part of the night chasing deserters and bringing them back to camp. "Why!" said he, "how the deuce could I teach these men all I know about military science if they are all the way from here to West End?"

The men soon settled down quietly under their discipline, all worked smoothly and the ten days were made what the Colonel announced they were to be—a period of instruction. And he applied himself to the schooling as rigorously as he did the men. The ludicrous predicament in which he had found himself on arriving had shown him that there were some further requisites for a Colonel besides a uniform and a sword, and he devoted himself vigorously to mastering the manual of arms and the more elementary evolutions. The first dress parade was rather awkward, like the previous display, but both men and commander improved very perceptably each day, and at the close of the ten days they presented the appearance of a well drilled regiment. Their dress parade was the feature of the day at Long Branch while they remained. All the company at the hotels poured out to witness it; carriages crowded around the encampment as far as any view could be obtained, and the pageant was one such as is rarely witnessed—Mr. Fisk, as ever, still being the great centre of all the curiosity and attraction.

Many rumors were afloat as to grand occasions that were going to be during the stay of the Ninth at the Branch. The Governor was going to spend several days there out of special compliment to the regiment, and join in its festivities and be its guest, as it were. General Grant, who has a cottage here, was to smile upon the encampment, and many distinguished men were going to be present with their ladies. But all these rumors ended in disappointment. Governor Hoffman did indeed make a flying visit to the encampment, but declined even to review the regiment, saying he preferred to see dress parade, and returned to the city the same day.

These little silent, negative slights were felt rather keenly, and it was then fully realized that great as was the attention the regiment attracted it was chiefly from causes not at all flattering. To compensate for some of the disappointments a grand ball in honor of the Ninth was gotten up at the Continental Hotel. The regiment took its meals at this hotel during its whole stay. It was announced that various distinguished citizens and military men were to be present at this ball. The appointed night came on. The dining hall was speedily metamorphosed into a grand ball room very tastefully decorated. The hour for the ball to open arrived, but with it came none of the distinguished individuals whose presence on the occasion had been foretold on rather apocryphal authority. When the Colonel arrived and made his usual inquiry " Well, how goes everything?" he found the burden of the occasion still rested on him. Nothing daunted, he proceeded to open the ball quite as contented as though all the distinguished guests wished for had been present. The ladies were largely in the minority on the occasion, so the soldier boys had to act as wall flowers. The music was very fine, there being some fifty pieces in the band. The affair passed off quite pleasantly and all had a good time, but it lacked what its promoters would have been most glad to have—the smiles of the *élite*.

The last dress parade was on Sunday. When the manual had been gone through with, the order " Parade—rest!" was given and with the men in this position the Colonel addressed them as follows :

" *Officers and soldiers of the Ninth Regiment :* By this time to-morrow evening there will be nothing left of Camp Gould but the ground on which our tents now stand. To-morrow we shall be on the march and therefore I avail myself of the present opportunity to address you. This is our last night in camp and I cannot dismiss you without expressing the pride and satisfaction I feel at your conduct. You have behaved well as soldiers and I am proud of you. You have behaved well as citizens and I thank you. During the ten days you have been encamped I have not received a single complaint from any quarter from the residents of Long Branch or from the visitors; and considering that we left New York nearly seven hundred strong and have had an average of about five hundred men per day here, this is more than I expected. I certainly anticipated a little trouble from outside, but I rejoice to say that up to this moment I have not received a single complaint. Gentlemen, this is something to be proud of and I cannot find words to express my thanks to you one and all. The few days I have spent here have been more to me than so many months. I have learned to know you better and have realized the responsibility of my position.   Gentlemen, I am proud to command such a regiment and it shall be my study to make the Ninth the model regiment of the National Guard.   Once again I thank you for the attention you have paid to your duties and in view of the progress made I am sure none of you will regret the time spent in Camp Gould."

As the day for breaking up of the encampment and returning to the city approached, various rumors were afloat as to the compliment of an escort being extended to the Ninth by some one of the National Guard regiments on its arrival in New York.   Some even had it that the aristocratic Seventh was to show Colonel Fisk this courtesy.   In due time the Plymouth Rock reached her pier bringing the boys of the Ninth for her freight.   A dense crowd packed all the available space in the vicinity of the pier and it was nearly an hour before the police could clear sufficient room for the regiment to land and form a line.   But in all the crowd there was no escort of honor. The Ninth was alone.   Among all the regiments of the National Guard, "none so poor to do her reverence."   Such a graceful act would have been highly appreciated by both Colonel and men, but as none cared to offer it they felt quite able - to paddle their own canoe.   The regiment formed and started.   Everywhere on their line of march, up Chambers Street, Broadway down 23d Street to the Grand Opera House—the crowd was as dense as at the pier.   Sidewalks, windows and every point from which a view of the Colonel could be had, were packed with people anxious to get a sight, but every face wore a peculiar kind of smile that no other regiment excites. The Colonel sat his noble horse well and made a fine appearance. He was as self-conscious as when he used to ride a broomstick, to his mother's great amusement. As he passed the large hotels on the line of march, the little nervous care he took to have everything about his position, carriage and appearance exactly to his liking, showed that he understood the chief cause of all this curiosity and whence that peculiar smile. At length the Grand Opera House was reached and the march was ended. With a few characteristic words from the Colonel, producing a laugh as he rode along the lines, the regiment was soon dismissed, evidently to the great relief of both Colonel and men, for it had been scorchingly hot and they had all suffered much from the heat on the homeward march.

The next public appearance of the Ninth was at a ball at the Academy of Music in February. The "Charity Ball" having become one of the great events of the season at the Academy, and the Americus Club having had a very grand affair in the way of a ball at the same place, Colonel Fisk thought the Ninth should not be behind the times in this respect and so shortly after the two others had occurred the grand Ninth Regiment Ball was announced as the next thing in order in that line. But the Charity Ball and the Americus Club were not shorn of their laurels. The Ninth had a nice time pretty much to themselves—the whole air of the occasion being the same as characterized their ball at Long Branch.

The Plymouth Rock having been brought into service for the purposes of the regiment last year, and a change being desirable for this, it occurred to the Colonel that it would be a nice idea to take his regiment up to Boston by his Sound steamers, and create a sensation at "the Hub" by displaying his splendors at the celebration of Bunker Hill on the 17th of June. With this view he indited the following letter to the Mayor of Boston :

New York, April 5th, 1871.

Hon. William Gaston :

Dear Sir—This will introduce to you Major J. R. Hitchcock, Captain A. G. Fuller and Lieutenant A. P. Bacon, officers of my regiment and the committee appointed by the board to visit your city and confer with you in regard to a proposed trip on the 17th of June *proximo*. They are empowered to make all arrangements in behalf of the Ninth Regiment, and I would respectfully ask that the hospitality of the city be extended to the regiment.

I am, with much respect,

JAMES FISK, JR.,

Colonel commanding.

The Mayor laid the matter before the City Government, when considerable discussion arose, in the course of which Alderman Cowdin said he understood Colonel Fisk did not intend it should cost the city a dollar, the compliment only being desired. Alderman Plumer said he did not know anything about the regiment but did know something of its Colonel, and he did not think it·would be creditable for the city to do anything in relation to the matter. The subject was then "laid on the table" by a decisive vote and given no more consideration. How the letter was regarded by the Bostonians may be accurately inferred from the following comments of the Boston *Daily Advertiser :*

"The action of the Colonel of the Ninth New York Regiment, in asking for an official reception of his corps by the City of Boston, marks a new era in the history of effrontery. Such compliments are generally supposed to be tendered by the host, rather than asked for by the guest; and when the would-be guest lets it be understood that 'it shall not cost the city a dollar,' the transition from the sublime to the ridiculous is at once reached. When the City of Boston tenders her hospitalities she does it on no mean scale, and will be slow to enter into any arrangement which smacks of those silver-plate presentations wherein the recipient pays for the present."

Notwithstanding this rebuff, the doughty Colonel was not in the least moved from his purpose but went forward with his preparations, utterly indifferent whether he was welcome or not. Boston had *got* to see him in his elegant uniform and mounted on his proud war charger. He even manifested a greater contempt for the Boston " City Fathers " than they had manifested for him, by addressing the Mayor a second letter, as follows :

New York, April 27, 1871.

Hon. William Gaston, Mayor of Boston, Mass. :

Dear Sir : On the 5th inst. I addressed to you a letter, asking an extension of hospitality to the Ninth Regiment,

New York State National Guard, which letter, I understand, was delivered to you by a committee of the regiment and referred by you to the Board of Aldermen. I infer from the published proceedings that the letter, which was simply designed to obtain your official permission for the visit of my regiment, was misconstrued into an application for special favors at the expense of your city, a perversion for which there was no warrant and no excuse. The reason of my application to you was that (as I was informed) the law of your State did not allow the entry of an armed force without the sanction of the Federal Government, or of the Chief Magistrate of the State or city to be entered. Having waited a sufficient time for your decision, and my regiment not having received from you the courtesy of a reply, I have applied, in the name of the regiment, to His Excellency the Governer of the Commonwealth for permission to enter your city, and he has most courteously and promptly granted the request. I beg, therefore, that you will relieve the Common Council from further consideration of the subject, as their action or inaction is a matter of perfect indifference to the gentlemen under my command.

I have the honor to be your obedient servant,

JAMES FISK, JR.,

Colonel commanding.

The reply upon which this little triumphant flourish was based, expressed the Governor's surprise that such permission should have been thought necessary, it being the first instance of such a request, and stated that, though he regarded it as a wholly unnecessary formality, he willingly granted the permission asked for. This crumb of comfort, small as it was, served the Colonel's purpose of coming out from behind his indefinite phrase with flying colors, snubbing his snubbers, and informing the city fathers of Boston that they were a very stupid set.

Having thus mercilessly crushed and humiliated the Puritan magistrates, pricked the bubble of their arrogance and pretension, and made them feel how very insignificant they and their actions were to the great and good like himself, the redoubtable Colonel proceeded with his preparations for entering the citadel of "the modern Athens" with his "armed force," determined that Bunker Hill should not be robbed of its crowning honor nor the intellectual citizens of "the Hub" be deprived of the rare privilege and pleasure of seeing the great Prince Erie mounted on his splendid black war horse, preceded by his unequalled band of one hundred musicians and followed by his regiment of braves, no matter how long-eared the proclivities of their civic rulers. But when the preparations were all completed and the day drew nigh for the departure of the gallant Ninth upon its pilgrimage to the monument that commemorates defeat, the Colonel suddenly found himself thrown up against the contumacious Mayor and Aldermen again in a most unexpected manner, and was forced to eat humble pie in the shape of having to ask further favors of the men to whom he had said, with sublime military *hauteur*, "your action or inaction is a matter of perfect indifference to the gentlemen under my command."

The regiment was to be in Boston on Sunday. The Colonel was familiar with Boston sentiment as to the proper manner of keeping the Sabbath, and manifested a commendable regard for that sentiment by resolving that while in Boston he and his would do as Bostonians do. Accordingly he had put it down on his programme marked out for the visit that on Sunday the regiment, with the one hundred musicians and the black war horse, would march from their hotel to the Common, there to hold such religious services as to their chaplain should seem good. But the Common is under the special ward of the Mayor and Aldermen and right well do they guard the sacred trust. Those two keys said to have been received in direct line from St. Peter are not more reverently held by Pius Ninth than is the open sesame of this revered enclosure by its depositaries. At the eleventh hour Colonel Fisk learned that he could not march his regiment upon that Boston Common, even to say their prayers, without permission from the very men whose ears he had recently boxed so contemptuously. To most men this situation would have been somewhat embarrassing. To Colonel Fisk it was only comical. It is one of his characteristics that what would be matter for embarrassment to most men in their false modesty, he regards as only a good joke and laughs away with the classic interrogation "How is that for high?" With the magnanimity of true greatness, he bore the Mayor and Aldermen no malice for the past, and the difference of the parties in worldly station, he thought, precluded all possibility of there being on this occasion a feeling of anything like embarrassment—that infallible sign of low breeding. Therefore when he learned the necessities of the case he experienced none of the qualms of vulgar natures, but immediately sat down boiling over with humor, seized his huge gold pen and indited the third epistle of James to the Bostonians, to wit :

New York, June 2, 1871.

Hon. William Gaston, Mayor of Boston:

Dear Sir : As I am informed that your city ordinances prohibit the entry of any regiment upon Boston Common without permission from the Mayor, I respectfully request permission for the use of the Common by the Ninth Regiment, N.G.S.N.Y., on the 17th instant for a dress parade, and on the 18th for public religious services.

Very respectfully, your obedient servant,

JAMES FISK, Jr., Colonel.

The reception of this letter was the occasion of quite an unwonted flutter in the City Hall. It was immediately laid before the Aldermen and its effect upon that body was magical. Their candle so ruthlessly blown out by the previous letter, was suddenly blown into new life and light again. The aldermanic dicky, which wilted completely and bowed its head in shame under the scathing snub of April 27th, was instantly given several vigorous jerks and bidden to stand up straight and stiff once more, and the municipal body suddenly exhibited signs of a resurrected self-respect after the month of humiliation with its nose upon the Erie grindstone.   But

> " Alas for the rarity
> Of Christian charity
> Under the sun!"

The Boston Aldermen displayed a sad poverty in contrast with Mr. Fisk's great wealth in this highest of the Christian graces.   Unlike him, they could not forgive and forget, but felt sulky and were disposed to nurse malice in their bosoms.   On receiving this evidence that they were of some little consequence, even to Prince Erie and "the gentlemen under his command," they became unduly elated by so great a compliment and were determined to make their importance felt.   That Boston Common, whilom the pride of "the Hub," the object to which Bostonians delighted to call the attention of New Yorkers before the days of Central Park; that Boston Common with its big elm, upon which they used to hang witches "in good old colony times;" that Boston Common with its Frog Pond whereon all Bostonians sent out their first ships across summer seas and first experienced the peculiar sensation and phenomenon of seeing stars by daylight during their earliest graceful performances on skates; that Boston Common with its "hoop skirt" gate bearing the State arms with the motto "*sub libertate quietem*"; that Boston Common with its parade ground whereon all Bostonians have played marbles and cat and ball, and expended their weekly allowance of pennies upon giberalters in their youth, where Webster made his last speech, where Gilmore first used cannon as a musical instrument, whence little red balloons and big black balloons had often gone up, to the infinite glee of little Bostonians and their nurses, where pin-wheels had whizzed and every species of pyrotechnic had fizzed, gyrated and gone out after its kind, to commemorate many a "glorious Fourth,"—that sacred Boston Common, said these pious venerating Aldermen, was not to be lightly profaned by the tread of unholy feet and the entrance of an armed force of Gothamites. While discussing the matter they had quite a little tempest in a teapot, repeated the sneers indulged at Colonel Fisk when considering his first letter, and that part of the request asking for the use of the Common on Sunday for religious exercises was refused on the ground that such a Colonel with such a war horse, such a band of musicians and such a regiment, would draw together a large crowd of the lowest and most disorderly element in the city and result in a desecration of the Sabbath and the Common.

When the Colonel was informed of the treatment his last request had received, he suddenly forgot the nature of the matter under consideration, put on his most warlike expression of countenance and indulged in expletives not generally deemed religious. Determined to bring these aldermanic noses to the grindstone again and win another triumph over the Boston magnates, the big pen was again called into requisition to indite a telegram:

New York, June 13—9½ P.M.

To his Honor the Mayor of Charlestown, Mass. :

I am at this moment in receipt of a telegram from Boston announcing that the Ninth Regiment are denied the privilege of holding religious services in any public place in Boston except the street, on Sunday next. Will you allow the regiment to march on Sabbath morning to your hospitable city, and there hold religious services in such suitable place as you may designate? If Monument Square or the grounds surrounding Bunker Hill Monument are subject to your control, allow us to suggest one of those places. Please answer by telegraph at earliest moment, in order that a committee may confer with you on Thursday.

JAMES FISK, Jr.,
Colonel Commanding.

But the result of this flank movement was not so brilliant as the previous one, for it not only gave no opportunity to snub his snubbers, as the Governor's reply was made to do, but it drove a new arrow of mortification, and led to further forgetfulness that the subject was a religious one. The Charlestown Mayor placed the matter before the Aldermen and after considering it they

Resolved, That the board esteems it a pleasure to grant any military organization all the courtesies and civilities becoming an intelligent community. But in considering the request of Colonel James Fisk, Jr., for permission to hold religious services in the open air with his regiment on Sunday the 18th instant, while we respect the object of the request, we feel that the crowd and confusion necessarily attending a parade would certainly ill accord with the proper observance of the Sabbath. And, therefore, as a matter of order and regularity we deem it inexpedient to grant the permission desired.

As soon as this resolution was passed some enthusiastic individuals, thinking this conduct to visitors ungracious, commenced scouring the city in search of some place to tender to the valiant Colonel, that he might not be turned away without saying his prayers. After great effort a vacant patch of land, too poor for earthly use, was found and made the subject of the following telegram :

Charlestown, June 15, 1871.

Colonel James Fisk, Jr., commanding Ninth Regiment N. Y. N. G., New York :

Near the foot of Bunker Hill, and approximate to the spot where the British hosts landed to make their assault upon the redoubts, ninety-six years ago, there is a suitable lot of ground for your regiment to worship on Sunday, the 18th instant, which is tendered you by

MANY CITIZENS OF CHARLESTOWN.

Either "many citizens" was too indefinite an address to reply to, or the Colonel was too much disgusted with the Puritanic spirit he had fallen upon to waste more of his valuable time upon such antediluvians, for the tender of "many citizens" was not accepted, and the Colonel was forced to set out on his pilgrimage ere the religious needs of the regiment were provided for.

The regiment left New York by special steamer for

Fall River on Friday afternoon, June 16th, and reached Boston on the morning of the 17th. They were received by a fine military escort, the first compliment of the kind they had ever received under their new Colonel, and marched to the St. James Hotel. After breakfast they resumed the march through Boston to Charlestown, took part in the celebration of the battle of Bunker Hill, marched back through Boston to the Common, went through a dress parade, then returned to their hotel and were dismissed to amuse themselves as they pleased. Everywhere on their march from the moment they arrived a large crowd awaited them. The Colonel, mounted on a splendid black horse, was of course the chief centre of attraction. All faces were marked by the peculiar smile which Mr. Fisk's appearance in public ever evokes, and as he rode along there were frequent faint demonstrations of applause of the kind that borders on the doubtful ground between compliment and jeer. In the evening the band, which had attracted much attention during the day from its large number of musicians and the presence of Levy, the renowned cornet player, gave a concert on the Common. It was a beautiful evening and a vast crowd gathered to listen, and was of such an appreciative class as to join in with a chorus of jews-harps at the most effective parts of Levy's beautiful cornet solos. The band played beautifully and the Bostonians, though priding themselves on their musical culture, were forced to confess they had nothing to compare with it.

Sunday morning came, and it was announced that the vexed question of religious services had been settled. The regiment was to be formed in Franklin Square, fronting the St. James, and the chaplain to deliver his sermon from the balcony of the hotel. But alas! after his many trials and disappointments, in relation to the matter, it seemed as though the very elements had joined his enemies and were opposed to Mr. Fisk's saying his prayers in Boston, for a severe rain storm set in and, for a third time, his plans for religious services were defeated. Trying as this third rejection of his devotions was, the Colonel's religious fervor remained unabated, and he was still determined that he would say his prayers somewhere before he left Boston. His Opera Bouffe company having recently performed at the Boston Theatre, he was on such terms with the manager of that establishment as to be able to secure it without difficulty for his present purpose. Therefore it was decided that the stage of the Boston Theatre, whereon his Aimée had yesterday entertained an audience in comic opera, should be the altar from which should be offered the thrice rejected prayers. A long string of omnibusses formed a cordon round the St. James Hotel, the gallant soldiers of the Ninth were packed into them and driven away to the Boston Theatre. Brief as was the notice and unpropitious as was the weather, the vast auditorium was filled with spectators. The regiment took seats in the body of the house, while the Colonel with his staff, chaplain and band took positions upon the stage. The band played so effectively and a cornet solo by Levy was so stirring that the audience broke out with applause. This the chaplain promptly and severely rebuked and then proceeded to deliver a sermon. This ended, the Colonel, in undress uniform and white kids, arose and said:

Soldiers of the Ninth Regiment and Officers of the Staff:

On the morrow, if God spares us, we shall get back again to our own city, or, at least, to the city where you belong, for I can scarcely say *our* city, because I belong in Boston. This is my residence. I hardly can express to you the feelings which I cherish toward you all for the manner in which you have fulfilled all your duties as soldiers on this occasion. You have again occasion to feel proud, in every sense of the word, of your entire behaviour from the time you left New York until now. I can only thank you in all kindness, heartfelt kindness, that you have done now as you always have done since you have been under my command; that you have again taken a great interest in the performance of your duties, and that you have, as usual, shown your willingness to carry out every wish of your superior officers. It is always with pride, when we have been anywhere, that in after times when I have met any with whom we have been associated, that I hear of the proud name in which the regiment is spoken of. I felt certain of our reception in Boston. I felt assured of your conduct. I know what the result would be. But a very unfortunate mistake, or accident, has occurred with regard to the authorities of the city of Boston—a mistake I would gladly have avoided. The hospitalities we wanted extended to us were those that I

felt we would be sure to get, and the only thing that has
gone wrong was the occasion which has made it necessary
for me to offer an apology to the Mayor of the city of
Boston, in behalf of my regiment, when passing in review.
We did not know that he was to review us. I saw him
just in time to salute him myself, but the regiment was
unable to salute him, for there was not time to pass the
word down the line. It was a respect which 'we owed to
him in his position as chief magistrate of this city, and it
is right that the regiment should apologise; and, therefore, when these remarks are registered, as they will be
to-morrow when we have returned to our homes, he will
hear that we have apologized to him for a mistake which
was not ours; we should have been notified. (Applause
from the spectators.) I wish to speak of the kind manner in which the military of Massachusetts have received
us, and to thank the citizens of Massachusetts and those
of other States for the exceedingly kind welcome they
have accorded us. It was the only welcome we wanted.
(Applause.) The matter of our hospitalities and expenses
were borne by friends. Hospitalities, in the strict sense
of the term, we can carry out ourselves; but the spirit
evinced by the people of Massachusetts, as we passed
along its streets, could not be purchased. It must come
from the heart; from the good feeling they bear toward
us, and I thank them, and I know that you all thank
them for it. In the future, when we have occasion, and I
think we shall have, of turning from the city of New
York, I shall yearn toward Boston, for I think the good
feeling displayed by the citizens on this visit would bring
us all back here the next season, instead of anywhere
else. Therefore, when we go from Boston, I will say for

myself and my regiment that we shall carry back nothing but the kindest spirit toward this good city.   There should have come up no "ism"; there should have come up nothing to say that we should not worship God how and where we pleased.   It was a mistake.   Nobody meant wrong toward us, and I was sorry to see that the question was agitated at all.   I do not believe that the signers of the paper said to have been sent in to the Boston City Government, requesting that the Common should not be opened to us, felt any differently toward us than did the 100,000 or 150,000 people who welcomed us so warmly.   We will cherish no bad feeling against them. I do not believe they cherish anything against us.   Again let me thank them for all they have done for us.   It speaks well for us to exhibit ourselves in full ranks to-day after the hard labors of yesterday, and reflecting on the fact that a leave of absence was granted from 9 o'clock last night to 1 o'clock to-day.   I am told that, except those who are upon the sick list, every officer and private is present here this afternoon, and I am proud of the Ninth.   Because why? whether under military rule or otherwise, they feel a pride in their organization.   They take pride in its good behavior, take them where you will. You have planted another peaceful battle on your flag. Thanking you for the spirit in which you have carried out your instructions, and that you have done what is right, and discharged your duties with a degree of merit to which you always aspire, I will retire.   (Applause.)

The ceremonies in the theatre over, the regiment were again disposed of in the omnibusses and driven to the depot, where they took the cars for home.   Despite the

drenching rain an immense crowd had gathered to witness the departure and cheered heartily for the parting
guest as the long train passed out of the depot.

Sympathy had grown rapidly in favor of the Colonel
and his regiment during their visit of thirty-six hours.
The evident commendable earnest desire of the Colonel to
manifest the highest courtesy to every one and pay the
most scrupulous respect even to every Boston prejudice,
the marked gentlemanly bearing of every man in the
regiment, which was noted by every one, the genuine
pleasure which the splendid music of the band had afforded, all conspired to turn the tide in favor of the visitors and create a feeling that they were treated too curtly
by the municipal authorities. "He laughs best who
laughs last," and the silent rebuke which the bearing of
the Ninth while in Boston gave to the absurd action of
the Aldermen in refusing the use of the Common for religious services, was a triumph of the proudest kind, and
the visit may well have been gratifying to them and their
Colonel, despite the preliminary affront

The Ninth had hardly recovered from the sea-sickness
of their very stormy homeward voyage and ceased to talk
of their pleasure trip, when they were suddenly summoned to arms for a more serious purpose than a holiday
parade. July 12th, 1871, will go down as a historic day
in the annals of New York, because of the terrible riot
that occurred on that date, and the Ninth wrote its fame
upon the same page of history in the blood of three of

its members, though perhaps it gained a greater ephemeral notoriety from the part played by its Colonel on that memorable day.

The Governor having ordered out the militia to protect the procession of Orangemen and suppress riot, Colonel Fisk was early at work rallying his command, little dreaming what a serious record the day would bring forth. The men of the Ninth that first reported at their armory were immediately sent out by the Colonel to hunt up the rest and hurry them to headquarters. But Colonel Fisk now experienced some difficulties from the many irons he had in the fire. Being the owner of one of the ferries to Jersey City, he received orders from the Governor to stop running it, to prevent Jersey Orangemen from coming across. He left his armory and went to his Grand Opera House to give directions for carrying out this order, but before this matter was settled he received word that his regiment had formed and was on its way to the scene of anticipated trouble and immediately started to join it. It being very hot, he had thrown off his coat while in the Opera House and, in his eagerness to be at the head of his men, thought not of such trivial matters as dress, so the doughty Colonel was seen hurrying up Eighth Avenue in his shirt sleeves and swordless. A son of Mars in such guise naturally excited the merriment of the bystanders, and caused some jeering remarks. Arrived at the head of his command he borrowed a sergeant's sword, less glittering and costly than his own but equally serviceable, and assumed command. In the attack of the rioters upon the troops the Ninth was the regiment to suffer most severely, three of its men losing their lives. When the troops returned the fire the mob rushed in every direction to get out of range. The space between the Sixth and Ninth Regiments being the readiest escape for many, a crowd rushed through, and as Colonel Fisk stood here at the head of his regiment in the way, the mob ran against him and he tumbled over. Not having anticipated anything so serious as this, his nerves were somewhat disturbed by the unexpected event, and not liking that kind of play he got up and ran into the first place that presented itself. Thinking all the fury of the mob now concentrated upon himself, he felt insecure in his first hiding place and therefore ran out into the back yard, jumped over the fence and went on jumping fences till he had passed several back yards. He then ventured to run through a passage way to Twenty-ninth Street, and after looking carefully up and down the street, and seeing no one near, he ran across the street through another passage way to another back yard and then commenced jumping fences again. At length he came upon an Irish woman in one of the back yards, who was at first frightened at his appearance, but who, on hearing the pitiful story of his great danger, got him an old hat, coat and pair of pants. Disguised in these, and having colored his moustache with a blacking brush, he ventured out upon the street and, starting in the least frequented direction, wandered about like Ulysses till he espied the carriage of his *fidus Achates,* Jay Gould, coming up the avenue. He hailed the driver and the carriage stopped, but Gould looking out did not recognize the Prince and Colonel in such disguise, and fearing he might be some dastardly Hibernian, ordered his coachman to drive on. The fugitive Colonel succeeded in making himself known, however, and was taken into the carriage, driven to their Twenty-third Street Ferry, there got on board a tug boat and hastened to Long Branch, where an interviewist of the New York *Sun* next found him in sumptuous apartments sweetly sleeping on a luxurious lounge, surrounded by a bevy of females and "a beauti-girl was fanning him."

Of the many wild rumors flying about on that terrible day, the wildest were those relating to the Colonel. He had no sooner fallen over when the crowd ran against him than the rumor started that he was mortally wounded, riddled with bullets, and torn in pieces by the infuriated mob. This was soon modified by the report that he was badly, though not fatally, wounded, and that the house to which he had been removed was kept a dead secret, lest it should be torn down by the mob. Next, the Colonel had received only a painful wound in the ankle, and was quite safe from all harm. And so the modifications went on till the interviewer found him drinking cobblers at Long Branch, hurt, as to his ankle—not at all.

The last time the Ninth ever marched under command of its far-famed Colonel, the last time he ever appeared conspicuously before the public and drank deep draughts of that delight, so keen and sweet to him, which came from making a sensation and centering the gaze of the multitude, was on the occasion of the reception given the Russian Grand Duke Alexis on his arrival in New York, November 21, 1871. The military display on the occasion was very fine and elicited the Duke's highest admiration. When the Ninth appeared with its unequaled band and the Colonel whose form and face were known to all, the crowd sent up such a cheer as greeted no other regiment that day. It was obviously personal to the Colonel himself and seemed a sincere demonstration of popularity with the throng. Royalty impressed him with nothing like awe. He was perfectly at home on his magnificent horse, and gave the Duke the military salute with perfect nonchalance and self-possession, and royalty lifted its chapeau to Mr. Fisk.

In the evening he extended the Duke the compliment of a serenade by his superb band. The square, streets, and every available place in the vicinity of the Clarendon Hotel were densely packed with people. A small space for the band was kept clear by a strong cordon of police, and two calcium lights threw their intense light upon the musicians and shed a spectral glare over the whole scene. After the salutatory pieces were played, the Colonel was invited into the house set apart for the royal guest and presented to the Duke.   He chatted with him in the free-and-easy, unembarrassed manner he wore among his Erie associates, and in the course of his remarks said: "I extend to you the hospitality of all I own in America."

On Saturday he had been in the Yorkville Police Court on a charge of libel preferred by his former mistress; on this Tuesday evening he was in the most distinguished company in the land! Such were the strange extremes that alternated so rapidly in his wonderful career.

The scene that followed Mr. Fisk's exit from the royal presence was a fitting climax to the long series of striking, sensational *tableaux* with which his life was crowded as was never another private citizen's.   In front, and far up and down the streets on either side, was a dense mass of humanity gazing in dazed wonder.   Close by his side was Europe's royalty, which he was entertaining; while in the background, looking down upon the wild scene from the hotel, was genius that had often moved all that is most elevating in the soul, those whose names are symbolic of all that is refined and elevating—the divine-voiced songstress, Nilsson, and her American sister in the divinest of the arts, Kellogg.   In the centre of this scene stood Mr. Fisk, one corner of his military cape thrown back over his shoulder, displaying his large diamond pin glittering brilliantly under the calcium light.   He was never in higher spirits or felt more in his element.   The cup sweetest in all the world to him was flowing to the brim.   He lighted his cigar and talked glibly and gleefully to all around him.

K

His band sent out its most delicious strains. Levy made his cornet do its best service; the multitude rent the air with applause, which was warmly joined in by the Duke, who had come out upon his balcony to look and listen. The curtain falls upon this scene and there closes the long list of sensational *tableaux* that, commencing on a peddler's cart in the quaint New England hamlet, ran the circle of the world's greatest variety with astounding rapidity, and ended with a multitude of many thousands in front, and the world's most favored and distinguished forming the side and background. The last piece is played, the calcium lights are turned out, the dense throng breaks up and scatters, the Duke retires to his apartments, Mr. Fisk is shut from view till seen lying in state at the tragic close, the last sweet strains of his band die away upon the midnight air to be waked no more till they march before his lifeless form with solemn tread, playing

"Funeral marches to the grave."

MANIPULATING JUSTICE.

CHAPTER XIV.

MANIPULATING JUSTICE—THE N. Y. SUPREME COURT—STRANGE JUDICIAL INCONSISTENCIES—NOW YOU SEE IT AND NOW YOU DON'T—THE LAW'S DELAY—RECEIVERS—A GREAT NAME TARNISHED—RICH PREY MAKES TRUE MEN THIEVES.

Of all the wonderful power Mr. Fisk obtained and of the many remarkable things he did, the most astounding, as well as the most dangerous and significant, was the control gained over the Supreme Court, First District, and the deeds he was able to do by its open aid and connivance.

There are eight judicial districts of the Supreme Court in New York, each presided over by a different set of judges; yet the power of each judge extends over the whole State, so that in this Court a man living in Buffalo may bring a suit in New York. Of course this whole system rests upon the assumption that the different judges, being each of the same power, will treat each other's proceedings with courtesy and respect, for if they wantonly or lightly exercise their authority they might go on issuing orders, injunctions and processes subsequent to each other *ad infinitum* and no issue ever be reached. When Judge Barnard granted his first orders and injunctions in the Vanderbilt-Erie war, the party with which Mr. Fisk trained took advantage of this possibility of abuse of power, and got subsequent injunctions and orders in various districts tying up all of Judge Barnard's proceedings. These orders were promptly disregarded by Judge Barnard as being anomalous, monstrous and beyond a judge's right or power. The question came up in the General Term of the Supreme Court in June, 1868, in one of the Vanderbilt cases and the decision was unanimous against such a power in a judge, and in giving the opinion of the Court Judge Cardozo said:

"The idea that a cause by such manœuvres as have been resorted to here can be withdrawn from one judge of this court and taken possession of by another, that thus one judge can practically prevent his associate from exercising his judicial functions; that thus a cause may be taken from judge to judge whenever one of the parties fears that an unfavorable opinion is about to be rendered by the judge who, up to that time has sat in the case, and that thus a decision in the suit may be constantly and indefinitely postponed at the will of one of the litigants only, deserves to be noticed as being a curiosity in legal tactics,—a remarkable exhibition of inventive genius and fertility of expedient to embarrass suits which this extraordinarily conducted litigation has developed. Such a practice as that disclosed by this litigation, sanctioning the attempt to counteract the orders of each other in the progress of the suit, I confess is new and shocking to me, and I trust that we have seen the last in this tribunal of such practices as this case has exhibited."

The chief managers of the legal tactics alluded to in these words, tactics for the anti-Vanderbilt party with which Mr. Fisk was identified, were the members of the distinguished law firm of Field & Shearman. The senior member is Mr. David Dudley Field, one of the fathers of the New York Code, a man with a name famed in England as well as at home, who is put down in the Cyclopædia as " a great law *reformer*," the brother of Mr. Cyrus Field who laid the first Atlantic cable, and a man of highest social and professional standing. Mr. Shearman is one of the few thorough read lawyers among the younger members of the New York bar, a man of eminent professional standing and the superintendent of the Sunday School in Henry Ward Beecher's Church. Dudley Field, a son of David Dudley, is the third member of the firm. At the time of the first legal scandal raised by the Vanderbilt-Erie war, the opinion entertained by this firm as to the moral and professional character of Judge Barnard had been placed beyond any doubt. Mr. Shearman had already published an article in the *North American Review*, portraying this very judge in the most derogatory terms, as a man utterly devoid of the legal attainments or moral character befitting his position; David Dudley Field was at that very time actively exerting himself to bring about the impeachment of this same judge, as being notoriously corrupt, a scandal and disgrace to the bench; and the opinion which Dudley Field, the son, had of the man was proven in one of these very cases by evidence taken before the judge himself showing that he had attempted to bribe the judge to sign an order by offering him money if he consented and threatening his impeachment if he refused.

When Mr. Fisk first became connected with the Erie Railroad, and in the multitude of suits commenced soon after his advent, the party with which he was identified was bitterly and scathingly denounced by Judge George G. Barnard as a band of "thieves, scoundrels and rascals who had infested Wall Street and Broad Street for years," and they were finally driven out of the State by him.

The next scene occurs some six months after the opening scandal, this record of the firm of Field & Shearman, and the foregoing words from Judge Cardozo. And this scene finds Judge Barnard in the most intimate relations with Fisk and the very men whom, when we last heard him, he was denouncing as " thieves, scoundrels and rascals," granting at their request some of the most astounding orders that ever emanated from a court. Judge Cardozo is seen doing the very things which when we last heard him he declared himself " shocked " at the very idea of, and " trusted he had seen the last of it in this high tribunal"—taking cases, not from another district merely, but from a fellow judge in his own district, and under circumstances far more aggravating than those in the case which he had himself so severely reprobated and declared beyond the power of a judge only a few months before. And the firm of Field & Shearman is disclosed as having suddenly ceased their warfare upon the judge whom they had denounced as too corrupt to be tolerated, and now all the suits of their distinguished railroad client are dragged before this very judge by hook and by crook, by precisely such manœuvres as the judge had declared wholly without warrant and illegal, had treated as sufficient grounds for disregarding proceedings, and been sustained in his course by the decision of his General Term. In the Albany & Susquehanna war, Barnard (who had been the first to deny the right or power) and Peckham followed each other with counter injunctions morning after morning, each one tying up all the other had done, till the law fell into utter contempt and was wholly unheeded.

The numerous suits commenced against Fisk to enforce the contracts entered into on his behalf on Black Friday and which he repudiated, were brought in the Court of Common Pleas, probably for the express purpose of avoiding Barnard; but when they were all commenced, that judge coolly issued an order commanding all these suits to be transferred from the Common Pleas and brought before him. This order was appealed from as being quite beyond his power. The question came up in the General Term after much delay, and Barnard being disqualified from sitting in review of one of his own cases, there were only two judges to pass upon it. Judge Ingraham promptly decided that Barnard had exceeded his authority and that the suits could not be taken out of the Common Pleas in the manner attempted. Cardozo was not ready to decide, so the case had another long delay. Being at length forced to dispose of the question somehow, Cardozo gave no opinion at all on the subject, but merely failed to concur with Judge Ingraham. Under the rule in such cases, where the Court is divided, the question went to the Second (Brooklyn) District. Here it was promptly decided that Barnard had no such authority as he had assumed. Thus, after a year and a half of "the law's delay" under the manœuvring of Field & Shearman and their now favorite Judge Barnard, these suits came back to where they were commenced, and the test suit was decided against Fisk, despite an attempt to bribe the jury.

In the early days of the Union Pacific Railroad, Mr. Fisk wanted to purchase a large amount of stock by paying only a certain per cent. of the value down (as is generally done on original subscriptions), that he might have an important voice in its councils. This offer, was declined and he was permitted to have only so much stock as he would pay the full value of at once. This offended him and he was bent on being a thorn in the side of the great corporation. He purchased some half dozen shares of the stock and then commenced a suit against the company to compel them to make known its affairs to him as a stockholder. In the course of the suit of course it was made necessary to have the books of the company for inspection. The officers declined to give them up. Fisk got an order to seize them and a score of men were set to work with sledge hammers to batter in the huge safe of the company in the wall of their office in Nassau Street. The proceeding caused much excitement in the vicinity, but the hammering was kept up and finally the heavy plates of iron yielded and the safe was opened. The company were so indignant at this outrage under the protection of the Courts that they removed their headquarters from New York to Boston, and thus one of the greatest corporations in the world both in wealth and importance was literally driven out of New York by Mr. Fisk and the insecurity which they felt in the Now York Courts.

Some English owners of upwards of 60,000 shares of Erie stock sent them to the officers of the company for transfer before the books were closed for election. Messrs. Fisk and Gould seized every one of these shares and got an order from Judge Barnard sustaining them in the seizure, which was nothing but a daring robbery. Legal proceedings were commenced by the owners, but the case came up before Barnard and he put it down for trial *after election*. The first object of the owners—to vote on their stock—being thus hopelessly gone, they were next concerned lest they should lose their property entirely. Judge Barnard, at the instigation of Fisk and Gould, had appointed a receiver who had taken possession of the stock. One of the parties being a foreigner, a suit was commenced in the United States Court in the matter, the stock meantime remaining in the hands of the Barnard receiver. When the suit had been delayed as long as possible and was likely to come on and be decided in a way to take the property out of the custody of the Barnard receiver, Mr. Fisk's lawyers served a notice of discontinuance of the suit in the United States Court, and recommenced proceedings in the State Court, intending to travel over this same course of delay again. It was soon found that this dodge would not work and the matter had to be left to the United States Courts. When it came on for trial, all the Erie clerks who were important witnesses in the matter had suddenly disappeared, reported to have gone to Europe, and Jay Gould when on the stand could not seem to remember anything. This farce soon leading to very hot water, and an order being issued for Jay Gould's arrest for contempt, the desired witnesses and books were forthcoming and Mr. Gould's memory suddenly became excellent, and the stock was finally returned.

A receiver is an officer of the Court appointed to take charge of property in litigation to see that no harm comes to it and that the interests of neither party suffers pending proceedings. He stands in the place of the Court and is supposed to be indifferent to the two parties, favoring neither. Judge Barnard's first act in favor of Messrs. Fisk and Gould was to appoint Jay Gould himself a receiver of the Erie Railway upon Gould's own petition, he being the president of the road at the time and the leader of one of the hostile parties.

In the Albany & Susquehanna war, James Fisk, Jr., was the active leader of one of the factions, yet when a receiver of that road was petitioned for in Fisk's own suit, James Fisk, Jr., was the disinterested and impartial receiver whom Judge Barnard thought proper to appoint for the responsible trust and to represent the Court. And when a receiver of the stock of disputed legality in the same case was asked for, Judge Barnard appointed a man so exceedingly impartial and disinterested that he subsequently voted on the stock in favor of Mr. Fisk, contrary to the wishes of the only man who could by any possibility have had any right to vote on it at all, and for this impartial and disinterested service, his fee was the modest sum of $15,000!

It is à long road that has no turning, and at length events began to indicate that these legal scandals and outrages have reached the length of their tether. All at once, the great firm of Field & Shearman found their reputation for professional honor hopelessly blemished, their social status sadly weakened, and a name that was near the pinnacle of lasting fame suddenly sunk in disgrace and fouled with mud flung by their own hand. They were made to realize that, even in New York, there are some things which may not be done with social and professional impunity.

The following is the sworn statement of Jay Gould of lawyers' fees paid by the Erie Railway. for the single year 1868:

Eaton & Taylor	$39,998 30
D. D. & D. Field	31,289 10
David Dudley Field	12,000 00
Field & Shearman	5,000 00
William M. Evarts	15,000 00
C. A. Seward	24,000 00
E. W. Stoughton	15,500 00
John K. Porter	22,000 00
William Fullerton	11,000 00
John E. Burrill	21,000 00
James T. Brady	6,000 00
A. J. Vanderpoel	10,000 00
Brown, Hall & Vanderpoel	1,000 00
Edwards Pierrepont	30,000 00

Martin & Smith............	$12,500 00
J. C. Bancroft Davis...	10,612 00
Levi Underwood	11,602 00
John Ganson ....·..	15,000 00
Ganson & Smith....	2,031 50
C. N. Potter....	7,000 00
Dimmick & Whitney.....	5,000 00
J. N. Whiting	2,500 00
William H. Morgan	2,177 80
Cortlandt Parker	3,100 00
Peter Cagger ....,..	2,000 00
Samuel Hand .... ·....	1,000 00
L. Seymour....	1,250 00
J. —. Bosworth....	1,000 06
Chapman & Martin....	1,000 00
Isaac W. Scudder....	1,000 00
John Hopper	1,500 00
—— Devlin....	1,000 00
—— Lane.... ....:...	1,000 00
H. Harris....	1,000 00
Lyman Tremain.....	700 00
Rumsey, Jones & Robie....	750 00
David Rumsey....	500 00
Bradley & Kendall....	500 00
Spencer, Thomson & Mills....	500 00
L. Zabriskie....	500 00
	—————————
	$330,510 70

David Dudley Field, Field & Shearman, and D. D. & D.
Field, being practically one and the same firm, the amount
paid this one office in a single year was $48,289.10.

" Rich prey makes true men thieves;"

and this exhibit abundantly verifies Mr. Fisk's characteristic assertion, that " the lawyers lap up Erie money as
kittens lap up milk."

CHAPTER XV.

JOSIE AND THE GUM SHOES—ANOTHER MIDNIGHT ARREST—
MISS MANSFIELD—EDWARD S. STOKES—THE SOFT SPOT IN THE
HEEL OF ACHILLES—HINC ILLÆ LACHRYMÆ—TOUCHING
SCENES—PUT ME IN MY LITTLE BED—SMOULDERING FIRES—
THE VOLCANO BREAKS OUT—THE ASSASSINATION.

The last new episode in Mr. Fisk's career was of a nature totally different from all its predecessors, seeming more like a chapter from the Iliad, while the others savored of the Arabian Nights. Its opening act caused his name to figure conspicuously in the papers for a few days; its last laid him in his grave.

Saturday night, January 7th, 1871, the footsteps of a young man were dogged about the streets for several hours, till he was finally caught at the Hoffman House, and arrested on charge of heavy embezzlements from the

Brooklyn Oil Refining Co., of which he was part owner and the secretary. He was forced to lie in jail over Sunday, but readily secured bail on Monday, when the examination disclosed that his arrest, though nominally at the instance of another man, was really instigated by Fisk, and was delayed till Saturday night for the express purpose of rendering it impossible to secure bail in time to avoid remaining in jail over Sunday. It also appeared that there was a modern Helen in the case, that slighted love accounted for the milk in this cocoanut, and that the object was, not to punish embezzlement, but to gratify revenge and inspire terror.

Miss Helen Josephine Mansfield, a beautiful Boston girl, was born December 15th, 1847. Her father died when she was quite small, and her mother married a man named Warren for her second husband. In her seventeenth year she and her mother went to California to join Warren, who had preceded them there, and was an editor of a small journal in San Francisco. Here she met Frank Lawlor, an actor, married him in September, 1864, lived with him about two years, when he obtained a divorce, without opposition on her part, both living in New York at the time. The decree was signed by Judge Barnard. She met Mr. Fisk in the winter of 1868, at the house of Miss Anna Wood, in 34th street. She was quite poor at the time. Mr. Fisk was deeply smitten with her at sight, and immediately lavished upon her all the kindness for which he was noted wherever his affections were enlisted. In a few weeks she that had been almost needy was lavishly supplied with silks and diamonds, surrounded by luxury, her every desire indulged. The flight of Erie officials to Jersey City soon followed, and she shared all the trials, excitement and fun of Fisk's memorable exile, occupying the finest suite of rooms in Taylor's Hotel. Not long after the return she had become possessed of sufficient money through Fisk to purchase the brown stone residence, 359 West 23rd street, near the Grand Opera House and Erie offices. Here she lived in the most luxurious style, bountifully supplied with everything that a Sybarite could wish, or wealth unlimited procure. She had the grandest turnout that appeared in the Park, enjoyed the pleasures of Long Branch, and was a conspicuous specimen of a certain type of beauty. At her house some of the most important and peculiar legal papers in Erie tactics are supposed to have been drawn up by Field & Shearman, and there Judge Barnard was suspected of holding extra midnight sessions of the Supreme Court for Erie's special behoof. Mr. Fisk doted upon her, called her his dear "Dolly" and "Dumplins," made her his *confidante* in all the secrets of the Erie ring, and often wrote or telegraphed her during the day when anything occurred so specially pleasing to him that he wished to feel her rejoicing with him before he could see her to tell her at evening. There was no other place like Josie's for him in his social hours. There he lived, there he invited his intimates to dine, there was his elysium.

JOSIE.

HELEN JOSEPHINE MANSFIELD.

Among those who in time became frequenters of Josie's elegant parlors was Edward S. Stokes. He was born in Philadelphia in 1841, but moved to New York with his family when a youth. He was born and bred to an excellent social position, and when about twenty-one years of age was married to a lovely New York girl. By birth, training, connections and tastes he was a gentleman; but under the pestiferous influences with which Wall street impregnated New York atmosphere, he gradually swerved from his early associations and habits, became a speculator and lived the usual life of a gay young New Yorker. It was in this latter course that he became acquainted with Mr. Fisk and formed a business connection with him in the Brooklyn Oil Refining Co., one of the many companies in which Fisk was interested, and which secured large and very profitable contracts for furnishing supplies to the Erie railroad. At this time Mr. Stokes also met Miss Mansfield, and he, too, found a force in her charms. Being an exquisite in dress, fine looking, very debonair and fascinating in his manners, the attraction between him and Josie was mutual and he became an *habitué* of her parlors and was favored with her smiles to such an extent that Mr. Fisk began to remonstrate. This she resented, and after one of the disagreements in consequence, she sent her benefactor a note discontinuing *his* acquaintance instead of Stokes's, and ordering him to remove from her house everything belonging to him, leaving behind not so much as his over-

L

shoes. This note naturally affected the stout heart not a little, and was said to have affected him to tears.

"TEARS, IDLE TEARS"—FOR JOSIE.

The Admiral thought that if Stokes, his friend and business associate, knew that his visits to "the bower where the woodbine twineth" were displeasing to him—a man of so much power and consequence—they would be discontinued, so he ingenuously took the note that "pirsed his hart" to Stokes, told him all, and, with tears in his eyes, said, "See here, Ned, she wont even let me leave my gum shoes in the house!" Stokes endeavored to make light of the matter and said all would soon come round right again. In vain ! Nothing would satisfy but a positive promise to "keep away from that bower." This, to Mr. Fisk's great surprise, being refused, he next tried a command and a threat. This worked no botter, and the Admiral returned to his marblo palace with clouded brow.

> The heart that once on Erie's walls
>   The soul of greatness shed,
> Now sits as sad in Erie's halls
>   As if that soul were fled.
>
> So sleeps the prido of former days;
>   So glory's thrill is o'er
> When Josie, in her altered ways,
>   Throws gum shoes out the door.
>
> No more to fleets and buttons bright
>   The heart of Erie swells ;
> Tho chord alono that wakes at night
>   Its tale of ruin tells.
>
> No charm hath now tho French ballet,
>   Thrown in with Opera Bouffe,
> To chase tho deepset gloom away
>   That sighs 'neath Erie's roof.
>
> Tho joy of all thoso former wiles
>   Its whilom power hath shed.
> Prince Erie weeps for Josie's smiles
>   And sobs, "My gum shoes, Ned !"

Tho Admiral now resolved that tho man who had dared to thwart his wishes in this matter should feel the mighty weight of his crushing power. Soon Stokes was informed of tho rescinding of certain verbal contracts for large amounts which ho had with tho Erie Railway. Next he was asked either to sell out his sharo in the Brooklyn Oil Refining Co., or buy out the other owners. He accepted the latter alternative and an agreement upon price was fixed between him and Fisk; but the other owners would not assent to the arrangement made by Fisk, so it fell through. From these and other indications, Stokes knowing he had incurred the displeasure and enmity of Fisk, sent him a note asking for an interview at Delmonico's, that they might reconcile such an unworthy difference. The Admiral responded to the appointment, and on reaching the *rendezvous* remarked to Stokes, "I thought I could cut nearer a man's heart than any one in New York, but you go plump through it." The interview promised little result, the one thing that would satisfy Fisk being just the one thing that the other would not promise, and therefore Stokes proposed that they should leave it to Josie to decide between them. Fisk jumped at the proposal. He had to drill, with the Ninth that evening, and left the famed restaurant saying to Stokes, "Meet me in Josie's at half past ten."

At the later interview the parties holding the same determination, Josie declined to decide between them, seeing no reason why they should not all be friends, neither concerning himself about the doings of the other. But Fisk was inexorable in the stand he had taken and said, "It won't do, Josie! You can't run two engines on one track in contrary directions at the same time." The interview was prolonged till the small hours of the night, and was said to have been attended with more tears, but ended at last without any change of the situation. The proud Admiral, chagrinned that the decision was not quick in his favor, now resolved to abandon "Dumplins" forever and wreak his vengeance upon his triumphant rival. The next step in the matter was the arrest of Stokes on the charge of embezzlement, when all the facts as related came out in the papers. The charge was speedily dismissed as unsustained, and the whole affair was quickly smothered, it proving to have stirred up a more than usually troublesome hornet's nest. Josie knew more about Erie matters, and also certain doings of the Tammany Ring, than the Erie managers and Tammany Sachems could then afford to have made public. The price of her silence in regard to them was, the discontinuance of all hostility to Stokes, and a full liquidation of all his rights, legal, equitable and pecuniary, and this the said interested parties obliged the Admiral to accept.

The next day after the above facts appeared in the papers, Fisk addressed a characteristic letter to the *World*, denying many of the statements and reminding that paper of the "sacred mandate," "Thou shalt not bear false witness against thy neighbor." But the most amusing part of this communication was not in the body of the letter itself, but in the

"P. S. I only wish, where your article states I burst into tears that you gave the truth. Years ago, before the world battled me so fearfully, I have a vague recollection that emotions could be aroused which would call forth tears, but that is many years ago, far back, before energy had taken such complete hold of us all, and before ambition swayed the minds of men as it now does. But the memory of those days is lasting and I can recall that when night came a mother's hand was laid upon my head, and I was taught to repeat a simple prayer and then I heard the words, 'My son, I must put you in your little bed.'

"J. F., Jr."

The rod which Stokes held over the head of his enemy in the possession of so many damaging secrets of Erie and Tammany, was a tempting one to wield, and he was inclined to make the most of it. He made claims upon Fisk which the latter declared exhorbitant. Finally the matter was referred to Clarence A. Seward (a son of the Hon. William H.), and in his hands were placed certain letters that Fisk had written Josie in his doting hours, and which contained the secrets that so seriously implicated the two Rings, and also a prominent and highly respected firm of Boston bankers. Mr. Seward delayed his decision till Stokes grew very impatient, and then awarded Stokes $10,000 (only a small portion of his claim), handed the compromising letters over to Peter B. Sweeny for safe keeping, and started on a tour to Europe. Stokes complained bitterly of this award as a fraud, and it was insinuated that Mr. Seward had been bribed by Erie money. However, Stokes took the $10,000, but did not regard the matter as settled and waited for opportunities.

The next move was by Miss Mansfield, who sued Fisk in September to recover $50,000 which she claimed to have entrusted to him to invest for her in their halcyon days. In this suit it was sought to introduce certain affidavits of Miss Mansfield and Stokes, rehearsing the substance of the compromising letters that had slipped out of their possession. It was of vital importance to Fisk and Erie that these affidavits should be suppressed. Erie's Judge Barnard was just then out with Fisk and the Rings, and, despairing of success before any of the New York judges, recourse was had to the old dodge of going over to Brooklyn, where they had a facile tool in Judge Pratt. By making one Potoon a party to the case, and alleging that he was a resident of Brooklyn, the Brooklyn Judge was secured jurisdiction in the case and speedily granted an injunction against using the affidavits or publishing the letters. It finally turned out that there was no such person as Potoon in existence, so the Brooklyn Judge lost jurisdiction and the case came back to New York to be decided by Judge Brady.

During the delay incident to these proceedings Miss Mansfield commenced another suit against Fisk for libel, bringing it in the Yorkville Police Court. A colored boy named Richard E. King, who had been long in Miss Mansfield's employment, was induced by Fisk to leave her, and then to make an affidavit to the effect that he had heard Miss Mansfield, her cousin Mrs. Williams, and Stokes talking together and laying plans how they could make money out of Fisk. After making this affidavit, the boy King disappeared, and could not be found. The publication of this affidavit was the ground of the libel suit on which Mr. Fisk was arrested and gave bail. The case was first called Saturday, November 18, 1871. On that morning, Fisk appeared in naval uniform, and there was a great sensation in and about the court room. Owing to a mistake by her lawyer, Miss Mansfield left early, and was not present when called as the first witness, so the case was adjourned one week. Saturday morning, November 25th, the sensation was repeated. Fisk, Mansfield and Stokes were all present. Fisk left early, but Miss Mansfield took the stand, and was under examination several hours. She maintained the most impertubable self-possession throughout, enduring the severe cross-examination of Fisk's lawyers without the slightest confusion or loss of temper. Her bearing challenged the wondering admiration of every one present. Her examination was not finished when he case was adjourned for another week. But instead of proceeding the following Saturday, it was adjourned from time to time till the eventful Saturday, Jan. 6th, 1872. On that morning Fisk did not appear, but Miss Mansfield was again called to the stand, and so bitter was her cross-examination, so searching and mortifying were the questions relative to her condition when she met Mr. Fisk, &c., &c., that all her remarkable nerve and fortitude gave way and she burst into tears. This is supposed to have excited the revenge of Stokes, who was present at the time, and was himself next put upon the stand and made to answer some very disagreeable and difficult questions. Altogether, the day seemed to have damaged the bright promise of the previous day's examination very materially, and their feelings in the matter must have been very much aggravated by the fact that the day before Judge Brady had rendered a very unexpected decision in the case before him, sustaining Judge Pratt's injunction against the publication or use of the affidavits or letters. Things looked as if Fisk was getting the best of them everywhere. They knew, too, that he had been exerting himself to get Stokes indicted for an attempt at blackmailing in instigating these suits. In this state of feeling they parted at the court house, Miss Mansfield and her cousin Mrs. Williams going in one carriage to her residence in 23d street, Stokes and his lawyers taking another carriage to Delmonico's restaurant, corner of Broadway and Chambers street, where the three took lunch. While they were there, the spider-eyed Judge Barnard came in and said to the district attorney, one of Stokes's lawyers, that the Grand Jury had found an indictment against Stokes for an attempt at blackmailing. Stokes is supposed to have heard this remark and been rendered desperate by it. He saw the waters closing around him on every side. Years of a reckless, gay, exciting life were showing their harvest of thorns and thistles, and had already made his black hair prematurely gray. He had sacrificed family, good name, wife and child, for pleasures that "in their triumph die;" a once fine fortune had dwindled away in an unequal contest, and he now saw himself falling into the power of his enemy. He left his lawyers hastily, hired a coupé and was driven to the Hoffman House, where he lived; after going to his room for a few minutes he was driven down Twenty-third street, and was seen sitting in the coupé before the Grand Opera House, looking up to Fisk's window. By some unknown means he learned that Fisk was going to call at the Grand Central Hotel at about four o'clock. With this knowledge he was driven down Broadway a short distance beyond the hotel, got out of the carriage, paid the hackman, walked back to the Grand Central Hotel, went up stairs and took his position at the head of the staircase leading to the ladies' entrance. He had not long to wait. A few minutes after four o'clock Mr. Fisk's carriage drew up before the ladies entrance; he deftly alighted, crossed the sidewalk with his usual air, in the height of spirits, as if this life were all a charm with nothing beyond it, passed through the door and ascended seven steps to the first landing when he looked up and saw Stokes standing above with something in his hand. As his eyes caught that something it was discharged and he fell, crying "Oh!" He got partly up when another shot was fired and took effect in in his arm. He was carried up stairs, and laid upon a bed, and the doctor of the hotel was immediately at his side. After the shooting, Stokes threw his pistol under a sofa in the ladies' parlor, descended to the main hall and endeavored to escape by the back or Mercer street entrance; but the cry of "man shot!" being raised up stairs, the fleeing assassin was caught and held. An examination disclosed that one of the two shots had made only a flesh wound in the left arm, while the other had entered the abdomen, five inches above the navel and two inches to the right of the median line. The latter was at once perceived to be probably mortal. The news spread like wild fire, and in a few minutes was known all over the city. A crowd thronged the hotel, and in a short time Jay Gould, William M. Tweed, David Dudley Field and other intimate friends of the wounded man had gathered in the room where he lay. After his wounds were dressed he made an *ante mortem* statement of the circumstances of the shooting, identified Stokes, who was brought before him, as the man who shot him, and then made his will. He remained calm and bore himself with excellent nerve, seeming to suffer little pain. About 10 o'clock the opiates administered began to affect him and he slept till about 4 o'clock Sunday morning, when he woke, said he was "doing nicely," asked for some water, and soon fell asleep again. About 9 o'clock he woke again and was now evidently sinking rapidly. He remained unconscious and easy till a quarter to eleven, when the mysterious change came calmly over him, and the man of sensations was dead.

As if giving the last touch of dramatic propriety to this modern Iliad, precisely a year had passed in its performance before the public. On the first Sunday of 1871 the curtain rises upon a young man secured in jail for the day by a mean trick, the victim of hell-born revenge, while the pursuer rolls the morsel of triumph under his tongue *con amore*, and glories in the fancied terror of his abused power. On the first Sunday of 1872 the prison door again closes upon the same young man, but he is the slayer now, and seems to glory in the notoriety of his cowardly act, while he who then felt triumphant and pan-oplied in a power that secured him from danger, is shot down like a dog, without a moment's warning, unsuspect-ing, and renders up his life, in turn the victim of his own revenge.

CHAPTER XVI.

Mr. Fisk's private life was on the same sumptuous scale of grandeur and luxuriance as his career in the business world and the acts which made him known to the public. His residence was at 313 West Twenty-third Street, next door to his Erie castle, and nothing that wealth could bring was spared in its accommodations and supplies. He kept a stable of fine horses, seeming to delight more in a fine, large turnout than in a fast team. He was often seen in the Park or on Fifth Avenue, with a beautiful four-in-hand, and sometimes six fine horses, three blacks on one side and three whites on the other. Not unfrequently he held the reins himself, which he could do in a style that few owners of a turnout can boast. On his large drag or coach, were four colored men in livery, two footmen behind, and the driver and assistant in front. No other turnout in the city created anything like the sensation his did. His summer retreat was at Long Branch, and here, as elsewhere, during the season, he appeared in the grandest style, had the most striking turnout, and attracted universal attention.

No man would go farther or spend more for revenge than he if he felt himself wronged; but, on the other hand, no man was more kind hearted or ready than he with his means, when he thought he could do good, help the deserving, or relieve suffering. He was quick to appreciate a favor and never forgot it. All his immense business affairs were attended to as so much play, seeming not to weigh him down with any care or trouble. With half a dozen enterprises on hand, any one of which would be all that most men could attend to, he seemed as free from care as a school boy, dashed off his duties with astounding rapidity, and was facetious and full of fun all the time. No being was ever more self-sufficient and self-reliant. He satisfied himself and acted upon his own ideas. If others liked what he did, it was well; if not, it was equally well. He wanted everything in his power, and depended upon nobody that he could not command. He was not harsh or offensive, but the reverse, in the exercise of his authority; yet all about him must tacitly acknowledge it. He was so perfectly affable with every one, whether of high or low degree; his manner, was so full of that hail-fellow well met style to every one with whom he came in contact; ho had such strong sympathy for the merry element of life and was so constantly full of fun, ho was liked not a little by the army of *employés* and retainers that surrounded him in his Erie offices, his theatres, his regiment, and his navy.

Mr. Fisk was married quite early in life to Miss Lucy D. Moore, of Springfield, Mass. When he came to New York sho remained in Boston, preferring that for her residence. Sho lived in a stylo that was a fitting counterpart of her husband's, like him, was very generous of the ample means at her disposal, and has made not a few hearts happy and grateful by her kindness. Sho had a beautiful villa at Newport, and her turnout was the grandest that appeared on Bellevue avenuo. Despite his eccentric career their relations were always pleasant. Tho news of tho shooting was telegraphed her in Boston. Sho loft immediately and reached him the next morning about seven o'clock; but he never spoke or seemed to recognize any one after her arrival. His will left all his property to her, except $100,000 to his sister, an annuity of $3,000 to his father and mother, and annuities of $2,000 each to Minnie F. Morse and Rosie O. Morse.

Monday, January 5th, 1872, tho morning papers announced that his funeral would tako place that day at the Grand Opera House, where his body would lie in state. Hours before tho appointed timo, one of the largest crowds ever drawn together in New York had gathered in the vicinity and every place that might afford even a passing glimpse of the coffin was packed with people. From the moment the doors were opened to the throng, a swollen stream of humanity flowed in and past to get a last view of the face till time forbade its longer continuance. The brief funeral services over, the solemn procession was formed. At its head, after the necessary force of police, was the band in which he had taken so much pride and which existed only through him. Laboring men from all the varied industries with which he had been connected turned out in full force. The brigade in which he was Colonel was ordered out to pay the tribute due his rank, his own Ninth regiment forming the guard of honor. Behind the hearse came his favorite black charger, and then the long line of carriages containing his family, the Erie officials, and those with whom he had been intimate. The band touched the wild strains of the "Dead March in Saul," and the procession started through the street packed with humanity, passed the Fifth Avenue Hotel, the balcony and every window of which, as well as of all the neighboring houses, were crowded with spectators. The cortege wound slowly through Madison Square, turned to the East, and reached the New York and New Haven depot, where the coffin was placed in the funeral car. The train drew out, and James Fisk, Jr., had passed away from New York forever, leaving it as he had lived in it—the centre of a profound sensation.

There seemed a weird propriety in the tragic close.

EDWARD S. STOKES.

Dramatic harmony could hardly have made it otherwise. A tragic end was almost to be expected for a career that scrupled not to cross men in matters that exasperate the most desperate passions, and there had been not a few occasions in it where perhaps his violent end would have drawn to him no pity; but the manner and circumstances of his death turned to the man a current of sympathy that else he never would have had. A strange influence rested upon all the crowd and all realized anew and more vividly the awfulness of sudden death, a violent sudden death. No one defended the morality of his nature or denied that the world and society could but be greatly the worse for every such career; but the mysterious power of death to silence censure and open the heart to tho'consideration of redeeming traits was intensified by the cruelty of his murder, and lead many to admit for the first time that his charity, kindness of heart and mental endowments were all on a scale commensurate with his moral deficiencies. Many kind, noble-hearted acts were freely told of him now. And might it not be, too, that he had in some degree been made the scapegoat of moral obliquities not wholly his? Was he not a legitimate outgrowth of the prevailing morality of New York? The legal tactics that scandalized the country in his name were not his work, but that of men of the most eminent professional and social standing, hired for the purpose. The judicial fiats that robbed many men of their rights and dues, were not issued by him, but by Judges whom he found on the bench of the Supreme Court. If infamous bills passed the Legislature for his special behoof, they passed by the votes of the people's chosen, and were signed by the Governors of the State. The crucible of death cleared him of much that had been heaped upon him where others were more to blame, more false to their higher trusts. The grave open to receive him, men's minds leaped forward to the judgment of history and saw that he only lived, openly and without disguise, much as those who passed for his betters and held positions of honor, lived and acted in secret, adding to their crimes one he never wore—hypocrisy.

How giant-like his mental powers and executive abilities were, the duties left vacant by his death and the influence of the event on many great interests, made impressively manifest. Who could step into his place and discharge all his multifarious duties? A dozen men were needed, and then nothing would move as he made it move. The news of his assassination produced a sensation second only to that of President Lincoln's throughout his own land and in Europe. It had a marked effect upon the London Stock Exchange. The effect may not have been complimentary, but it at least bespoke his abilities. He had many of the mental (and moral, too) traits that made a Bismarck, and had he been an educated man, he would undoubtedly have led an equally prominent career in a different field and written his name upon the history of his country as one of her most remarkable public men.

The last railroad journey, the funeral train that bore him back to his early home at Brattleboro, attracted an interest that attaches only to a remarkable man. At all the stations along the road over which it passed, crowds gathered, eager to catch a glimpse of anything connected with the man and the final tragedy. It was near midnight when the train reached Brattleboro. A night more drear, more weirdly in keeping with the occasion, could not well be. Snow covered the landscape, the mountains towered above in their gloom, and a cutting, desolate wind sent a shiver through the multitude waiting amid the wild scene for the coming back of one whose boyhood and early life had run beside their own, who had gone out from them to lead a career that excites in them a peculiar wonder, because of their knowing more intimately than others how small the beginning—coming back for the last rites at their hands. He was taken to the Revere House, where we early found him, and the circle is complete. He has been out, made the world know him as few are ever known by sheer force of their own abilities, and has been brought back to be buried at the age of thirty-six.

With the gray dawn of Tuesday morning, January 9th, 1872, picturesque vehicles of all variety of non-descript patterns begin to pour into the quaint village of Brattleboro, all heavily freighted with people of the country round eager to witness the last ceremonies over the man who has made so much noise in the world. Many were there who,

as children, in middle life, or even old age, had looked upon him with something of wonder when his form was
familiar to them in his earliest career. The tragic close
has impressed them with an awe, a wonder, a shudder, unknown to the denizens of the city where it fell. Voices
are hushed to their lowest tones; movements are slow and
careful, as if in fear of disturbing Death. Something akin
to stupor rests upon them all, as if unable to comprehend
how such things can be, as though doubting if-it be
real. The gold-mounted rosewood casket is placed in a
position for them to pass by and look upon the face of the
dead. He lies in his elegant full uniform of a Colonel,
with his beautiful sword beside him. They saw the beginning, they have seen the end. The awe pervading the
throng deepens and becomes more dread. Brief and simple services are held, and the last procession, plain and
wholly unostentatious, is formed and winds through the
street, over the bridge, up the steep hill, to the grave.
It is a bleak, dreary day, and the plain, unornamented,
treeless burial ground is in keeping with the day. It is
at the southern border of the village, upon a bluff rising
abruptly from the mellifluous Connecticut, with Mount
Mantasket towering up gloomily, just across the river,
in New Hampshire. Snow covers the landscape, and the
vehicles in the final procession are sleighs. The casket is
lowered to its place in the ground, the first shovelfull of
earth grates down upon its lid; the grief-stricken wife,
sister, mother and friend, are led away, the officers of the

Ninth are called into line and given the "order—march!" and James Fisk, Jr., is alone for his long rest.

Homely and desolate though the graveyard be in itself, it commands a view rarely equalled in surpassing loveliness. Here summer is charming in beautifully-nestled mountain scenery, and whispers only of quietude, happiness and purity; here the tints of autumn leaves are of unrivalled brilliancy and variety, clothing the entire landscape in a grandeur that feasts eye and soul; here winter is most impressive in its drear and solemn majesty. Here, amid scenery in strange contrast with the incidents of his life, yet in perfect keeping with many of the impulses of his heart, returned to the dust as it was the man whose career was one of the most remarkable of which the world has any record.

THE END.

APPENDIX.

THE ENJOINED LOVE LETTERS.

One week from the morning Mr. Fisk died, the following letters, except the last two, were published in the New York *Herald* as the ones over which there had been so much controversy in the courts. They contain no such important revelations as the public had been led to expect. Among them are none revealing any Erie or Tammany secrets, nor could it reasonably be expected that any such would ever see the light again after once passing into the hands of Peter B. Sweeny. There is in them nothing compromising any one but their author, nor him in any way for which he would have cared in the least. It is absurd to suppose that these are the letters that gave Stokes and the woman their fancied power, or whose possible publication made so many minds uneasy, and against which Mr. Fisk fought with such vehemence and determination. Private letters such as these are the best reflex the world ever gets of a man's real heart and nature in his best hours, moods and impulses; and it is Emerson (is it not?) who says that every man has a right to be judged by his *best* moments.

The first letter was written on his visiting card, in the winter of 1867–8, and ran:

Mrs. Josie Lawlor, 42 Lexington avenue:

Come. Will you come over with Fred and dine with me? If your friends are there bring them along. Yours, truly,

J. F., Jr.

Have not heard from you as you promised.

On the back of the card was:

Come. Fred is at the door. My room, 8 o'clock. After many good looks I found Mr. Chamberlain. The understanding is now that yourself and Miss Land are to go with me, say at half-past 9 o'clock, and the above gentleman is to come at 11 o'clock, as he has some matters to attend to which will take him until that time. Answer this if you will be ready by half-past 9 o'clock.

Yours, truly,   JAMES FISK, Jr.

Soon after Josie had arrayed herself in silks and fine jewelry, wishing to dazzle her benefactor, as Cleopatra dazzled Cæsar by being borne into his presence as a bundle of old rags, from which she emerged in all her splendor, she called at the Erie office, and, of course, made a decided sensation among the clerks and attendants. It must be remembered that Fisk was then unknown to the public, had not attained to autocratic power, was only a director under Drew and Eldridge, and could not then afford to disregard public sentiment. The next day he wrote:

Strange you should make my office or the vicinity the scene for a "personal." You must be aware that harm came to me in such foolish vanity, and those that could do it care but little for the interest of the writer of this. Yours truly,

JAMES FISK, JR.
5TH AV. H.

Dolly : Enclosed find money. Bully morning for a funeral.

J. F., JR.

Dear Josie : Get ready and come to the Twenty-third street entrance of the hotel and take me down town, and then you can come back and get the girls for the Fulton dinner to-day.

Yours truly,   SARDINES.

SHE IS GOING OFF ON A JOURNEY.

Dolly : The baggage sleigh will call at one o'clock, and you can leave in my charge what you see fit. You have no time to lose.

J. F., JR.

My people are partaking of New York, in the shape of " White Fawn" and two or three other different matters. I may not be able to see you again to-night. If not, will take breakfast with you— the best I could do. Yours truly,   JAMES.

February 5, 1868.

Dear Dolly : Get right up now, and I will be down to take breakfast with you in about thirty minutes. We will take breakfast in the main dining room down stairs.

Yours truly,   JAMES FISK, JR.

Wednesday Morning, Feb. 6.

A NOTE ENCLOSING MONEY.

Have the kindness to acknowledge. Yours truly,

Feb. 22, 1868.   J. F., JR.

GOING TO THE OPERA.

Dear Josie : I have got some matters to arrange, and cannot call for you until it is about time to go. I will be there twenty minutes before 8. Be ready. Yours truly,   JAMES.

Feb. 26, 1868.

Dolly: Enclosed find $50. Sleep, Dolly, all the sleep you can to-day—every little bit! Sleep, Dolly! I feel as if three cents' worth of clams would help me some. Yours truly, J. F., Jr.

MONDAY MORNING.

I am going to the San Francisco Minstrels with my family. If Mr. L. was here I should ask him to take you. Shall see you to-morrow evening. Yours truly, J. F., Jr.

This is a playful allusion to his having to play the family man, and implies that it would be in keeping if Josie could appear at the same place under escort of her divorced husband.

Dolly: Enclosed find ———. I am wrong, but I am bothered. It will come right. When I don't come don't wait. You shall not be placed as you was to-night again. Yours truly,

Wednesday Evening. JAMES FISK, Jr.

Have the kindness to acknowledge. J. F., Jr.
Feb. 22, 1868.

187 WEST STREET, Tuesday, Oct. 13, 1868.

My Dear Josie: James McHenry, the partner of Sir Morton Peto, the largest railway builder in the world, Mr. Tweed and Mr. Lane will dine with us at half-past six o'clock. I want you to provide as nice dinner as possible. Everything went off elegantly. We are *all* safe. Will see you at six o'clock.

JAMES FISK, Jr.

MONDAY, Aug. 2, 1869.

Dear Josie: Send my valise, with two shirts, good collars, vest, handkerchiefs, black velvet coat, nice vest, patent leather shoes, light pants. I am going to Long Branch to see about the calerye. Enclosed find $25. Be back in the morning. J. F., Jr.

ST. JAMES HOTEL, Sunday, Oct. 18, 1869.

Dear Josie: Enclosed you will find $143. Yours truly,

JAMES.

Josie wished a competence for life settled upon her. Fisk refused, and she sent him a letter severing their intimacy.

SUNDAY EVENING, Feb. 1, 1870.

My Dear Josie: I received your letter. The tenor does not sur-prise me much. You alone sought the issue, and the reward will belong to you. I cannot allow you to depart believing yourself what you write, and must say to you, which you know full well, that all the differences could have been settled by a kiss in the right spirits, and in after days I should feel very kindly toward you out of memory of the great love I have borne for you. I never was aware that you admitted a fault. I have many—God knows, too many—and that has brought me the trouble of the day. I will not speak of the future, for full well I know the spirit you take it in. "You know me," and the instincts of your heart will weigh me out in the right scale. I will give you no parting advice. You have been well schooled in that, and can tell chaff from wheat, and probably are as strong to-night as the humble writer of this letter. The *actions* of the past *must be* the right way to think of me; and from them, day by day, I hope any comparison which you may make from writing in the future will be favorable for me. A longer letter from me might be much of an advertisement of my weakness, and the only great idea I would impress on your mind is how wrong you are when you say that I have "grown tired of you." Wrong, wrong! Never excuse yourself on that in after years. Don't try to teach your heart that, for it is a lie, and you are falsifying yourself to your own soul.

No more. Like the Arabs, we will fold our tents and quietly steal away, and when we spread them next we hope it will be where the "woodbine twineth," over the river Jordan, on the bright and beautiful banks of Heaven. From yours, ever,

JAMES.

Finding from this letter that Fisk was not yet her slave and that she could not gain her object, she went to see him and they quickly made up again.

FEBRUARY 10, 1870.

My Dear Dolly: Will you see me this morning? If so, what hour? Yours truly, ever, JAMES.

WESTERN UNION TELEGRAPH COMPANY, }
WORCESTER, Mass. }

To H. J. Mansfield, 357 West Twenty-third street:
On the 3 o'clock train from Boston. Shall be in New York at 12.

J. F., JR.

10TH OF MARCH.

Dear Dolly: Enclosed find $75, which you need; do not wait dinner for me to-night; I cannot come. Yours truly, ever,

JAMES.

My Dear Josie: Enclosed find your request. I will send to the Fifth Avenue for the things. I cannot go to the house as much as I would like to. Yours, JAMES.
May 6, 1870.

C. OFFICE, May 31, 1870.

Please send me the diamond brooch and necklace, my dear.

JAMES.

AUGUST 1, 1870.

My Dear Josie: I send you letter I found to my care on my desk. I cannot come to you to-night. I shall stay in town to-night, and probably to-morrow night, and after that I must go East. On my return I shall come to see you. I am sure you will say, "What a fool!" But you must rest and so must L The thread is so slender I dare not strain it more. I am sore, but God made mo so, and I have not the power to change it.

Loving you, as *none but you*, I am, yours ever,

JAMES.

AUGUST 4, 1870.

Dear Josie : I found on my arrival at my office that the following despatch had passed West last night:

E. S. Stokes, Buffalo and Saratoga Springs:
Pay no attention to former despatch. Come on first train. RANE.

Of course *it means* nothing that *you are aware of.* But let me give you the author of it and my authority, and you will see how faithfully they have worked the case out after my departure last evening. Miss Peiris drove directly to Rane's office; from there to the corner of Twenty-second street and Broadway, where the above despatch was sent, and from there to Ruilley's. A third party was with them, but who left them there? Rano and Peiris, why should they need Stokes? "Comment is unnecessary"—a plotting house and against me. What have "I done" that Nully Peiris should work against my peace of mind. Yours, truly, ever,

JAMES.

P. S.—Since writing the within I understand a despatch has reached New York that he is on his way. JAMES.

Josie, still failing to secure the settlement of a competency for life upon her, has now discarded Fisk for Stokes.

AUGUST 19, 1870.

Enclosed you will find $400 for your little matters. You told me when I saw you last you would send me your bills, which I would be pleased to receive, and they shall have my attention at once. Your letter would require a little time to prepare a right answer to, so I will answer it more fully by to-morow, when I can look it more carefully over. I am very happy to know that you have acted from no impulse in leaving me, but that it was a long matured plan. I hope you have made no mistake. Yours truly, as over,

JAMES FISK, JR.

NEW YORK, Oct. 1, 1870.

Mrs. Mansfield : There can be no question as to the authority of the letter which was handed to me yesterday by your servant, in this respect differing from the epistle which you say you received from Miss Peiris, and which, in your opinion, required the united efforts of herself, Mlle. Montaland and myself. Certainly the composition should be good if these parties had combined to produce it. But the slight mistake you made is evident from the fact that the letter referred to was never seen by me, and I presume Mlle. Montaland is equally ignorant of its existence, as it is not likely she troubles herself about your affairs. I can scarcely believe that she assisted Miss Peiris in composing the letter. and the credit is therefore due to Miss Peiris for superior talent in correspondence. As far as the great exposure you speak of is concerned, that is a dark entry upon which I have no light, and, as I fail to see it, I cannot, of course, understand it. I have endeavored to put your jumbled letter together in order to arrive at your meaning, and I presume I have some idea of what you wish to convey; but as your statements lack the important element of truth, they cannot, of course, have any weight with me.

You may not be to blame for entertaining the idea that you have shown great kindness to Miss Peiris and others, and that they are under great obligations to you for favors conferred. The habit of constantly imagining that you were the real author of all the benefits bestowed upon others would naturally affect a much better balanced brain than yours, and in time you would come to believe that you alone had the power to distribute the good things to those around you, utterly forgetful of him who was behind the scenes entirely unnoticed. Can you blame, then, those from whose eyes the veil has fallen, and who see you in your true light as the giver of others' charities? I would not trouble myself to answer your letters, and I do not consider it a duty I owe you to give you a final expression of my opinion. In venting your spite on Miss Peiris (with whose affairs, by the way, I have nothing whatever to do) you have written a letter, in answering which you afford me an opportunity of conveying to you my ideas respecting the theories which you have taken every opportunity to express to those around you, and which many people have considered merely the emanations of a crazy brain. I could not coincide with this view, for crazy people are not inclined to do precisely as they please, either right or wrong, and so long as they are *loose* I consider them sane, and therefore I could not put that construction on your conversation.

As for Miss Peiris being "a snake in the grass,'" I care but little about that. She can do me neither harm nor good. I have done all that has been done for her during the past year. She comes to me and says: "Sir, you have been my friend; you have assisted me in my troubles, and I thank you from the bottom of my heart." This is a full and sufficient recompense for me for any good I may have done her, and she can return. If she be a snake in the grass, I know full well her sting is gone and she is harmless. But what think you of a woman who would veil my eyes, first by a gentle kiss, and afterward, night and day, for weeks, months, and years, by deceit and fraud, to lead me through the dark valley of trouble, when she could have made my pathway one of roses, committing crimes which a devil incarnate would shrink from, while all this time I showed to her, as to you, nothing but kindness, both in words and actions, laying at your feet a soul, a heart, a fortune, and a reputation which had cost, by night and day, twenty-five years of perpetual struggle, and which, but for the black blot of having in an evil hour linked itself with you, would stand out to-day brighter than any ever seen upon earth. But the mist has fallen, and you appear in your true light. I borrow your own words to describe you, "a snake in the grass," and verily I have found thee out, and you have the audacity to call your sainted mother to witness your advice to me. "A dog that bites," &c., &c.

You accused her of leading you on and of ever standing ready to make appointments for you. The tone of your letter is such that you seem willing to shoulder the load of guilt under which an ordinary criminal, would stagger. I believe you have arrived at that state when no amount of guilt will disturb your serenity or prevent your having sweet dreams, and we still shall see you crawl "a snake in the grass."

How I worship the night I said, "Get thee behind me, Satan!" The few weeks that have elapsed since that blessed hour, how I bless them for the peace of mind they have brought me! Again the world looks bright, and I have a being. You imagined I would pursue you again, and you thought I would endeavor to tear down the castle you had obtained by robbery. God knows that if I am an element so lost to every feeling of decency as to be willing to link itself with you I will foster it, so that it will keep you from crawling toward me and prevent me from looking on you as a snake, as you are, and from raising a hand in pity to assist you should trouble again cross your path. So I have no fears that I will again come near you.

I send you back a ring; and, were I to write anything about it, the words would be only too decent for the same, were they couched in the worst of language. So I say, take it back. Its memory is indecent, and it is the last souvenir I have that reminds me of you. I had a few pictures of you, but they have found a place among the nothings which fill the waste basket under my table. I am aware that in your back parlor hangs the picture of the man who gave you the wall to hang it on; and rumor says you have another in your chamber. The picture up stairs send back to me. Take the other down, for he whom it represents has no respect for you. After you read this letter you should be ashamed to look at the picture, for you would say, "With all thy faults I love thee still," and what would be merely the same oft-repeated *lie*. So take it down. Do not keep anything in that house that looks like me.

If there are any unsettled business matters that it is proper for me to arrange send them to me, and make the explanation as brief as possible.

I fain would reach the point where not even the slightest necessity will exist for any intercourse between us. I am in hopes this will end it.

JAMES FISK, JR.

James Fisk, Jr.: That your letter had the desired effect you can well imagine. I am honest enough to admit it cut me to tho quick. In all tho annals of letter-writing I may say it eclipsed them all. Your secretary made a slight error, however, in supposing that Mlle. Montaland was mentioned. The only prima donna I had referred to was "Miss Peiris." As you say, Mlle. has nothing whatever to do with my affairs. I have always respected her, and only thought of her as one of the noblest works of God—beautiful and talented, and *your choice*—never referring to her in my letter in thought or word. I freely admit I never expected so severe a letter from you. I, of course, feel that it was unmerited; but as it is your opinion of me, I accept it with all the sting. You have *struck home*, and, I may say, turned tho knife around. I will send you the picture you speak of at once. The one in the parlor I will also dispose of. I know of nothing else hero that you would wish. I am anxious to adjust our affairs. I certainly do not wish to annoy you, and that I may be able to do so I write you this last letter.

You have told me very often that you held some twenty or twenty-five thousand dollars of mine in your keeping. I do not know if it is so, but that I may be able to shape my affairs permanently for the future that a part of the amount would place me in a position where I would never have to appeal to you for aught. I have never *had one dollar from any one else*, and arriving here from the Branch, expecting my affairs with you to continue, I contracted bills that I would not otherwise have done. I do not ask for anything I have not been led to suppose was mine, and do not ask you to settle what is not entirely convenient for you. After a time I shall sell my house, but for the present think it best to remain in it. Tho money I speak of would place me where I should need the assistance of no one.

The ring I tako back as fairly as I gave it to you; the mate of it I shall keep for company. Why you could say I obtained this house by robbery I cannot imagine; however, you know best. I am sorry that your associations with me was detrimental to you, and I would gladly with you (were it possible) obliterate tho last three years of my life's history; but it is not possible, and we must struggle to outlive our past. I trust you will take the sense of this letter as it is meant, and that there can bo no mistake I send this by Etta, and what you do not understand she will explain.

NEW YORK, Oct. 4, 1870.

After tho departure of Etta to-day, I wasted time enough to read over once more the letter of which she was the bearer from you to me, and I determined to reply to it, for the reason that if it remained unanswered you might possibly think I did not really mean what I said when I wrote; and, besides, I was apprehensive that the friendly talk carried on through Etta, at second hand, between you and me, might lead you to suppose I had somewhat repented of the course I had taken, or of the words I had penned. It is to remove any such impression that I again write to you, as I would have the language of my former letter and the sentiments therein expressed stamped upon your heart as my deep-seated opinion of your character. No other construction must be put upon my words. I turn over the first page of your letter; I pass over the kind words you have written; have I not furnished a satisfactory mansion for others' use? Have I not fulfilled every promise I have made? Is there not a stability about your finances to-day (if not disturbed by vultures) sufficient to afford you a comfortable income for the remainder of your natural life? You say you have never received a dollar from any one but me, and you will never have another from me, until want and misery bring you to my door, except, of course, in fulfilment of my sacred promise, and the settlement of your bills up to three weeks ago, at five minutes to eleven o'clock.

You need have no fear as to my sensitiveness regarding your calling on any one else for assistance, as I find the word "*assistance*" underlined in your letter to make it more impressive on my mind. That of all others is the point I would have you reach; for in that you would say, "Why, man, how beautiful you are to look at, but nothing to lean on!" And you may well imagine my surprise at your selection of the element you have chosen to fill my places (Stokes). I was shown to-day his diamonds, which had been sacrificed to our people at one-half their value, and undoubtedly if this were not so the money would have been turned over to you, that you might feel contented as to the permanency of your affairs. You will therefore excuse me if I decline your modest request for a still further disbursement of $25,000. I very naturally feel that some part of this amount might be used to release from the pound the property of others in whose welfare the writer of this does *not* feel unbounded interest.

You say that you hope that I will take the sense of your letter. There is but one sense to be taken out of it, and that is an "epitaph," to be cut on the stone at the head of the grave in which Miss Helen Josephine Mansfield has buried her pride. Had she been the same proud-spirited girl that she was when she stood side by side with me—the power behind the throne—she would not have humbled herself to ask a permanency of one whom she had so deeply wronged, nor would she stoop to be indebted to him for a home which would have furnished a haven of rest, pleasure and debauchery without cost to those who had crossed his path and robbed him of the friendship he once felt. The length of time since I had seen her and the kind words she spoke left my mind ill prepared for the perusal of your letter at that time, and it was not until after her departure, when I was seated quietly alone, that I took in the full intent and meaning of your letter, and felt that it was "robbery," and nothing else.

Now, pin this letter with the other. The front of this is the back of that, and you will have a telescopic view of yourself and your character as you appear to me to-day; and then I ask you to turn back from pages of your life's history, counting each page one week of your life, and see how I looked to thee then, and ask your own guilty heart if you had not better let me alone; and instead of trying to answer this letter from your disorganized brain, or writing from the dictation of those around you to-day, simply take a piece of paper and write on it the same as I do now, so far as we are now, or ever may be. "Dust to dust, ashes to ashes. Amen."

J. F., JR.

OCT. 19, 1870.

Madame: Enclosed I send you bill of Harris receipted, and I also beg to hand you $126.29, being the honest proportion of the Bassford bill which belongs to me to pay. I should have made the word "honest" more definite, for had not Mr. Bassford to put the dates to the bill, as he had received instructions from Miss Mansfield to have the bill all under the date of June 8, 1870, although ($146.26) the amount of the goods, as bought by you or your agent, was spent at a much later date. I should not suppose you would care to place yourself in the light that this bill puts you, knowing as I do the instructions that you gave Mr. Bassford. I had supposed you "honest," but I find that a trace of that virtue does not even cling to you. I am, yours,   J. F., JR.

DEPARTMENT OF FINANCE, ERIE RAILWAY,
 NEW YORK, Oct. 20, 1870.

Madam: You know I would not wrong you, and I would take back all my acts when there could be a shadow of doubt that you was right and I was wrong; and let me speak of the other harsh letters I have written. I wrote them because you had wronged me positively, because you had placed between me and my life, my hope and my happiness an eternal gulf, and I felt sore and revengeful, and on those letters I am now the same. It would be idle for me to write aught about them or about *us*. When I could talk to you there, you did not listen. I presume it to be the same now.

The entire connection is like a dream to me, a fearful dream, from which I have awoke, and, while dreaming, supposed my soul had gone out; and the awakening tells me I am saved, and, from the embers of the late fire, there smoulders no spirit of revenge toward you, for you acted right, and the *wrong* only came to me from you because you did not act sooner, and I would not believe that any power on earth would make any question of money influence me or come between me and the holy feeling I once had for you. I sent John to Bassford's, and they told him what I said, or he told me so, that you left word that the dates of the bill should not be changed. But what does it matter whether it is so or not? I cannot *feel* that you would do it, and something says to me, this was one of the things she was not like. So I pass it by, and if the letters of last night or to-day are not like me you can wash the bad act out from your memory, and leave but the one idea that I want to do my duty and fulfil every unsettled relic. At least in my heart rests no remorse, for the memory is too deeply seated, and I would cherish all that is good about you, and forget forever the bad. Of late you have thought different from me (this may be imaginary on my part), for which I think you give me all the credit you can.

We have *parted forever*. Now, let us make the memory of the past as bright and beautiful as we can ; for on my side there is so little to cherish that I cling to it with great tenacity, and hope from time to time to wear it off. You *know* full well how I have suffered. *Once* you knew me better than any one on earth. To-day you know *me less*. It is the proper light for you to stand in. It is *all* you desire on your side. It is all you deserve *on mine*.

This letter should remain and be read only by you. Should you see fit to answer it the answer will be the same way kept by me. There has been a storm. The ship, a noble steamer, has gone down. The storm is over and the sea is smooth again.

Little ships should keep near shore ;
Geater ships can venture more.

" My ship is small and poorly officered."

I am yours, ever, &c., &c.,   J. F., JR.

P. S.—I would have liked to have answered your letter in full, but, as you say, I have not a well balanced brain, and I know I could not do justice to a letter of that kind, so refrain, and content to let the sentiments of it " know and fret me."

Oct. 25, 1870.

Why should I write you again ? Shall I ever reach the end ? There comes another and another chapter, until I get weary with the entire affair. I would forget it, and no doubt you would the the same. The mistake yesterday was almost the mistake of a life time for me. Who supposed for an instant that you would ever cross my path again in a spirit of submission and with a contrite spirit. You have done that you should be sorry for, and I the same in permitting it. This cannot be, and I shall write you the final letter, and I shall see you no more. I told you that much yesterday evening, and still I write it to you again. Yes, for the reason I treated you falsely last night, and I left you with a different impression, and I would put that right. You acted so differently from your nature that I forgive you, and even went so far as to bring my mind to bear how I could take you back again. First, the devil stood behind, and my better reason gave way for the moment, and I came away, telling you I would see you no more. When your better character comes in contact with mine we are so much alike that much of what is said, like that last night, had better been unsaid.

All now looks bright and beautiful, and my better nature trembles at ideas that were expressed last night. But that I should have left on your mind an idea that you could control me is erroneous. There are truths in this affair, and they must be spoken. You have gone from one element and have taken another (Stokes), and for you to turn back, either when you are situated that way, or when even you could say that clement had gone, should make no di'erence to me. It was you that took the step, and you should and shall suffer the consequences. Supposing the part you took last night and yesterday afternoon was one of truth, if not, and I—— [Here this letter is torn].

Again, if you was not dealing from your heart in what took place, and I hope it was not true, then there are no consequences and no suffering for you to endure. Why, it has been many a long year since I could say to myself that I had committed such a folly. To find another like yesterday would bring me back almost to childhood. To imagine that I should have again crossed your threshold, and crossed it, too, deliberately, knowing that the same facts existed that had given me all my trouble, and made me this sorrow—why, it is devilish.

I told you that I had passed the realm where I had forgiven you all the sorrow you had made me, and that I would not murmur; I would not find fault with all that I saw. I would fain tear your image from my mind, and I will. Why, I thought all night last night and all day to-day of your saying, "I would rather be a toad," &c., &c. Was that written to apply to me? I should say so. Yes. Who knows what you would not conceive? No one but yourself. And I must weigh you carefully, for I have nothing but a great character to deal with, and I must meet things carefully. You might suppose you could love two, and perhaps more elements, and make them hover near you. Certainly you did last night, and, for shame, I was one of them. But it will *never* occur again.

For once let us be honest. You went that road because it looks smooth and pleasant, and mine looked ragged and worn. Now, a mistake cannot be found out too soon. Travel further along, and don't try to turn so soon. I can see you now, as you were last night when you talked of this man (Stokes); and do not deceive yourself —*you love him.* Yesterday there was nothing but the breaking up of strong pride and the giving way of willfulness. Cling to that one. Leave me alone, for in me you have *nothing left.* Why ask me to weaken yourself with him? All this you must study; but I pledge you to-night that I will not countenance even your impression on my mind until the door is closed behind him forever. For what you can gain from me you probably cannot afford to do that; so let me advise you—nourish him and be careful. Nothing is so bad for you as changes. He loves you; you love him.

You have caused me all the misery you could. Cling to him. Be careful what you do, for he will be watchful. How well he knows *you cheated me.* He will look for the same. And now, as I know precisely how you stand from your own lips, I will treat him differently. Although you would not protect him, I will. While he is there, and until his memory is buried forever, never approach me, for I shall send you away unseen. Ever be careful that you do not have the feeling that you can come back to me, for there is a wide gulf between you and me. I would not hold a false hope out to you. I shall not trouble you more in this letter. You have the only idea I can express to you. You know when you can see me again, if ever. The risk for you is too great. Loving and suited as you are, cling to him for the present, and when you nature grows tired of that throw him off. And so along until it is time for you to be "put in your little bed" forever, you must rest contented. Don't begin plotting to-morrow. Take to-morrow for thought, and be governed by this letter, for the writer has much of your destiny in his hands.

Despite the estrangement, Josie could not bear to let such a man slip away from her. She continued to ask favors and keep herself before him by various means.

NOVEMBER 1, 1870.

Miss Mansfield : I have taken the steps for the corn doctress' removal to a southern clime, where her business should be better, as vegetables of that class thrive more rapidly there than on our bleak shores. I presume it will take from two, or say four days, before I get the passes, when they will be sent to you. Should she call on you say to her to come back in four days and you will have them for her. I sent you a package by Maggie for what you desired on Saturday evening, with a little surplus over for trimmings, which I hope you received. I am of your opinion regarding not only Dr. Pape, but all of the doctors. You are well; let nature take its course. You are in too good health to tamper with a constitution as good as yours. This is important for your consideration.

Yours truly, JAMES.

NOVEMBER 10, 1870.

Enclosed find $300. Please use. I am very sorry we could not have arrived at a more satisfactory conclusion last night. I did all I could, and the same feeling prevails o'er me now. With careful and watchful manner you should look at all our affairs. You should make no mistake. You told me I should hear from you when you came to a conclusion. Therefore I wait upon your early reply, and until then I must of course pursue the same course I have for the last six weeks. I hope we shall mutually understand each other, for the thing could be made, as should be made, satisfactory to you.

I am yours, JAMES.

Josie received $1,000 with this memorandum:

Erie Railway Company, Treasurer's Office, November 7, 1870, receiving desk—$500.

WM. H. B.

Erie Railway Company, Treasurer's Office, November 10, 1870, receiving desk—$500.

Wm. H. B.

Please acknowledge receipt.   JAMES.

NOVEMBER 11, 1870.

Enclosed you will find the order on Miss Guthrie, which have Etta or you present and it will be all right. Mr. Comer gave them an order nôt to deliver anything only on my written order to stop the "opera bouffers;" but present this enclosed order and it will be all right. Mrs. Reher was here this morning and I gave her transportation for self and Michael to Charlestown by steamer.

Enclosed you will find box at theatre in order to get the same, as it was sold. I have convinced myself that I desire you and yours to come.

Please answer the note, that I may know you are to come.

Yours, truly,   JAMES.

NOVEMBER 12, 1870.

Enclosed find the letters. I was not aware Miss Jordan was to come until I saw her pass the gatekeeper; but that is nothing astonishing, as she is one of our regular customers. Of course I did not send her the box, for she is not in a mood that I presume such civilities would be received from Fisk, Jr. I am glad you was pleased. I would have been glad to have you seen "Les Petit Faust." 'At the "Duchesse" we used old clothes and scenery, while in "Faust" all was new. We play "Faust" this afternoon. Shall I send you a box? And on Monday night we give the world "our diamond," "Les Brigands," all new.

Surely the world is machinery. Am I keeping up with it? is the question.   Yours truly,   JAMES.

NOVEMBER 14, 1870.

Dear Dolly : Do you really wish to see a "brigand" at your house to-night? If so, what hour, or from what hour and how late should I call? For I might be able to come at 8, or perhaps not until 10. Say what hour, and how late is your limit after the time you first say.

NOVEMBER 15, 1870.

Enclosed find box for to-night. Should you find you cannot use it, send it back to me later. Do you feel as I said you would this morning? The box, of course, is for whoever you may invite.

Yours ever,   JAMES.

NOVEMBER 16, 18—.

Dear Dolly : Don't feel that way. Go riding, and to-night, darling, I will take you to rest. I shall go out at half past 3, and you can safely look ahead, darling, for rest. It will come, and we shall be happy again.   Yours truly,   JAMES.

THE LAST LETTERS.

Nov. 18, 1870.

Shall go to the race to-day, and this evening I am engaged until late, and I am afraid you would get tired waiting for the ring of the bell or the ring of the door. So I will not ask you to wait my coming unless it be your wish, in which case I will come as early as I can. Yours, &c.

Enclosed find the Leidunnor Ball. Yours truly, J. F., Jr.

MONDAY MORNING.

Not time to come up. J. F., Jr.

Apocryphal.—From the Tribune, Nov. 25.

ERIE RAILWAY COMPANY.

JAY GOULD, President. JAMES FISK, JR., Treas.

Office of the Company, New York, ————,

Dear Dolly : To-night we play "Les Briggans." It is too jolly. When you past me at the gait last night without looking at me my heart was pirsed. JAS. FISK, JR.

JOSIE'S LAST BROADSIDE.

James Fisk, Jr.—Sir : You and your minions of the Erie Railway Company are endeavoring to circulate that I am attempting to extort money from you by threatened publication of your private letters to me. You know how shamefully false this is, and yet you encourage and aid it. Had this been my intention, I had a whole trunk full of your interesting letters, some of which I would blush to say I had received. If you were not wholly devoid of all decency and shame, you would do differently, knowing, as you do, that when your own notes to my orders are brought into the courts, your letters acknowledging your indebtedness to me, you will appear all the more contemptible and cowardly. You are no sooner apprised of my proceedings against you than I am served with an injunction order requiring me to surrender up all the letters you wrote me and prohibiting me from talking about them. This, indeed, looks to me like a "Field" movement worthy the great and distinguished Erie lawyer. Do you, in your sane moments, imagine that I will quietly submit to the deliberate and wicked perjury in swearing to these injunction papers? (and to the credit of New York, I am glad to say you were obliged to get them in Brooklyn). Unfortunately for yourself, I know too well the many crimes you have perpetrated. Was it not only recently you bought over my servants, a negro boy, Richard E. King, also my cook, and bribed them to perjure themselves to aid you in your villainy? I have the sworn proof of what I tell you, and more. You surely recollect the fated Black Friday —the gold brokers you gave orders to to buy gold, and then repudiated the same, because, as you said, they had no witnesses to your transactions. There was one I recollect in particular, a son of Abraham, who had the courage to swear out an attachment against the Grand Opera House for what was justly due him, and how you and Jay Gould ruined the poor victim by breaking up his business, and having him arrested and imprisoned for perjury. And at the time you premeditated this crime, you well knew he held your written order to buy gold, and you were the perjurers. You are aware, in the papers you served on me, you swore to what was wicked and false, for it was only a few days previous thereto you sent Mr. Hubbell to offer me inducements to give you an order on Peter B. Sweeny for my original affidavit and your letters to me, which documents Sweeny got possession of, as they compromised him and other Tammany magnates in the division of the Erie Railway plunder. But I positively refused to give the required order. Knowing your doings as I do, do you wonder I object to you and your minions practicing the same upon me?

It is an everlasting shame and disgrace that you should compel one who has grown up with you from nothing to the now great Erie Impressario to go to the courts for a vindication of her rights, which you refuse to adjust for reasons you too well know. It is only four years ago since you revealed to me your scheme for stealing the Erie books; how you fled with them to Jersey City, and I remained there with you nine long weeks; how, when you were buying the Legislature, the many anxious nights I passed with you at the telegraph wire, when you told me it was either a Fisk palace in New York or a stone palace at Sing Sing, and, if the latter, would I take a cottage outside its walls, that my presence would make your rusty irons garlands of roses, and the very stones you would have to hammer and crack appear softer under my influence. You secured your Erie palace, and now use your whole force of Erie officials to slander and injure me. It is, indeed, heroic, and worthy the hero of the memorable 12th of July last.

I write you this letter to forever contradict all the malicious, wicked abuses you have caused to be circulated, and at the same time fully state that I am willing to leave all matters in dispute and difference—and forever settle any further controversy—to our respective counsel, Samuel G. Courtney, Luther R. Marsh, and William A. Beach. If they cannot agree, I am willing William M. Evarts shall decide between them. However, I only make this proposal to place myself in the proper light and spirit.

If you feel your power with the courts still supreme, and Tammany, though shaken, still able to protect you, pursue your own inclination. The reward will be yours.

I am, with what respect you are best able to judge,

HELEN JOSEPHINE MANSFIELD.

COLONEL FISK'S MONUMENT.

THE marble monument erected to Colonel James Fisk, Jr., by his widow, in the cemetery at Brattleboro, Vt., was unvailed on Decoration Day. The Veteran Association of the Ninth Regiment, with the famous band, the officers and about one hundred members, all under command of Major Fuller, left New York City the day previous, and were present at the ceremony. The monument was made in Italy, of the choicest marble, and cost, with the solid marble fence-posts and steps, about $33,000. The base itself weighs five tons. Upon it rests the body of the monument, on the four corners of which are life-size figures of Victory, History, Music and Science. One side bears an admired likeness in relief of the deceased Colonel. At the base of the plinth which rests on this pedestal is a grouping of *immortelles*, while further up are garlands of laurel with ends tied in the centre of each side of the shaft. After appropriate addresses, the monument was elegantly decorated with natural flowers, the band meanwhile playing suitable airs.

www.ingramcontent.com/pod-product-compliance
Lightning Source LLC
Chambersburg PA
CBHW021729110726
47902CB00005B/1403